Fate

Fate

Mary Jane

Writers Club Press
San Jose New York Lincoln Shanghai

Fate

Writers Club Press
an imprint of iUniverse.com, Inc.

For information address:
iUniverse.com, Inc.
5220 S 16th, Ste. 200
Lincoln, NE 68512
www.iuniverse.com

DISCLAIMER:
It is, of course, impossible to spend the night within the confines of Disneyland.

ISBN: 0-595-18985-7

Printed in the United States of America

This book is dedicated to you, personally.
Buy this book.
Tell a friend.

CONTENTS

Foreword

There will be those of you who do not believe the following story. If you fall into this category, I implore you not to give it a second thought: I won't be offended, I promise. These things just happen, after all. To be honest, if I hadn't experienced it first hand I probably wouldn't believe it, either. Alas, like a UFO abductee or Used Car Salesman, I'm cursed with being perpetually disbelieved whether I tell the truth or not.

All I can do is assure you, from the depths of my heart and hard drive, that everything that follows is completely true. I have not embellished, I swear. If I am guilty of anything it's toning down the craziness which I experienced nearly first hand. Oh, sure, I occasionally insulated the facts with a glaze of pleasing prose for dramatic effect, but that is not embellishing. What's the difference you may ask? The difference between embellishing and what I've done is like the difference between a mortal and a venial sin. If you need help differentiating those two, call the Pope.

Anyhow, just read the first few pages with an open mind, OK? I'll tell you a little more about myself later…

ACKNOWLEDGEMENTS

A slightly different version of this story has appeared twice before:

First, as a screenplay called ***Man with a Mission***, with story credit to myself, Chris Carriveau and Joe Lunne.

Second, as my final project for a Masters in English from Cal State Dominguez Hills, mentored by Dr. C. Michael Mahon.

My debt to all three of these individuals is substantial.

Prologue: The Day Before

Lying flat on his back and staring at the ceiling, Christian Whitney has been rambling eloquently on the topic of his pre-pubescent trauma for over 30 minutes when the watch on his wrist chimes three. This reminds him that his time is running short and he should get on with what he's really come here to talk about, but like a sculptor trying to liberate his subject from solid marble the difficult bit is deciding where to start.

Christian is a few months shy of thirty with short, uncontrollable black hair and soft dark eyes. He's too tall for his weight, looking like a man put together with spare parts from producing basketball players and starving children. He shifts his weight uncomfortably in his full recline, his lower back aching mildly. He laces his hands behind his head and contemplates the patterns on the ceiling as his ancient ancestors may have contemplated the patterns in the stars. With all this contemplating to do it's no wonder he completely fails to begin talking about what he came here to talk about.

Courage, he tells himself. Courage is required in the face of an uncertain future. He's been living with his delusions and misconceptions and above all The-Thing-He-Came-Here-To-Talk-About for so long he can barely conceive what it will be like to suddenly be without them. It's possible it could be worse than his life is right now; he doubts it, but it's possible. It could be better—God, how he hopes it will be better. He just needs the courage to take the first step, confident the others will follow along in due course. So he takes a deep breath and puts that first metaphorical foot forward.

"But, enough about my childhood," he begins. Truer words, Christian wits to himself, have rarely if ever been spoken. "I came here to talk about something that's been bothering me for awhile; 14 years, 3 months and 28 days, to be exact. You see, my problem is I've always felt I was born into this world for some reason." He hangs on that last word for a long, long time, stretching the nuances of it until they clatter on the floor in shards. "And not for some off the wall, 'make people happy' or 'work for world peace' kind of reason. Something...specific." Christian again holds out the tones of his finale, wringing every single ounce of meaning from the eight letters thus arranged.

Christian could make a living off nuance if he would stop misusing it so overtly.

"But I'm getting ahead of myself. I haven't ***always*** felt this way. Just since the aforementioned 14 years, 3 months and 28 days ago. It was Saturday, I was in bed but still awake, straining to hear Chevy Chase announce he was live from New York in the living room with my parents, when..." He pauses, shifting uncomfortably again. His mind is staring into the precipice of his future, unformed and indecipherable. Apparently, the following steps do not stay on the heels of the first step as well as he'd imagined. He hasn't told a soul about his life-defining delusion; not yet, anyhow, he can back off and continue with his pleasant if somewhat distorted and unhappy life. All at once a sense of potency he'd never imaged overcomes him; at this one instant he truly is in control of his destiny. He can remain outwardly normal and traditionally successful, or he can carve out a more deviant yet honest life from the ethereal unknown.

Wow.

He gives indecision a few more seconds of freedom and joy and then, older and wiser, pushes over the edge into the exhilaration of free fall.

"Well, when I heard this voice. Not Chevy Chase's, mind you, but this other voice, very nasal, sort of pushy, calling my name from thin air." Christian shifts position again, rearranging his long frame. "'Christian,' it said, and I remember this part word for word, 'you have been chosen for a mission in life.'" He swallows deeply, his sense of potency quickly being replaced with one of sheepishness and embarrassment, but he can't hold back now. "'Should you choose to accept it, you are to begin searching for the Holy One, a person identifiable to you by his or her ability to answer a Sacred Question.' He then told me the Question, its Answer, and He wished me luck."

One thing about turning points in life, they surely take the wind out of you. Christian feels spent, ridiculous, and satisfied. He regains his breath, fights off a persistent fatigue, and continues weakly, his voice getting softer and softer until it's barely audible. "Yup, He wished me luck. Which made me mistakenly think God is a good sport. No one, not in over 14 years, has ever come close to answering the Question. No one. Ever. I guess I came here because I'm losing hope and I need someone to tell me it's OK to stop trying." He's whispering now. "Because I don't think I can keep living like this."

There. It's done, all of it. He turns his charcoal eyes to his listener, sitting in the shabby chair on the other side of an hourly hotel room. This working woman, her chocolate skin shimmering in the harsh light of a naked bulb and her long stringy hair hanging carelessly in her face, snores lightly with her chin resting on the palm of her hand. In her disordered slumber she has slumped in the chair, revealing immaculate white underwear under her bright red micro-dress.

Christian doesn't blame her for losing consciousness. He has a fairly realistic self-image and realizes listening to him is not the easiest task in the world. Still, this is his dime, so to speak, and he doesn't immediately sense he's getting his money's worth, so he clears his throat. No reaction from the woman, whom he'd guessed was 10 years his senior when he'd picked her up on Sunset but now looks much, much older. He gets up and shakes her shoulder, causing her arm to fall out from under her chin. The sleepiness in her eyes turns to panic, not remembering what hotel room she's in or with whom.

Now, under normal circumstances, falling asleep on (or under) a customer is a bit of a no-no in her profession, cause for an avalanche of apologies upon awakening, occasionally even resulting in a lowering of her sliding scale for services rendered. Her manager doesn't like that, and usually makes her feel sorry she's done it, but she considers herself an honest business woman and feels her clientele deserves her best if they're paying for her best. Now, though, as the surprise subsides and reality embraces her, she feels at a loss for the appropriate reaction beyond smoothing her dress down over her hips and legs.

From her point of view, it hadn't started out as the best night anyhow. She'd awoken with a headache about the size of a Buick Roadmaster, and from her first strut on the boulevard those damn heels she has to wear were digging into her Achilles' tendon and doing a cluster fuck on her toes. Then this skinny geek (Christian) pulls up in a Beemer and says he just wants to talk. A very standard John line, she's heard them all before, she can tell you that, but this crazy bastard had actually meant it. They walked in the hotel room, he takes off his shoes, lies on the bed and starts babbling about his mother and his kid friends and just leaves her standing there, dumbfounded, not even undressed. Ridiculous. She doesn't need this aggravation, this job can be enough of a bitch on its own normal course, and whom does this maniac think he is, anyhow? But she sat down in the chair, not like he was offering her room on the bed or anything, so she sat in the chair and listened as long as she could. She doesn't even remember where the hell he was when she fell asleep, and is far too fed up to care.

Basically, she doesn't know if she should apologize or swear loudly. There just aren't enough instructions given out for the living sometimes, too many situations without proper guidelines. So, like any other sentient being she has to wing it and accept whatever consequences that may bring.

"Wake up!" Christian says to her. "Are you awake?"

"Oh yeah, honey." She decides to try a medium apology. "I'm sorry…"

His glare doesn't soften, but he does let go of her shoulder. "Is a little of your attention too much to pay for?"

"Oh no, it's just…" and that's it. That's as far as her mind has processed this thought, and it doesn't want to go any further. All she's left with, without the protective shell of humanity, is honesty. "It's just, this listening stuff isn't really my forté. Couldn't we just do it? Then I'll be on my way, and you'll be…"

"I don't want to do it."

Cold as ice, this one is. He and his penis just must not get along too well, she figures.

"That's not what I need," he continues.

"That's debatable, honey."

"What I need is someone to justify my whole God damned life!"

"Justify your life." Christian sits down on the bed again, looking even more pitiful than when he'd picked her up. He's not actually attractive, she decides, due mostly to his miserable attitude. His features are good enough, acceptable, presentable. His eyes would even be considered attractive if they showed any indication of life. But nope, the demeanor, the posture, the drooping eyelids keep him from putting his best foot forward. But, again, she feels a certain obligation to try to spread a little joy into every client's life, even one that keeps his manhood from coming out to play. So she continues with as little contempt as possible. "OK. Now, I heard the first part. Those little friends of yours were way outta line, especially…what's his name?"

"Joe," Christian replies without looking up. He's trying to burn holes in the carpet with his eyes.

"Oh yeah, Joe! What an asshole...but I'm here to tell ya, ya can't whine forever, ya know?" Christian does not look like he knows. She continues anyhow. "Sometimes, ya just gotta pull yourself up by your own scrotum and get on with it."

"I'm trying to," Christian says, smiling weakly. "Tomorrow, I'm abandoning it."

"It, sugar?"

"My mission."

She begins to feel as if she missed something important. "Mission?"

"Yes, mission!"

She shakes her head. "I think I missed that part. You know, I've been pulling 12 hour shifts, so I'm a little shagged..."

"You missed everything!" Christian falls back on the bed in anger and self-pity. This evening certainly isn't going as he'd imagined. His imagination had told him all he needed to do was confess to one other human being and he'd be free. Now he's told the tale in all its gruesome detail and it hadn't been heard. Does that count? Is his soul emancipated? It sure doesn't feel that way. He is, to say the least, a little disappointed. "I lay my soul bare and you can't even be bothered to glance at it."

His companion feels back on familiar ground again. "Now honey, I ain't never seen a bare ***soul*** before; go ahead, bare that little tiger again."

"Again! I wouldn't..."

She moves over to the bed, in what she considers to be a very seductive yet reassuring manner. You can't be too aggressive with these nerds, she's learned, it scares the altitude right off 'em. "Aw, babe, a lot of men don't get it right the first time, don't you worry yourself none..."

Christian sits up and pushes her away forcefully. She is both surprised and insulted. "You want to hear this or not?" He shouts at her.

"Yes," she answers indignantly and dishonestly, sitting on her chair again.

"OK, once more, from the top. God talked to me one night, and..."

"God talked to you? How depressing."

"He talked to me, and revealed to me my mission in life, to find a person who can answer the Question for me, and I've..."

"Oh honey," she says mournfully, shaking her head slowly, "you are screwed up, ain't ya?"

Christian looks like she'd slapped him. "Yeah," he replies, lying back again. "Yeah, I am."

OK, this has gone just about far enough, the hooker thinks. His eyes are closed; I can probably slip outta here before he starts crying or something. She looks at her watch; time is certainly up, after all.

But she doesn't go. Christian has never enjoyed many natural advantages with women, but his bouts with helplessness have a way of being at least vaguely attractive, appealing to dormant maternal instincts or some such thing. She goes over and sits next to him on the bed, running her fingers through his hair. "I'm sorry honey. I didn't mean it." He doesn't respond, but he also isn't sobbing yet or anything. She decides she would leave if she had her money, but since she doesn't she stays. She starts humming softly; she's learned that white men want black women to hum to them, though she doesn't know why. Maybe it was in ***Gone with the Wind*** or something, who knows, but you do what you gotta do.

While humming and stroking his head, a question occurs to her. "How do you know you're not looking for me, Sugar?"

"I already asked you. It was the first thing I asked you on the street."

She doesn't recall him asking her anything special, but she isn't at her best this evening, after all. "I missed it?"

"No worse than thousands of others."

Fair enough, she figures, checking her watch again. "Look, isn't there someone more qualified to be hearing this?"

He rolls his head in her direction, opening his eyes. "You've got ears, don't ya?"

"You know what I mean."

Christian launches into a well-rehearsed response, as he'd been expecting this question. "I can't stomach any textbook logic from a flaming intellectual asshole like myself." He sits up in bed, scaring her onto her feet. "I know it's irrational to wander around asking complete strangers idiotic questions in search of my destiny and I know I'm not taking responsibility for my life, I know…" His anger gives out on him, leaving only exasperation. "I know tomorrow things will change; I'm leaving all this behind and I just wanted to flush these thoughts out of my system. I don't want a diagnosis or words of wisdom, I don't want to be showered in Freud, Jung or Skinner, I just want a hug."

A surprise ending, if ever there was one, to both of them. But Christian really wants to hold onto someone, so stands up slowly, keeping his eyes fixed on his companion. As graceful as two supertankers maneuvering near each other in a shallow harbor, they move together and embrace for a long moment. And, slightly to his surprise, Christian does feel a little better as he holds her against him, the thrill of closeness taking away his ability to think about anything else in his life. He remembers the glimpse of brilliant white cotton he'd had earlier and is momentarily aroused by the memory. She seems to notice the change in his nether regions and smiles; Christian is immediately embarrassed and disengages from her embrace. He takes two twenty-dollar bills and a ten out of his wallet and hands them to his temporary employee. "Thank you."

"Thank you, honey," she says, surprised yet again (and hurt, yet again) by his rejection of his erection making a connection injection for her inspection.

"Will you take the sheets back, for the deposit?"

"Sure, baby."

And he walks out of the room, into the dingy hall and the dingier night beyond. The hooker hustles the sheets to the counter, in a hurry to get back to her profession and forget about this bizarre, kinky experience.

Out on the street Christian walks quickly past the homeless and hopeless people of downtown, late-night Los Angeles. He glances at the restless sleeping form of a man of at least 70 years using the steps of a pawnshop for a pillow, wondering how far he is from that sort of fate. He wonders what, exactly, holds him safe and separate. Confidence lies in his intellect, Christian being convinced his mind will always be employable, but where does this sense of self-confidence come from? It's not written into the Constitution or anything, Thou Shalt not Lose Everything You Own and Everyone you Love if you Score Over 1300 on the SAT's.

A few steps further on he suddenly decides there's also nothing in the Constitution saying one must have a reason for every feeling one clings to, every idea one bases one's life on. And thank God for that.

Under a moonless sky, when you're in the right frame of mind, and if you squint a little, downtown Los Angeles can actually look rather serene and peaceful. Christian steps lightly through the night. He's careful not to show any signs of anxiety, knowing the elements who might want to separate him from his wallet or other possessions can sense fear better than dogs hear a bag of potato chips being opened. So he walks casually, but not too casually, as not to appear to belong in the neighborhood. He pushes his hands deep in the pockets of his brown suede jacket, enjoying the silken smoothness of the lining.

He passes two kids wearing Raider's gear in a doorway when the irony of his previous thought hits him. Thank God for what? What had God ever done *for* him, exactly? He couldn't think of an example. He credited his parents for the fool decision to give him life. The trees and the lilies are the result of random pollination and survival of the fittest. His trusty dog, if he had one, which he doesn't, he could also account for with natural selection and/or the breeding efforts of fellow humans, depending on lineage.

So, what does that leave?

Sure, He had given him this challenge in life, this chance to excel, but seemingly He had also given him every opportunity to fail, which Christian had indeed managed to do. A familiar frustration just burgeoning on anger bubbles up from his bowels into his stomach. Questions of practical theology always have this sort of effect on him, and yet like a car crash or Madonna video, he can't turn away.

About twenty steps past the garage protecting his transportation, he stops and wheels around. If he had a quarter for each destination he's absent-mindedly walked/driven/dogpaddled past, he would be a rich man. Of course he is a rich man, at least relatively well off, but he could be filthy and swimming in lucre if he received those additional quarters. Christian claims his deep purple BMW from an attendant whom he eyes with suspicion while tipping five dollars. A stench of violation hangs in the air of his car; Christian does not like to leave it with strangers, especially strangers in the heart of downtown late on a Thursday night. He presses a button or two and rolls down his windows.

The city streets are rising up to meet him and the wind is prevailingly at his back, but still his mind is uneasy and his stomach queasy. There's not much left to think about, so he continues to think about the old topics: why his life's such a mess, why he's so damned unhappy, why he's not content with the things everyone else he knows is content with. In a flash of either genius or indigestion, he has a revelation of sorts and nearly rear-ends a Miata. What it comes down to, basically, is the curse of self-awareness, Christian's damnable ability to see every side of an issue. Christian can, when provoked, see a situation from every conceivable angle.

Here's an example: If he greets his neighbor while picking up the morning's *Times*, he can see he was being polite while the neighbor was behaving rudely for not responding; or the neighbor was only responding to his own particular mood and chemical balance and sex life and could do nothing other than not respond no matter how good Christian's intentions; or the neighbor is an accurate amalgam of society and therefore it is Christian who has made things worse for himself, the neighbor, and the world in general by his glib attempt at personal interaction.

Very illuminating, it is, to have this sort of omniscience (or is it omni-point of view?), but Christian is the worst type of deity because he couples his omniscience with a complete sense of impotence. He can see all, but can't do shit about anything.

Once on the freeway his thoughts lighten a bit, or perhaps are merely diluted by the twin thrills of acceleration and luxury. The machine at his command feels like an extension of himself, and he can almost feel the asphalt being ripped asunder by his own mighty feet, mile after mile. His body molds itself to the genuine leather upholstery, his eyes see out through the headlights, and his superiority over the other man-machines on this road is undeniable. Perhaps the basic problem with life is that very little of it is at all like the experience of driving a fine example of German engineering. If life were like driving a BMW above the posted speed limit, war would become pretty undesirable and people would be good and kind to each other.

Unless, of course, there's some guy who insists on driving slowly in the fast lane, or refuses to let you merge, or who borrows your BMW and returns it with the needle pointing to empty. How quickly a utopian idea crumbles. Still, Christian enjoys driving. While driving he thinks of tomorrow, and he smiles.

At home all too soon, he pulls into the garage, past his Realtor's "SOLD" sign on the front lawn. At the touch of a button he's admitted to his home; at the touch of another the automatic garage door closes off the outside world and has the fluorescent lights dim and die on another day.

Day 1: Friday

Chapter 1—The Lawyer's Lament

How many times can a man reconsider, he wonders. Christian has, of course, considered the question before. Instead of just reconsidering whether or not to revamp his life, Christian first has to consider whether or not he can yet again entertain second thoughts and still have any pretense at being a man. Or is there even any need to have such pretense? What difference do society's mores and standards make to a person anyhow, or is it his own standards and values that cause him to…

Sometimes, whole days can go by like this with Christian working his way backwards in a topic searching for the root cause of his neuroses before contemplating their effects. Correction, he tells himself, whole days *used* to go by that way, but not anymore. Today is The Day, the turning point in his life, and there's no better time to discard bad habits so whoop! there it goes. Christian decides to reconsider his decision right now, and by-pass all the other possible avenues of thought. Of course, the fact that he can immediately reconsider without fear of his manhood being called into question is a sign that he's already changed, so there's nothing to consider in the first place, let alone to reconsider.

Christian smiles. This day is starting out exceedingly well; or rather the afternoon is, as Christian slept in. He'd intended to get up early, but feels glad he decided to be well rested for The Day.

He glances around his well-appointed office. The leather chair, the oak desk, the incomprehensible modern art tastefully displayed on the walls. The bookshelves are filled with his personal law books, the ones he rarely needs or opens, but which look so darned good on their shelves and impress the hell out of clients, especially those who "have never needed a lawyer before." Now, Christian is not really a lawyer. He has the degree, passed the bar, and gets to put the little initials at the end of his name, but he has never tried a case. He's filed his share of motions and all, but mostly he handles the affairs of those too old, too lazy or too stupid to do it for themselves. Not a particularly difficult job, a little law, a little investment management, a hell of a lot of money. But the law books are an integral part of the look, the image which makes his clients feel they and their money are safe with him. When he actually has to look up laws he uses the firm's extensive library down the hall, past the bathroom, before the lounge.

He's going to miss his office.

The middle drawer of his beautiful desk slides open at the slightest touch. He takes out a single sheet of lily white college ruled paper and places it on the desk, directly behind the brass nameplate his mother gave him when he graduated from Stanford. He's wearing his standard business attire, a dark expensive suit over a white shirt and a red tie; there are no casual Fridays in investment management. Meticulously he folds the paper in half and then slowly forms the wings of a paper airplane. His right thumb presses each fold carefully, insistently. His craftsmanship is excellent, but when launched the craft goes nose down and crashes immediately. With a wicked laugh Christian dismisses this air disaster from his thoughts and hits the intercom button.

"Yes?" His secretary Marie answers in her bright, cheerful, Friday early afternoon voice.

"Marie, I'm headed to the bank in Santa Monica. If I'm not back by three, get the file for Mr. Simpson off my desk, OK?"

"Yes, Mr. Whitney."

Christian fills his lungs deeply with the sweet, purified oxygen of this office complex; if he'd done such a thing out of doors, he'd probably either choke on a particularly thick piece of air or merely suffer from its toxicity. Out of his inner coat pocket he takes a plain white envelope, sealed. He takes the Monte Blanc off its holder and writes, "Marie: tell Simpson I quit, and thanks for the memories. Christian." He rises, pocketing the pen. Half way out of the office, he remembers a few more words are required. Leaning over his desk he includes the following postscript: "You'd best cash your bonus check (enclosed) very soon."

He walks out of his office, briefcase in hand.

CHAPTER 2—SORE EYES, SIGHTS FOR

The First National Bank of Santa Monica is a sight for sore eyes, something Los Angeles desperately needs. This is not just for aesthetics: smog induced eye irritation is the third leading cause of grumpiness in the area, behind Other Drivers and The Dodgers. The bank's facade is grand and towering, yet somehow inviting and reassuring: a place where you're proud to put your money and where you're convinced it will remain, safe, sound and multiplying, till you come calling for it. The white marble used to create the sense of importance is exceptionally contextual with not only the other large buildings in the area but also with what people expect of banks in general.

Christian likes banks, which is fortunate enough since so much of his occupation requires visiting them. This institution in particular is a favorite because it's a perfect distance away: far enough to take his BMW on the freeway but not so far as to disrupt any lunch or dinner plans he might make. The sea breeze usually clears the air by mid-morning, leaving the sun a definite spot in the sky instead of a generalized glow. Salt air is stronger than any amphetamine, bringing life into the old and infirmed, hope to the most cynical, and energy to the most thoroughly lazy.

In other words, providing all the reputed advantages of ginseng at a small fraction of the cost. Or perhaps at a great multiple of the cost, when you consider real estate prices in towns with the word "Beach" in them.

In any case, Christian's conscious mind is oblivious to the wonders of the breeze today. The rejuvenating effect is strong enough to have him bound up the steps, but his mind nervously concentrates on the task at hand which ironically requires masking his nerves until he's again alone in his car. Then, in private, he can get nervous, scream, shout, throw up, whatever it takes.

Perhaps this is a good moment to mention Christian is here to embezzle a mid-sized sum of money from this particular bank and one of their clients.

For that reason, Christian tries not to think about a couple of key words (crime, embezzlement, imprisonment), but it's difficult to *not* think of things once they occur to you. It's rather like being unwillingly erect: trying not to think about it just focuses the mind and intensifies the problem. He keeps his head down, avoiding eye contact with all patrons (especially security guards) and takes his place in the common feeder line. He's at least ten customers away from reaching a teller, and wonders if he can avoid hyperventilation till then or preferably after.

The clock on his wrist chimes three.

A little voice in Christian's head suddenly comes to life and says, 'Wait a minute, you're a changed man!' After all, one of the things Christian has decided to give up is morality. It's never done a thing for him, after all. His strict moral code had kept him from taking advantage of rich, assholic clients who certainly deserved it and had kept him from the private parts of several women. What sort of thing would do that, would make his life miserable (or perhaps more miserable) with no clear return? No, it's right out, leaving only the new, amoral Christian behind. Not evil, mind you, just not all that concerned with what consequences his actions have on fellow humans, the environment, the economy, whatever. His plans for the day, then, should not cause him pause.

Stand up straight, man! he says to himself, mentally anyhow. Do what you want, let everyone else look out for him or herself.

Unfortunately, Christian's knees are not listening to his rousing speech and begin to shake. Their motion is imperceptible outside of Christian's trousers, but to his imagination it's like a billboard announcing his intentions to those in the bank, people watching on the security cameras, and any alien life forms monitoring humanity from a distance of up to six parsecs. On the backbeat his lower lip starts a slight quiver; his stomach completes the rhythm section by doing back flips in time. Great, he thinks, my body's doing the mamba; normal, uninteresting (i.e. non-criminal) businessmen do not do the mamba in a bank line. His riptide of emotion is also causing his penis to stiffen, another thing normal businessmen do not do on company time, or at least it's something Christian doesn't do on company time. Faced with these embarrassing truisms, he decides he needs to sit down for a few minutes, let the salt air clear his head, and then try the line again.

"Next, please!" a young woman at the far right end of the wall of tellers calls. Christian glances about and realizes she is talking to him; time sure does fly when you're doing the mamba. Unable to contemplate a way out without creating a dramatic scene, Christian points his proto-erection and its accompanying percussion toward the window. He wonders if he'll be able to speak when he gets there. He wonders if he'll still have bladder control then, too. To his chagrin he realizes this moment calls for the gritting of teeth and walking along a relatively straight line to the teller, so this changed man does what's required.

At the window he sees a woman who artists, photographers and poets would kill for the chance to paint, photograph or describe. He is struck first by her eyes, a turquoise blue (or green), amazingly clear, illegally penetrating. When she looks at you, as she is doing to Christian right now, it's almost immobilizing. Christian has to remind himself to breathe, lest he pass out at her feet, or more literally at the feet of her teller window. Her hair is a wild mass of strawberry blonde curls, tumbling beautifully along her long neck, past her shoulders. Her right breast is named Marilyn. She appears exceptionally tall but it could be the high stool she's sitting on. Christian is dramatically impressed and suddenly can't remember the English language, delaying long enough to cause her to look at him with a curious, intrigued, perhaps suspicious expression. Another part of his brain speaks up to remind him this is exactly the sort of look he does not want to attract today. If he had the time he'd curse fate for adding this woman's distractive qualities to his busy schedule, but he hasn't so reminds himself to do it later.

Tired of waiting, she speaks first. "Good morning," the goddess chimes, her voice lyrical but soft enough to cause her listeners to lean in to hear. She looks down at something out of Christian's line of sight. "May I…"

"Help me?" Christian finishes. As she is still looking away, Christian's brain is able to reengage, allowing him to launch into his pre-rehearsed lines for embezzling money from a bank. "Yes, I think so. I called this morning and talked to a Mr. McCarthy about the accounts of Mr. Thomas Goldstone. Mr. Goldstone has asked me to close out all of his accounts with you for him." He's on a roll now, even punctuating his "with you" and "for him" with conservative hand gestures. He opens his briefcase with a flourish. "Here is the letter granting me power of attorney, and…"

"And you are his…"

"I'm Christian Whitney, Mr. Goldstone's…" and Christian's mind goes blank at Marilyn's reaction. She stares right at him, eyes as large as dinner plates and her lower jaw hanging slightly slack, and she looks like she's lost her breath. He wonders if he has said something insulting to this perfect creature, or if the police already have an APB out on him. The first thought is slightly more frightening than the last, but neither can be considered pleasant.

Marilyn, unnoticed by Christian, is still working on taking care of his transaction; only her face has been suddenly transformed by pleasant surprise. She drops her already soft tones another level, causing Christian to lean his head almost to the ledge of the window. "You're ***the*** Christian Whitney?"

"I think so," Christian responds. He tries to think of what words to continue with, but Marilyn smiles with such warmth he doesn't even try to find words. Why make an obviously pointless attempt?

"I am almost speechless," Marilyn says, her hands typing wildly to disclose the nature of Mr. Goldstone's accounts. "Financial advisor," she says, nearly knocking Christian over with confusion. "You are Mr. Goldstone's," she explains.

Christian vaguely remembers the question and answer this comment connects with, so nods.

"***The*** Christian Whitney," Marilyn continues, with a slight giggle. Then she is immediately all business again. "Do you have any identification on you, Mr. Whitney?"

"Oh yes," he answers, pulling out his billfold.

"You do." Marilyn's professional demeanor resumes for a few seconds as she verifies his identity; when she looks up, it's with her incredibly disarming smile. "All seems to be in order, I'll just draft you a check…"

Christian nods mindlessly. What a wonderful woman, here, standing before him. Luckily his mind jumps back at the last minute and he tells her, "Cash. Mr. Goldstone specified cash. A bit of an…"

"Eccentric, eh?" Again, she smiles. If Christian had the presence of mind to remember any jokes, he'd certainly tell them to try to keep that smile turned on him. Unfortunately only his autonomic nervous system seems to be on line, no higher brain functions, so he stands there dumbfounded. "Let's see, his savings accounts, checking, money markets…that's just over three quarters of a million. I'll have to check with…"

"Mr. McCarthy. That's why I…"

"Called ahead. I'll be right back, Mr..."

"Whitney."

Marilyn smiles, Christian perspires. "*The* Christian Whitney." She stares at him for a long moment, and then walks away with a vaguely disappointed air. Christian watches her go, finding out to his complete satisfaction she is indeed very tall, nearly six feet, and is wearing stylish four-inch heels. An image jumps to mind, taking Marilyn in his arms and kissing her, finding her lips almost perfectly level with his own. The dream of every tall, skinny bloke is to find a tall, skinny, heel-wearing woman. Christian allows himself to be mesmerized by the soft sway of her body in its well-tailored pinstriped suit until a heavy jowled male teller at the window next door obstructs his view. He looks at Christian with a combination of contempt and disgust. "Don't get too excited by the "*The* So-and-so" bit. She's been around the bend for years now."

Christian takes offense at the remarks, but doesn't feel up to making a scene so mumbles his thanks for the unsolicited advice. The large teller dismisses Christian as another fool on a rush of self-confidence, about to be shot down.

The other teller had seen it happening for years, to everyone who walks up to Marilyn's window. Marilyn's mannerisms, her open and expressive face, her overwhelming body and, yes, especially the "*The*" bit, make men think she's flirting with them in an interested sort of way, and they always ask her out, and she always shoots them out of the sky. The teller had had his turn, when he'd first arrived here; since then, he's watched her turn down 20, 30 guys a day, day in and out. There ought to be a support group for men who've asked her out. He hypothesizes one of their meetings in his mind: 'Hi, my name's Mack, and I've been shot down.' 'Hi, Mack!' Of course, Marilyn messes with the women's minds also, but that'd require a different support group to fix. He doesn't know what impulse made him try to warn this one, when he's just one among many; he'd never tried to warn a victim before. And look what good it'd done: none. This nerd in a nice suit keeps staring after her like she's

Helen of Troy while nervously hopping around like a dog in heat. Yeah, let him find out for himself, then, nothing else for it, after all.

The teller misinterpreted Christian's behavior; he's managed to push Marilyn at least partially out of his mind because fear of being arrested again demands a majority of his attention. Doubts rush at him from all sides and quickly overwhelm him. His eyes haven't left Marilyn: her first stop is at the desk of a blue-blazered man talking on the telephone who scribbles his signature on the form Marilyn presents without pausing his conversation or reading the form. Marilyn moves elegantly onward. Christian's erection, fueled by the twin motors of lust and nerves, grows uncomfortably. Slowly, the sound of alarm bells grows and Christian fights the urge to turn and look for their source. Marilyn enters the vault, disappearing behind the eight-foot thick steel reinforced doors. Christian starts shaking uncontrollably as the bells grow louder and louder. He stares at the point in space where Marilyn has disappeared and is rewarded by her reappearing, carrying a heavy canvas bag. She walks directly behind a loan officer who passes out on his desk, bored, tired, and unneeded. Christian is about to scream from the intense ringing in his head when he hears testosterone charged, angry voices through a megaphone, "Come out with your hands up, come out with your..."

"Mr. Whitney?"

Christian opens his eyes. Marilyn is standing before him, looking concerned and deliciously beautiful. No bells, no police are anywhere to be seen or heard now that his overactive imagination is shut down. He tries a small chuckle with little success. "Sorry, it's been a long day."

"Well, here's Mr. Goldstone's money. Mr. McCarthy had everything arranged."

Christian exhales forcefully. "Thank you."

Marilyn motions towards his briefcase. "May I?"

"Please." He opens up the case and Marilyn begins stacking the bills neatly. She is extremely efficient, and the fact she will soon be finished causes vastly mixed emotions in Christian. On the one hand, he is stealing this money, and so needs to be on his way. On the other, he despises the idea of walking out of here without getting this woman's phone number. Of course, being a fugitive may well have a detrimental effect on his social life, such as not being able to call her for fear of it leading to his arrest. Despite years of male training to do otherwise, Christian decides to place some other goal above copulation and merely walk out of the bank once he has the cash.

"I'm afraid all the bills are non-sequential," Marilyn tells him. "All of our new money is spoken for..."

"At this time of the month," Christian finishes. "Believe me, that's fine."

She finishes stacking. The briefcase is full, but not overflowing. Perfect. "And if I could just talk you out of your signature there, then..." Christian leans over to sign, a brief glance confirming his suspicion that he can see her cleavage from here. "I can't believe I'm talking to ***the*** Christian Whitney!"

No no no, Christian thinks to himself, I'm not getting pulled back into this conversation again, places to go, beaches to sit on, money to spend. "Well, it appears that you are."

Marilyn's face falls like an amateur soufflé. "Yeah, I guess so." Christian hands the paper back and makes the mistake of looking her straight in the eye. The special, bubbly charm she'd been generously exuding has vanished, replaced by disappointment, anger and contempt. She hates him, or at least appears to. Why? Christian hopes it's because he's about to leave. He holds her angry and challenging gaze, its intensity having as strong a hold on him as her beauty had a few seconds before. He allows all his senses one more pleasant instant of Marilyn before his better judgment drags him away.

But it doesn't drag him very far.

He takes a step away from the window and Marilyn forms her bright red lips around the "n" sound in "Next," but Christian steps back before she can speak. Her sour expression gives way to one of cautious surprise.

"You know, I said I'd quit doing this, and I'll probably hate myself in the morning, but…" Christian means this literally, he is convinced he will hate himself for it, but he hears himself asking, "Do you just happen to know the more common name of Robert Leroy Parker?"

Without a moment's pause, she replies, "He's Butch Cassidy, isn't he?"

And, without warning, several things happen at once.

Chapter 3—You Can't Always Get What You Want – The Rolling Stones

Christian would like to enjoy the moment. After a short lifetime of searching, he's finally found The One. Like a wildly large majority of great, incredible, overwhelming moments in life, Christian had imagined it for years, had lived for it for all practical purposes, and yet failed to see it coming or to have any accurate perception of what it would be like. He can't recall what he'd thought it would feel like, exactly, but certainly not like this explosion of light and lilting rose petals cascading through his mind. Suddenly, it all makes sense. Christian had been on two searches through his post-pubescent life, searching for The One and searching for The One (from his God-given and hormonally driven quests, respectively). Somehow he'd completely failed to make the connection between the two until it happened: she's here, she's now, she's life and liberty and a whole truckload of happiness. A lifetime of standing still, staring deeply into her eyes, and lightly stroking her face couldn't possibly begin to be enough, yet Christian would be eternally satisfied with one perfect, gentle touch. He wants her, he wants her, he wants her.

But, as Mick Jagger so astutely pointed out oh so many years ago, you can't always get what you want.

A moment's happiness and satisfaction is not to be, due mostly to all the automatic weapons fire burning through the air. At approximately the same moment Marilyn scrambled Christian's body and soul by saying Butch Cassidy, a noisy and shrapnelly intense entrance had been made to Christian's left flank, and the gent has been firing round after round in all directions ever since. Somewhere behind Marilyn the private security officer monitoring the lobby camera hits a lone button, which notifies the police, seals the vault door, and locks all the cash drawers. Christian is busy enough maintaining bladder control while throwing himself sharply at the floor (and hitting it head on, mind you) to miss this detail, but it happened all the same. From the floor he can see very little. A little marble tile, the wood of the tellers' wall against the unwashed masses, and an occasional dust bunny, that's all. He is still facing the teller window (a bit lower than he had been previously) but his legs are unceremoniously spread-eagled behind him. The gunfire continues unabated for what seems like a long time before a chilly silence falls over the building. The gunman's audience remains patiently prostrate, awaiting orders and a chance to check for blood spots on their shirts.

The voice, when it comes, is calm and direct. "OK, ya all stay down and I swear I won't kill any more of ya than is absolutely necessary! Hey, you!" Christian hears footsteps pounding toward him accompanied by another burst from the semi-automatic, and hopes to any available celestial power the madman isn't talking to him. "Yeah, you!" He calls, standing immediately in front of Christian, who appreciatively notes the cheap sneakers of this killer are pointing away from him and therefore the voice is probably meant for someone else as well. "Blond hair, nice cheekbones, Marilyn. Since you're the only one still standing, give me some money."

A wash of thoughts vie for Christian's consciousness. Why is Marilyn still standing? Is she brave, stupid or just deaf? What will he, Christian, do if this gunman threatens Marilyn, the person he's spent 16 odd years looking for? Does he have the testicular fortitude to protect her? The gunman does a slow circle, presumably to check the room for heroes, exposing the entirety of his footwear to Christian's watery eyes. This adds another question to the list: why do those tennis shoes seem so familiar? The laces were inserted at the top eyelet, and then laced downward, so the knot is right next to the toe. Somewhere he'd seen someone do this before. His life had just passed in front of his eyes, so these memories should still be accessible in his short-term memory. He thinks he met the person either in romper room or law school; and that voice, resonating a few feet over his head, sounds vaguely vague and yet familiar as well…

And, he remembers. And without a cautious thought he calls out "Joe!" This brings a great deal more gunfire, a barrage of loud metallic pings being directed to the four winds, some of the shell casings hitting Christian's back and singeing his jacket. It sounds as if much of the bric-a-brac and art adorning the walls of the lobby is having a bad day also, and one of the glass walls of Mr. McCarthy's office shatters and splinters on those unfortunate enough to be inside. Christian wishes he'd kept his stupid mouth shut.

But, if you'll recall, you can't always get what you want.

"Who the fuck said that?" Joe asks, when he stops his random field of fire.

Well, this is not good, Christian thinks, but perhaps a little friendliness can make it right. "Joe Bridgers!" He screams to the whole institution, pushing himself up with his arms to begin rising to his knees. "It is you, isn't it!?"

Christian finds the barrel of the gun in his face. The heat from all its recent firing burns the very tip of his nose, leaving him to smell the cooking flesh directly and unforgettably. Fear overcomes his instinct to pull his head away, so the odor rises and spreads up his nostrils and deep into his lungs. "OK," Joe begins, slowly, calmly. "Is there anyone else you want to shout my name to, asshole?"

"Joe," Christian whispers, vibrato, in a mostly prone and completely frozen position. "It's me, Christian." He feels this isn't quite complete, given the circumstances, so adds, "Your friend, Christian."

The gun is removed from his face, causing a sharp but short-lived pain as it takes some skin as a souvenir. The barrel is replaced almost immediately by Joe's incredulous face, covered in nylon. He looks at Christian with a mixture of wonder and disbelief before his eyes alight and his teeth appear. "Chris Whitney! You still have those little weasel eyes, don't ya? Come on up here!" He helps Christian to his feet. They hug each other awkwardly, causing Joe to squeeze off several more rounds into the stucco walls. "Oh, sorry!" He calls to the crowd. "Sorry, folks!"

As previously mentioned, Christian had already realized he's made a mistake. It wasn't difficult; the extra shooting was a clue, the second-degree burn on his nose an added reminder, but it's only now that he realizes the magnitude of his blunder. Now that he's been recognized, Christian remembers exactly how little he's ever had to say to Joe and senses (correctly) he has even less to chat about at a time like this. Why did he say anything? There are theories out there (they practically abound, in fact) that everything in our lives happens for a reason, so perhaps there is a reason why Christian spoke up so inappropriately. Or perhaps he is stupid, as others have sometimes noted. Christian tries to remember, from his law school days, if chatting with a bank robber in the act can be construed as aiding and abetting.

By now the silence has gone on an awkwardly long time, so Christian opens with light conversation. "It's those laces of yours, man. I knew it was you!"

"Yup, it's me." Joe is about Christian's age, about Christian's sex, and 20 pounds over Christian's weight. Their divergence continues from there, picking up speed like a squirrel in an avalanche. To Christian's tall and wiry, there is Joe's short and stocky, bordering on pudgy. Where Christian is fair and blue eyed, Joe is a little swarthy and has tiny little gunmetal gray beady eyes. Joe's demeanor is over-the-top jovial; this generic engendering doesn't take a back seat for anything, not bank robberies, cocktail parties or funerals. Christian, of course, has trouble out-talking the potted plants at parties and rarely displays any emotion at all. In addition to his choice of identity hiding leg wear, Joe is wearing shorts with grease on them and holes in them, a dirty Nirvana T-shirt, and his short socks and tennis shoes, laced backwards.

They have been nodding to each other for quite awhile by now. "What's it been junior high?" Christian attempts, doggedly. "You're looking well."

"You too, Chris."

"Christian," he corrects, as politely as possible.

"Oh, yeah, I forgot." If I'd remembered, Joe tells himself, I would've left you on the floor. Joe finds few habits as distinctly annoying as someone who insists on being called by an excessively long name; he developed his passion about this habit from his acquaintance with Christian. Joe figures he probably has better things to be doing right now than reminisce. After all, traffic won't slow down the cops forever. "Well, we should get together sometime."

"Yeah, I'll call ya!" Christian replies, dishonestly and gratefully.

"But, right now, I'm in a bit of a hurry..."

"Oh, I know, I know." Christian, too, would like to leave the bank shortly. He wonders if there's any chance he can make a get a way with Marilyn; it seems unlikely. If there were any books out there on how to rob a bank, they would likely include the warning, "Don't try to pick up women while on the lam, especially employees of the bank you just robbed."

"So," Joe continues with little humor and considerable impatience, "I'll see ya later. Do you mind lying down again?"

"Oh, not at all! Good luck!" Christian slowly lowers himself to the floor. Today is certainly turning out to be quite a day, though not exactly the one he'd planned. He wanted to get up early, walk away from his distasteful job, steal a little money and leave the country, and now he's lying flat on cold marble near Joe's stinky feet. Not according to plan, but this little distraction will probably occupy the police long enough for him to get out of the country, so it seems Joe's appearance is all for the best. Besides, he recalls, you can't *always* get what you want.

Joe, for his part, is returning his attention to Marilyn. "So, did you find any money yet, honey?"

Marilyn clears her throat nervously. With a slight tremor in her voice, she says, "There's $780,540 in this briefcase."

Christian pops to his feet like well done toast.

"Is that enough?" Marilyn asks Joe.

"Wait," Christian whimpers while trying not to interrupt.

"Yeah, great, toss it over."

"No," Christian whispers, more as a wish than a command.

Marilyn smiles. "What a pleasure to be working with ***the***..."

"Wait!" Christian wails. Joe and Marilyn look at him, for the first time noticing his presence in the conversation. "You're giving him my money!" he continues, by way of answering their startled expressions.

"Mr. Goldstone's money," Marilyn corrects him.

"That's what I said!" Christian feels an all too familiar steaming pressure behind his eyes. He doubts his mythical Bank Robbing Manual suggests crying as appropriate behavior for bank robbers or embezzlers, and fights his tears off by squinting. Joe flashes back to their younger days; he'd seen that look a lot, and had exploited it to his benefit on many occasions.

Marilyn is getting a little tired of this entire situation. "Well, he asked for it."

"***I*** asked for it!" Christian protests.

"He has a gun."

"I have a gun!" Christian pats the bulge of a water pistol in his pocket. He hadn't really planned on bluffing his way through a bank robbery, but came as prepared as possible for any eventuality.

Marilyn tries again to finish the conversation. "I saw his first."

"That's true, she did," Joe adds, less than helpfully.

"I asked for it first!"

Marilyn summons up her remaining patience. "You see, Mr. Whitney, he's robbing the bank, so..."

"I'm robbing the bank!" Christian yells, causing several of the folks embracing the floor to glance at him in disbelief.

Marilyn, also, looks startled. "Really?" She flashes her disarming smile at him, and Christian is again mesmerized. He stares into her eyes and suspects he has to have her. When he manages to disengage from her gaze, the briefcase is gone and Joe is halfway to the door.

"Bye, buddy, take care," Joe calls in responds to Christian's guttural cry of alarm. "Bye, babe," he adds with a surprisingly lewd smirk. Christian fights momentarily between staying and going. He recalls Marilyn's smile. He remembers he's announced to many witnesses and security camera's that he's robbing the bank. He chases after Joe, now at the door.

"Boy, you sure had me fooled!" Marilyn calls after him. "Oh well, good-bye, ***the***..." until Joe's final burst of ammunition drowns out her parting words.

I get a real kick out of people sometimes, I really do. A bank robber's manual; what a concept! Damn thing should sell like hot cakes, if hot cakes actually sold like hot cakes, that is. Here's what we have so far:

- Don't try to pick up women while on the lam, especially employees of the bank you just robbed.

- Crying is not appropriate behavior for bank robbers or embezzlers. Squinting can help stop tear build-up/emission.

What a hoot. Maybe it should also include:

- Don't wear your best suit to the bank; that paint stuff they use to booby-trap the money plays hell on fine washables.

- Always go early; people are much less grouchy if you rob them before lunch.

- Check your weapons before arriving at the bank; nothing is more embarrassing than forgetting your ammo at home.

- Never, ever wear ebony tights instead of a nylon.

Ya just gotta love humans sometimes. They think up the wildest things. I don't know if Christian thought about the bank robbing manual while actually robbing the bank; I wasn't tuned into him in real-time. But I can accurately report that he **thought** *he thought about it while robbing the bank. He was pondering it in great detail when remembering the situation a few weeks ago, so if history has been amended it's on his head not mine.*

So there, now I've said it: I read people's thoughts. At one point in my life I felt self-conscious about this ability but now I've learned to accept myself for what I am. What I am is someone who can read other people's thoughts. What I'm not is a much longer list: I can't see into the future, I can't affect events from afar, I can't determine winning lotto numbers until I see them in the paper, just like your boring old selves. All I can do is sit in a room, clear my mind of ground clutter, and drift from one channel to another till I find an interesting head to live in for a little while.

I'll admit it's a neat trick, if you can manage it. I spent my puberty in the minds of men (and women) having sex; what did you do? When I want to go to Disneyland I don't buy a ticket, I just jump in the mind of someone on Space Mountain, saving me major money and I don't have to stand in line. When I hunger, I can share the sensation of eating at Spago's or Mickey-D's without ever leaving home. And, as you read this I can get the first truly honest feedback an author has ever received…

So, what do you think of the story so far?

That's what I thought. Don't worry, the disparate shards of this tale all fit together in the end, manufacturing a mosaic of startling shallowness and incredulity.

Sit back and enjoy…

Chapter 4—Singing Like Aretha

After a few more glorious moments of rapid random fire, Joe egresses the bank and turns immediately left. The day is glorious, and Joe feels at his best. He has always been pleased to find exquisite enjoyment from every career he's tried (to name a few: short order cook, 900-number operator, and now bank robber) and this one is turning out equally well. He takes a deep, refreshing breath of invigorating spring air and walks briskly towards his car.

Christian exits the bank moments later, anger and knee knocking fear competing for his attention. "Hey!" he calls after Joe, fighting to keep the tremolo from ruling his voice.

Joe keeps walking. His Pinto is parked down an alley over this way, engine running. That's the main advantage of using a piece of shit as a getaway vehicle; anything more attractive than his thrash-mobile with the motor running and door unlocked would've been stolen in a minute. Pintos in particular are good because people also tend to give you a little more room on the freeway.

"Hey!" Christian calls again, walking fast in Joe's direction. Unable to think of anything dramatic, he goes with the obvious. "You almost killed me!"

"Sorry." Joe doesn't look back, nor does he invest much conviction in his answer.

"Sorry!" Christian takes a few jogging steps after his prey. "You powder burn my hair and then say you're sorry?"

"Sorry I missed." Joe turns down the alley.

Christian fights a sudden tendency to feel ridiculous. Though he would like to blame this feeling on the obviously inane turn his crime has now taken, he knows it's more basic than that. Joe has always been the person to make anything Christian does seem at least ridiculous if not criminally insane. As a kid, every tree Christian wanted to climb Joe quickly denounced, demanding they climb the obviously superior one right next to it. As a teenager Joe immediately denounced any girl Christian looked twice at as the least desirable creature on the planet (irregardless of whether or not he ended up sleeping with her). Christian said taste great; Joe opined less filling. And the tragedy is, the real nitty gritty truth of the matter is, every time Joe spoke Christian not only listened, he believed.

It must be that history momentarily blinds Christian, because he walks around the corner and into the hard snub nose of Joe's weapon without slowing down. It's a race between surprise and pain to stop him from impaling himself on the gun completely. Joe's eyes have a certain wildness in them, hidden behind a compelling playfulness that few can resist. Compelling playfulness and a nylon, of course. "The question is, am I sorry enough I missed to take the time to correct the mistake?"

It's always been difficult to read Joe, but this time Christian can't figure out for the life of him if this is a joke. In any case, Christian picks this as another moment to reassert his new life style. He steadies his voice and his limbs, coughs briefly on the alley's stale air, and stares Joe in the eye. "OK, now if you'll just give me my money, then…"

Joe lets the gun go slightly limp. "You know, Chris…"

"Christian," Christian corrects, flush with strength of character and sensing victory around the next conversational bend.

The "-tian" part of Christian rattles inside Joe's skull like the beads of a maraca. Joe casually puts a new clip in his weapon and removes the safety; Christian stands there waiting for him. "You know, a man really shouldn't leave the holes in his life undarned, now should he?"

"All philosophy aside," Christian continues on, refusing to let the conversation drag, "we should talk about my money..."

Joe levels the gun at Christian's chest again. "Of course, 'murderer' is such a bitch of a rep to live with..."

Christian realizes this is the moment for resolve and personal strength; Joe isn't going to shoot him. Joe has nothing to gain by shooting him. Of course, Joe doesn't have all that much to loose by shooting him either. While his mind may be attempting a stiff upper lip, it doesn't have any tradition of self-confidence to fall back on and so resolve gives way to doubt which hands off to fear. Suddenly the new Christian takes a seat and lets the old one emerge. "But," he stammers, jaw practically out of his control, "And...my money..." And no more words, all energy being devoted to keeping his knees from buckling.

"And that's another thing, old friend. Why do you keep saying that? 'My money...'" Joe ponders that idea for a short moment, aware time is running out and a decision will soon be required. "This stash never belonged to you, did it?"

"Withdrawal," Christian manages in reply, nearing hyperventilation. "A small withdrawal..."

"So get your ass back inside, they'll give you some different money. You never could lie for shit, Chris..."

Joe looks down the sight of the semi-automatic, though he certainly has no opportunity to miss if he pulls the trigger. A voice in his mind nags at him, though. Not regret, not remorse, not one even remotely involved with his conscience; it's merely a worker in his over developed sense of self preservation, reminding him it's time to go. Christian has clamped his eyelids closed and given up breathing, figuring he may as well get used to it; not breathing, that is. Joe snaps his wrist 'round and stares at his watch; he lowers his gun and race walks to his car.

Christian takes his first breath in the afterlife, confused that the air quality is still just as chunky as it'd been on earth. Then an alternative explanation strikes him, and he opens his eyes to see Joe slamming the driver's door. "Christian," he exhales, figuring if he's going to keep on living he may as well try to keep it on his terms.

"Bye, Chris!" Joe calls, starting the car and backing right at his old, true friend. Christian steps out of the way to let him pass, unwilling to leap on the car like some damn stuntman. Besides, it is the ass end of a Pinto being offered to him, and no one wants to die in a gasoline fire. But as Joe smiles his way past, Christian calls out to him, "I'll turn you in."

Joe stops the car.

"They'll arrest me, and I'll sing like Aretha Franklin," Christian informs Joe. "Tell them your name, where you grew up, where your father lives… he's still there in the same little house in Thousand Oaks, isn't he Joe?" He pauses for breath, hoping he doesn't have to go on. Despite the fact that the car is still there and momentum is more or less on his side, he doesn't have a clue where to go with it. Joe would know, but not Christian; instincts are a gift he just has to live without.

After a indecisive second, Joe pulls forward again, stopping to let Christian hop in before backing out of the alley and directly into traffic without a glance, like a true Californian driver should.

Chapter 5—Christian Whitney

It should be no surprise he carries a briefcase, because Christian Bradley Whitney had been leaving rooms with baggage for as long as he can remember. Not always literally, mind you, but more psychologically. Never, not once in his life, has his brain taken the day off. It's constantly sticking its neurons in where they don't belong, thinking about everything and nothing all at once, remembering the slightest slight and the smallest minutiae of the day. Forget to say hello to Christian one day in the hallway in second grade, and he'll relive the horror of that moment through junior high. This may sound like hyperbole, but it's literally true, and he still thinks of it on occasion today, some twenty years later. He also turns the same microscope towards himself and analyzes each word and gesture of his life until he determines for certain whether or not that moment had been lived to its fullest and within expected margin of his morals, opinions and attitudes. This explains, almost without further effort, why Christian remained a virgin until he was 23: he just couldn't face thinking about *that* moment's conflicting emotions and mores *that* many times.

Where exactly this trait of psychotic self-awareness originated is difficult to determine. His parents were never particularly concerned with the opinions or actions of others or themselves, and lived reasonably normal lives from start to current time. Father, Benjamin G. Whitney, actually allows people to call him Ben and sleeps deeply through most every night, untroubled by memories of thoughts already thunked. Mother (Elizabeth Archibald Whitney) is a sensitive but practical woman who tried to teach her son the value of relaxing but failed miserably to get through to him. His father was a forest ranger in southern California until he retired, and his mother an elementary school teacher who spent much of her summers in boots and khaki, enjoying the beauty of nature at her husband's side. They had three children, Christian and two perfectly normal, healthy, well-adjusted twin girls.

Go figure.

For whatever reason, and it would take a trained psychiatrist years to work it out, there was tension between Christian and his parents practically from the womb. He was born almost a month late, refusing to cooperate with the timeline his parents had set out for him before they'd even been properly introduced. He refused to go to his first day of kindergarten, saying, "I like home. Why change now?" Christian's legs were no more than a dozen inches long, and the short pants his mother had dressed him in made him look like a character out of a Dickens's novel after a bath.

"But you'll have fun at school," his mother assured him.

"I have fun here," he replied.

"You'll learn such a great many things," his father tried.

Christian merely shrugged his shoulders non-committally. He placed all his weight on one foot and tapped the opposite set of toes energetically. He stubbornly refused to meet his parent's eyes by staring resolutely at the dancing toes going up and down, up and down. Many a stubborn child is undone by appearing to be on the verge of breaking down and giving in, if only his parent will give him a way to get there; Christian gave off no such signals. He appeared ready to stand there in the foyer for the rest of his life, all seventy to eighty years of it, continue standing there for a few decades after the passing of his parents from severe old age if that's what it takes to get his way.

Negotiations like this are almost entirely a matter of convincing the other party that you won't budge an inch, no matter how reasonable, how generous, or how compromising they may become. Christian, after an hour and a half, managed to convince his parents, and he stayed home from his first day of school. His mother finally convinced him to go on the next morn by letting him know the old ways were gone; he can stay home, certainly, but he'll have to help her in the garden all day long, a chore he'd shown previously he had no interest in. Parents may not manage to overwhelm their children's will, but they can usually outsmart them for at least a few years into life.

Christian's parents had met simply enough, at a dance in King City, California. Mom, all legs and breasts and beautiful, was standing against the wall next to her friends as the 'do began to be done. They were a tight group, young and ebullient and rating each man as he entered the main door. Most of the comments were not particularly complimentary.

"He's a complete nerd," Wanda offered on one particular individual. There were no dissenting votes.

"Not bad, if only he could walk upright," Jenny summed up another.

They were all drinking and smoking, flaunting these symbols of independence and liberation. The music was stuff that seemed cool for a few years, before the Beatles invaded and showed the American youth the error of their ways. Mom was mature enough to appraise people coolly, without malice or desperation. At the same time, she was immature enough to take pleasure from the fact her mother was probably worried she was out smoking, drinking, or worse. She smiled and took a long drink of her gin and tonic.

She didn't over react when Dad walked into the place with his mates. Her trained eyes walked over him and were vaguely pleased with what they saw: a solid two hundred and twenty pounds on a frame on the tall side of six feet, chestnut hair tossed carelessly to one side, dancing eyes when he smiled or laughed, as he's doing now, toward everyone, inviting the room to look in his direction, see what he has to offer.

"Hey, that's Ben," Wanda declared, putting out a cigarette.

"Who?" Mom asked.

"Ben," Wanda yelled into her ear. "I met him last week at that place we went one time."

"Where was I?"

"Grading papers."

"He's kinda cute; tall," Mom said, more or less to herself, but the music had stopped at precisely that moment. The entire room turned and looked at her, causing her to blush candy apple red. Ben looked too, and their eyes met in that silent moment, she blushing and smiling, he with a twinkle in his eye. With minor side trips (Ben had come there looking for Wanda after all, so there was that detail to work out during the night) the two of them had been together ever since.

Grading papers was still a common excuse for Mom throughout Christian's youngness. It seemed whenever he wanted anything at all from her (love, affection or Bactine) she was grading papers. This is completely inaccurate, of course, it almost never happened, but there is an undeniable tendency to exaggerate slights of all sorts and the maternal ones most of all. For example, the one time his parents made Christian go to bed without his supper (he had broken the lamp by rushing around the house like a maniac) is now stored in his memory as having been sent to bed hungry at least once a week.

And this is a sane person, mind you. Crazy brains are much worse.

Christian soon found that he loved school, once his mother had coerced him into giving it a try. He easily mastered any skill asked of him be it reading, writing or 'rithmatic, usually finding himself with plenty of time to spare as his other classmates were barely beginning to understand what was being asked of them. With this time he couldn't do anything except read, so that's what Christian found himself doing. He read voraciously, everything he could get his hands on, feeling the creeping tingle at the base of his spine during a mystery or laughing out loud (and annoying his teacher) with Erma Bombeck.

It's an old story, common and unsurprising: In books he found himself, found entertainment and companionship, and life. He had given other kids a chance, by the way, giving them the opportunity to like him. They didn't, of course; as I say, it's an old story; you've heard it all before. I'll leave it to your sordid imaginations to take a random sample of Christian's early disappointing interaction with fellow bipeds; as I'm sure you're aware, it wasn't pretty. So he turned to books and the books were happy to turn to him.

And then there was Joe. Christian and his other mates had reached their fairly peaceful standoff years earlier: Christian left them alone, and they left Christian alone, and everyone went about their lives. Then Joe arrived in town at the beginning of fourth grade, and he was something none of the kids in this small bedroom community had ever seen before: charismatic. Everyone, from the moment they laid eyes on him, wanted to be like Joe. And don't imagine this description doesn't equally fit for Christian: he fell for Joe as fast and as hard as anyone. Perhaps it's the fact that Joe is the person most like a literary character he had ever met, someone who fell out of the pages of Dickens or Fitzgerald, with a little S. E. Hinton thrown in for good measure. Christian did his level best to dress like Joe, walk like Joe, and basically be Joe, all with Joe's complete encouragement.

After all, it's good to have someone to take the blame when things go wrong, and this Christian found himself doing time and time again, at school, at convenience stores, you name it. Each betrayal, each opportunity Joe took to re-focus the blame onto him, came as a complete shock to Christian; his loyalty to Joe's cult of personality was strong enough that he kept coming back for more. Why did he feel a need for Joe's approval? Why do any of us feel the need for anyone's approval? These things just happen. In fact, Christian may well have kept returning forever if Joe hadn't hit puberty and started having less and less time for his micro-gang and more and more interest in gullible young women. Christian, abandoned, returned inside his head and to reading, and eventually came to see Joe for what he was: a manipulative little monster. Christian, never one to settle halfway, came to hate Joe through their junior high years, continuing on through high school, after which he had never run into him again.

Until today, of course.

Chapter 6—How to Drive Like a Californian

It is the Constitutional Right of each and every Californian to make U-turns at every intersection, begin applying the brakes mere millimeters from any required stop (and then roll through it), and weave in and out of lanes on the freeway to make the best possible time home. Joe, though, has no intention of waiting till the Pinto reaches the freeway to make good time, and is weaving about Santa Monica Boulevard like a drunken entertainer. Christian is gripping the window ledge and the dashboard with all his strength plus his fear and his force of will, hoping that at least one of them will save them from every impending accident fast approaching the cracked windshield.

Christian is too worked up to notice right now, but Joe's car is not exactly stock. The interior is standard: Detroit's finest red vinyl seats, skillet hot in the summer and dry ice chilly in the winter. The floor mats aren't standard, but it's not hard to find any car accessory with the Playboy Bunny symbol on it. He picked them up at the same auto parts store where he got the fuzzy dice hanging on the rearview. No, the unusual bit of the vehicle is in the electronic gizmos Joe had added on since acquiring the frame and engine and such. Different displays and dials and buttons on black boxes of all sizes and varieties, each sprouting wires of all colors from every corner. Black electrical tape is stuck on everything and hanging everywhere, holding the mish-mash more or less in place. Joe twiddles with a knob or two every now and then for reasons he feels no need to elucidate.

After all, he does have a few other things on his mind. He's driving like he means it. Joe is in the zone, the driving zone. He uses all lanes, he hits all lights, and he's in a terrible rush and yet will pass no car before its time. Each maneuver is crisp and decisive, poetry in mechanized motion. He's seeing more than just the road and opposing drivers, he can sense the interconnection between every car, pedestrian, stray dog and pothole. In his mind the rusty steed he pilots is pure energy so he can split every seam and ride the perfect wave.

Christian just thinks Joe's the luckiest bastard ever to live. He's always been the luckiest bastard alive, whether it's forgetting his homework and the teacher not asking for it or becoming intimate with any girl he's picked. In all previous moments of their shared existence this fact had annoyed many bodily fluids and solids out of him, but it's remarkable how being the passenger in an enemy's car can increase your concern for his well being. Christian, though boiling like a teakettle, is cheering Joe on unashamedly and rejoicing at each unlikely moment of survival.

During a clear moment in traffic, Joe rolls down the window and spits for distance. He turns his attention to his subdued passenger. "Look, there are some rules to this game, and I want to get the fucking rules straight right now." He clears his adenoids and spits again. "First rule: I get to say 'fuck' anytime I fucking feel like it; you got a fucking problem with that?"

Christian feels he probably does have a problem with that, but gets no further than, "Well…"

"Too fucking bad. Second rule: I'm on a damn tight schedule, so don't bother me right now, got it?"

"I haven't said a…"

"Good." Joe cranks the wheel sharply right, entering onto the 10 at the expense of several layers of rubber off the Pinto's original tires. He merges onto the freeway aggressively, and then settles into a 10 miles per hour over the limit pace. Another glance at his watch depresses him further. He takes a cassette tape from his jacket pocket, and after examining the label on each side picks one, pops it in the deck and hits rewind.

Christian watches the whole show with little comprehension. "What?" Christian asks.

"Shut up," Joe suggests.

"Why?"

"Shut up!" Joe glances at each axis of the car, his head resembling a Tilt-a-Whirl.

"When?" Christian inquires, spinning his head as well.

"Any minute now…"

The tape finishes rewinding and Joe hits play. His voice booms in the car, bass-less and full of static, directly from the lone speaker in the middle of the dash. ***"OK, dickface,"*** he begins, ***"this tape should be rolling exactly eight minutes after entering the bank, so you're now a mile from the 405."*** Both passenger and driver obediently glance at the fast approaching road sign, saying their car is indeed a mile from the 405 interchange. ***"If not"*** the tape continues, ***"take the next exit, left for three blocks, right at the 7-11, call yourself a shithead and turn yourself in."***

Joe looks annoyed. "Yeah, yeah keep talking…"

"Still with me?" his taped voice lilts. ***"OK, then, crank up the range finder, scramble the sensors, let's party!"***

Joe twiddles with a gizmo here and a knob or two there. Christian is almost emasculated by his curiosity, but refuses to give Joe the satisfaction of asking. What the hell, Christian asks himself, has this spawn of Satan done to this car? And how many batteries does it take to run it? And is it licensed by the State of California's Occupational Safety and Health Association? And…

"Hey, Chris, lock your door, will ya?" Joe more commands than asks, tapping on the small cylinder taped to the outside of the rearview.

Christian reaches towards the button, mumbling to himself, "My name is Chris…" and then receives a few dozen volts from the door lock. His teeth chatter and his eyeballs try to get out of his head.

Joe suppresses his urge to laugh, settling for an evil smirk. "Oh, I'm sorry. I gotta fix that short."

"Short!" Christian shouts, spittle ending up on the windshield. "What the hell do you mean short? In a door lock?"

Joe eases back into the slow lane. "That door lock activates the sensors on that sides of the car. When I'm clear for lane changes, I get a light here on the dash. We've also got radar front and back, so I don't even have to look out the windshield if I don't wanna." He smiles the smile that's infuriated people from here to Botswana. "And, I've got the fuzzy dice here, for luck."

"Who the hell are you, McGyver?"

Joe laughs for a hearty second then falls dumb. The silence is deafening to the passenger, music to the driver. Their differences don't end there: Christian can't think of a thing to add to the surrealism of today, and Joe's getting ready for the fun to start.

"OK, you should be at the La Cienega exit."

"Tell me something I don't know."

"And the cops should be entering on the ramp."

To his right, Christian indeed sees five highway patrol vehicles, shiny white Tylenol-looking machines with lights and gun racks, pulling onto the freeway. He instinctively pulls his head down below the level of the dash, to Joe's amusement. Noting his companion hasn't moved an arrogant inch, Christian settles for a serious slouch, only his hair visible to the outside world. "How the hell did you—"

"Just hang on, asshole."

"Now remember to drive the speed limit. They're looking for the speeding get-away you're not making. Just relax, they'll go on by."

With a slight straightening of the spine, Christian raises his eyes above the door and sees, indeed, the police cars have merged and are moving over into the faster lanes, pulling away from their Pinto. His spirits immediately lift. "All right! This is great!"

"OK, now sneak up behind 'em, close as you can."

"No!" Christian squeals.

"Hell yes." Joe's merry mood is gone and he stares intently through the glass at the road ahead. He resembles a great athlete, seeing the entire field and anticipating the opponents' every move. He checks the dash, finds his baffles are clear and eases his car to the left, behind the trailing CHP.

"They should all be in the third lane, so—"

"Yeah, I'm closing in." Not only is Joe nearly sucking on the bumper of the rear car, he also starts waving and making ridiculous faces at the driver. After a double take in the rearview, the driver slaps the hell out of his partner's arm. The partner turns around tactlessly and immediately goes for the radio.

"When he lights 'em, hit it."

The trail car turns on its lights.

"What?" Christian asks, but neither he nor Joe hears the words. Joe's right foot is pressed firmly to the floorboard and the Pinto springs forward like a stung steed. The tires beg for mercy as they're asked to immediately place the car in the fast lane. Joe is past three of the cops before they react; it's as if his passing turns on their blue and red spinners, and their synchronization would make the Rockettes green with envy. Joe pulls even with the fourth and lets off the accelerator, ruining the timing of the lead car, which is swerving into the fast lane to bump the Pinto into the barrier. The patrol bounces hard off the barrier instead and steadies itself in the side panel of a Cadillac merging on from the city. Joe punches his foot down again to keep pace with the accelerating patrolmen, giving Christian a legally significant case of whiplash in the process.

A Saturn in Joe's lane is getting larger by the breath. A female voice, which proves to be pre-programmed into the sensor package, begins to whisper in their collective ears: "Car, fore, 100 meters…50 meters…10 meters…"

"I hear ya," Joe snaps, manhandling the car into the third lane. The driver in the newly promoted lead vehicle involuntarily takes his foot off the gas; he's seen plenty of the Pinto safety test footage and wants no part of being further evidence of a poor gas tank design.

Christian had seen most of the same footage, and figured they were dead, all dead, corpsicles, ashes to dust and such. He presses his eyelids together tighter than intended by design and holds his breath, awaiting a death which had just been narrowly averted. A long dozen seconds later, he opens his lids to see the same dirty, nasty, putrescent Los Angeles he's grown so fond of. Relief replaces his sense of mortality, moving quickly to undiluted anger. "What the hell are you doing?" he inquires.

Joe is staring intently at the road and does not respond. The only answer Christian's reasonable query receives is from the feminine tones of the sensor package. "Car, aft, 75 meters…70 meters…"

"OK, now that you've got their attention—contingency plans call for a road block at the Harbor Freeway, so be ready for it."

"No problem, Jack," Joe responds, using his natural intensity to mask how damn much fun he's having.

Chapter 7—Joe Bridgers

Most people realize not all experiments are successful; that is, they don't always turn out as expected. A few will even see that you often learn more from the failed experiments than the one's which support your hypothesis. The thing which is almost always forgotten is many experiments are not supposed to be successful at all.

The parents of Joe Bridgers forgot all three of these things when deciding how to raise their son. They decided to experiment: to throw out the teachings of Dr. Spock and his similarly conservative contemporaries and do things differently. In their infinite ego, they never doubted they'd do things better by following their distinct path. Not for a second did they consider this experiment might fail, meaning they might not end up with the son they wanted, the one they envisioned each night as they fell asleep in each other's arms. A few years later, when things were beginning to indicate that perhaps (just perhaps, mind you) they were doing their son a disservice with their progressive thinking and the chance of failure had to be faced at last, they didn't back away. They stayed the course, trying (if anything) even harder to realize their vision.

Their experiment was to try to raise a child without ever, ever saying no to him. They decided upon this course of action the first night they met, on a blind date in college. After a long dinner at the Sizzler's salad bar chocked full of chit-chat (including excruciating detail about the weather), Lola allowed Hank to walk her back to the dorm. Step by step they strode home, walking purposefully. Too purposefully for Hank's taste; he wanted to take a slow and leisurely stroll home, full of significant, deep conversation and long, lingering looks into each other's eyes. But alas, it's more like the Bataan Death March than a romantic stroll and having to sprint to keep up with one's date seems to be a sure sign of the impending end of a rather unsuccessful first date: no kiss, no cuddle, etc., etc.

This is, of course, disappointing.

After four furlongs in thirty-three and a fifth, Hank is winded and at least half pissed off. This date is over, he knows it's over, and he doesn't feel any need to sprint the rest of the way to her dorm. This sense of fatalism causes him to take the greatest of all dating chances: speaking honestly. He slows down to a stroll, so Lola gets a sudden lead on him; he speaks to her back with emphasis: "You know something, Lola? This is ridiculous. I'm not race walking with you anymore."

Lola stops in her tracks. She hadn't expected him to like getting rejected, but most boys took it like men and went home when asked. This was a little different, surprising. "Who says we're race walking?"

"I do." He stares at her meaningfully. "I want to talk to you; if you aren't interested, then you can go on home on your own."

She considers this for a long, long moment. Something about this honesty trick is appealing to her, slowly working its way past her defenses. "What do you want to talk about?"

"About life, about love, about you and me." OK, he's given up on honesty again, but it's a fairly sweet line all the same, don't you think? She doesn't respond, so he decides to continue. "Lola, I want to be different when I grow up."

"Aren't you grown up now?" she asks.

"No, I mean when I really grow up, get married, settle down."

"How do you mean, different?" She's opening her arms a little bit, stopping the closed and unapproachable posture she'd maintained all night.

"Well, different," he says, smiling outwardly but with an inner panic. He's really done it now, dragged the spotlight onto himself and given himself one small chance to make an impression. This is good, except he doesn't have any material prepared. Thus, he grabs the first thing that comes to mind. "For example, I want to raise my kids differently."

She smiles sweetly, a first for this evening. "Me, too." Lola begins to walk again, but slowly, with Hank instead of in front of him.

"I think there's just too much thought control in parenting; you've got to give your kids a chance to think for themselves, to experience the world first-hand." Hank is on a roll, and Lola is hanging on every word. He doesn't bother to think, he just rides the wave out, making it all up as he goes and yet giving the impression he's held these beliefs since birth. "Making your own mistakes is how you learn, after all. Every significant experience I've ever had has been the result of self-initiated, self-designed effort."

She nods enthusiastically.

And that was it. She kissed him good night with both lips, and they've been together ever since; well, until the divorce, anyhow. They got married in a small private ceremony at her parent's house in Oxnard and were soon expecting the baby who would grow up to be Joe.

At first, everything was fine. They never said no to the baby, but then again the concept of language was a little beyond him. The baby only wanted to eat and sleep, and they allowed him to do both whenever he chose. He continued to grow and seemed well rested, so it was reasonable to conclude so far, so good. Their smugness was overbearing, and forced friends and family away, usually only after the third or fourth chorus of, "we're raising our baby better than you're raising your baby," was sung.

Then Joe started to crawl.

Keeping him from crawling off the top of the stairs, from crawling into the poisonous cleaning supplies under the sink, and from crawling up his mother's skirts without reprimanding him or crushing his individuality proved to be a definite challenge. Somehow he survived the accidents, and did (eventually) learn what's dangerous and what's safe in this crazy world of ours, and there were signs that things were going quite well for him. Joe began to walk and talk earlier than normal kids, and was developing a vocabulary, which could serve a child twice his age; this also caused some problems, as the following exchange between a three-year-old Joe and his mother demonstrates:

"Fuck."

"Now Joe," his mother began patiently, "it's OK for you to say that, but some people find it offensive, so you might…"

"Fuck."

"Now, Joe, you know…"

"Fuck."

So, you can begin to see what sort of experience Lola and Hank were getting themselves into. For years they hid their doubts from each other, assuming their partner was still confident in their chosen path and not wanting to be the first to sound the alarm. Surely enough, they were raising a genius; this, they expected. To their shock, though, their genius was of the amoral variety. That realization proved to be too much for them, and they divorced before Joe made it to junior high.

So a word of warning to all you experimenters out there: for every step forward humanity takes by the efforts of bold visionaries, there are at least three steps back caused by the bumbling of dim-witted egotists. Please at least try to figure out which one you are before undertaking your experiment.

Chapter 8—Throwing a Book

It had been a bad day already.

The Sergeant unlucky enough to have the cubicle nearest to Captain Smith's office was digging frantically through a swamp of paper and binders large and dense enough to impress any bureaucrat. Under the Captain's constant and unfriendly glare, he'd given up any sort of rational search plan and grasped desperately for each book, manual and stack of free range paper at once, knocking everything over and finding nothing.

Disbelief could not begin to describe Captain Smith's feelings at this point. On top of the festering cesspool, on top of the malignant rubbage tit, on top of the fresh layer of mold, mildew and shit that was claiming to be His Day, His Life, His God-Damned Existence on this Jock Itch of a Planet, this incompetent Sergeant can't find something as basic to their lives and happiness as the Contingency Plans. First his wife didn't want to screw on the patio this morning, then the toast was burned, and his dog had vomited on the seat of his Mercedes, and the traffic had been a bitch, and Mark and Brian weren't funny on the radio (those ass-holes), and the coffee was thick enough to patch roofs with, and now the first decent robbery of the year and not a damned dickhead in this whole rat infested building could find the simple little Contingency

Plans. According to his doctor, he should imagine his happy place right now, since high blood pressure is nothing to mess around with.

Fuck that.

"Well?" he asks the Sergeant impatiently and hopelessly. Obviously the peon can't find the Plan, if he found the Plan he'd jump up ecstatically and take it up to him, eager to please. But, Captain Smith asked anyhow in hopes of completing the humiliation he's raining down on his subordinate.

The Sergeant takes a deep breath and rises, resignedly, for a full shoulder shrug and the Captain's wrath. "You lost the Contingency Plan?" the Captain asks in a level voice, quite unfairly. Of course the Sergeant didn't lose the Plan, he'd never even heard of the damned thing until today, didn't realize there were set plans on what to do when there is a major crime in any sector of the city. This information is nice to know, but it doesn't help him out right now since one rarely answered "No" to one of the Captain's questions, especially when he's livid. The Sergeant nods, his eyes down at the orgasm of papers surrounding him and soaking into his shoes.

The Captain throws a book at him. Not ***the*** book, mind you, just any old heavy bindage of paper handy. Incompetence upsets his stomach horrendously, and his Maalox was an infinity of steps away in his briefcase. He picks up the microphone he'd wrenched from the dispatcher's grasp when he'd walked into the room. "Adam 13?" he asks, but doesn't wait for an answer. "There is no plan. Set up the roadblock wherever the fuck you are right now."

The patrolman in the field acknowledges receipt of this order, but Captain Smith doesn't hear. His anger has filled his head and is allowing nothing through. In disgust, he heaves the microphone at the hapless Sergeant and storms from the room.

Chapter 9—One of These Days—Pink Floyd

Meanwhile, back on the freeway, Christian rises up far enough to peer over the rear seat. "They're still there!" he observes out loud.

"What a stupid thing to say," Joe hisses. "Of course they're still there!"

This hits Christian squarely in the groin. He hadn't yet considered that Joe might really be winging this whole party and had no solid concept of how to get them the hell away from the gentlemen with registered weapons. He takes it upon himself to offer a few words of advice and encouragement. "Well, lose 'em!"

"What the hell!" Joe glances at Christian to make sure he doesn't look as crazy as he's acting and talking. "How! Oil slicks? Cloaking device?" He stares at the road and swings into the fast lane to pass a semi.

"Shut up!" He adds. And then he continues, "You really are even dumber than when I used to know ya, and Chris…"

"OK, miss the road block; take the Grand Avenue Exit."

Joe realizes they are in the process of passing the Grand Avenue Exit at this point, and makes a mental note to adjust the timing of this particular tape. Christian notices they are immediately next to the tractor of this tractor-trailer combination and hopes the exit on the far side of this obstacle isn't the Grand Avenue Exit, though he's been riding long enough with Joe now to know better. Joe urges the car faster and whips the wheel right an instant before his indicator light tells him it's clear. Since his sensors are a rather robust combination of electronic do-hickeys they let him know he shouldn't have done this with a crescendo of buzzers, bells and whistles, including Christian's contralto scream of alarm and fear. Once past the truck Joe has to slow slightly to avoid a Jeep Cherokee, then nudge the gas a little to clear the other imports barreling down on him in the slow lanes. He hits the lead collision-absorbing barrel at an angle, spraying water over traffic on the freeway and the street below. The car is now yawing badly, the outer wheels threatening to catch and flip them at the next instant. Christian's mind is screaming, "Turn into the direction of the skid;" Joe hears the synthesized voice from "One of These Days" by Floyd: "One of these days, I'm going to cut you to little pieces..."

And the guitars flare in Joe's consciousness, deafening and thrilling. The ass-end of the car fishtails back into line and they're flying 70 miles per hour down the shoulder of the off ramp. Joe gets all over the brakes, using his left foot for leverage. They merge onto Grand Avenue and squeal to a stop in the middle lane of traffic in the same motion.

"Sorry, I forgot, were you still in the fast lane? Oh well..."

"Way to go, Joe." Christian is shaking stoically, and fighting to retain bladder control.

"I lost the bastards, didn't I?"

True enough. Their smoking Pinto and a bunch of locals are waiting for the light to change, but not a single police officer. They can't even hear the sirens anymore; it's as if the sun is shining and more or less all is right with the world. The facts don't make Christian feel much better; not only is Joe right but Christian is traumatized ever after about taking freeway off ramps.

"OK, you should be at the stop light. Take a breath, then a left, then a right. You need to average about thirty to stay on schedule."

Joe moves over the two lanes effortlessly; the other drivers had seen his arrival and wanted no part of that action. They all gesture Joe onward with fear and a certain patient awe. Unimpeded, he accelerates smoothly to the prerequisite speed. Unfortunately, the light in front of them is red, about a dozen cars waiting their turns. "Car, fore, 40 meters…" the woman says.

"Uh, Joe…" Christian adds.

"I said to go 30, man," Joe answers while merging onto the sidewalk between an in-line skater and a couple walking arm in arm, who should probably have a room of their own anyhow. The pedestrians in harm's way scatter like popcorn kernels, giving Joe plenty of room to maneuver.

"OK, take the next right…"

"That's one way; wrong way!" Christian points out.

"So?"

"So if you turn you'll get a Porsche shoved up your nose and out your…"

Joe turns. The Pinto suddenly finds itself swimming upstream. The drivers of the defensive vehicles prove much bolder than the previous obstacles, probably having something to do with iron, insurance and air bags. Joe is forced to make his own way, utilizing every lane and scrapping every fender on his Pinto. In his wake, cars are turned to every compass heading, and no one makes it out of town early this Friday afternoon.

Talk about your modern tragedies.

"OK, right again, and you'll see the freeway."

"I'd love to live that long," Christian whimpers, hugging his knees to his chest.

"Shut up!" Joe repeats emotionally but without much hope. Still, it had to be said.

Chapter 10—I Love L. A.

The four Highway Patrol cars have blocked all four lanes of the 10, after several miles of slowing down traffic and avoiding the impatient. Luckily, the officers drive as if they're in rentals, so the process went rather smoothly from their point of view. The driver of the car in the fast lane, the Sergeant in charge, picks up his radio. "The road block is established just before the 5 and 60 diverge, sir," he reports.

"Good, get ready," Captain Smith's voice growls back. "They'll be there pretty damn quick."

With a quick nod, the driver signals all his fellow officers to get out and get ready. They jump up and out as if their cars are fashioned with ejection seats. Each officer takes energy and a sense of urgency from the others, creating a dangerous, panicked situation more than responding to one. Everything calls for action, and it calls for action now. They check their side arms; an odd combination of nickel plated service revolvers and blued Berettas with 15 round clips sliding home with satisfying clicks. Trunks are unlocked and the heavier weaponry readied, shotguns, and rifles from small bore through those more closely related to artillery pieces. Body armor is found and Velcroed into place around barrel chests and pot bellies alike, tight enough to restrict breathing. The rookies and other youngsters look to the veterans for clues on how to act, and are disappointed to see them looking vainly to each other.

Each hides his fear and excitement behind a rigid mask, their faces near a collective breaking point. All the cops sneak glances at the Sergeant, begging guidance, awaiting orders.

Blinded by their own thoughts, none of LA's finest notes the crowd gathering from the parking lot worth of vehicles they've stalled behind them. A veritable melting pot is dumping people out of their drivers' seats and onto the pavement. Every race, color, class, gender, preference, hairstyle and build is represented. They share only two things in common. First, they are Los Angelinos, participating in the daily experiment in cultural diversity, human interaction, and social climbing that is the Southern California Freeway System. All are welcome, and you're only judged by your willingness to exceed the posted speed limits and the cleverness of your vanity plates and bumper stickers. Second, they all are wearing gourmet athletic shoes. Even in uniformity there's diversity, as evidenced by the fact that all major brands are represented.

"Hey!" a tall Hispanic man in a suit and Reebok cross-trainers calls. "What the fuck's going on?"

The police snap their heads in his direction and immediately, collectively suspect they may have a problem. Their chiseled expressions don't change, though. The harshness of their demeanors fulfills the twin tasks of intimidating the public and steadying their own nerves.

"Yeah, you assholes, get outta the way!" a white '60's holdover in tie dye and Converse high tops adds.

The officers are torn between action and inaction, wondering if they've been sufficiently provoked to respond with force or threats. In indecision, they turn to their leader for guidance. The Sergeant sees the battle lines are being drawn with him in the middle, an aggressive human amoebae on his right, his nervous, critical and ambitious men on his left, all looking to him for decisions he hasn't been trained to make, for action he's never even imagined. His mind is suddenly flooded with images from John Wayne movies. John always rose to every challenge, in situations much stickier than this one. And James

Bond, escaping from certain death to derail the evil asshole's dastardly plan and then ball like a wild collie with the beautiful babe he'd saved from certain death three times in recent hours. Bond, Wayne, these are the bastards who set the impossible standards he'll be expected to live up to here and now; what a crock. This is the worst example of people not being able to differentiate between drama and reality. He feels a mass of eyes focused upon him and knows it's time to do something, perhaps even anything. Maybe that's the key; any decision is better than none at all. He turns to the slightly less hostile mob, his men: "Everyone get down behind your cars, they're coming."

"Damn right we're coming!" a young black woman in LA Gears shouts. The Aryan looking bloke next to her unconsciously flexes his prize wining biceps and adds, "God damn it, my hairdresser's waiting."

He wears Nike Air Pegasus.

The Reeboks guy steps a few feet in front of the throng. Some have greatness thrust upon them, and some step up and demand it. "Why are you hiding back there?" he inquires. Gesturing beyond the 50 or so people now following him, he continues, "Whomever you're waiting for will be slamming into these miles of cars you've stopped!"

This is a good point. The Sergeant gazes over the hood of his unit, parked at an unnatural angle on the freeway, and sees sheet metal and radio antennas to the horizon. One of life's unpleasant sensations creeps from his hairline down his face, his skin melting and running like slow burning paraffin. His nervous system is trying to tell him something: he may have made a mistake, and even worse, he may be the last person to realize it. He's an actor who's forgotten his lines, on stage with no place to hide. So like that actor, he decides to try his lone remaining option: improvise. "Now look," he starts with a steady voice.

The reviews are poor.

The LA Gear woman chimes in first. "This is as pointless as fucking your husband!"

"Just move your shit and go flashing somewhere else!" a swarthy gentleman in a gold lamé tracksuit and Keds shouts.

"Move all your asses!" the Converse high-tops bites off, tugging at his beard.

"Who the fuck..." begins Mr. Reebok, overcome with anger and unable to find further words to express himself.

The Sergeant stands up. "Look!" he calls, anger shorting out the buffering function in his mind and allowing his thoughts immediate access to his mouth. He uses his sternest command tones and bellows at the crowd, "Get back to your cars. Now!"

No one moves. It's as if their shoes are planted in the boggy Southern California asphalt. A light breeze blows across the freeway, cleaning the air ever so briefly, long enough for a quarter lungful. The Sergeant, feeling momentum is finally with him, or at least not against him, searches for the words that will bring this situation home.

Unfortunately, they're not there.

Nowhere is a word, phrase or guttural growl that'll help. With fumbling hands he unbuttons his holster and in a smooth arc raises his revolver to the sky and squeezes a warning shot straight into the smog.

The sudden clatter of mechanical clutter, magazines being slammed home, chambers cleared, rounds being encouraged into barrels, drowns out the reverberations of the warning shot. The Sergeant looks at the rabble he expected to scatter and sees instead every form of weaponry imaginable leveled at his head. Pistols, shotguns, knives, mace, pepper spray, automatic rifles and grenade launchers, they're all at the ready, held by people whose expressions indicate they mean business.

Chapter 11—Blue Suede Shoes—Vanna White

"OK, things should be pretty damned cake by now, no cops, light traffic."

"Yeah, I hear ya." Joe is annoyed. His unparalleled success thus far is making him feel pretty darned pleased with himself, but his own offensive voice on this tape won't let him enjoy the moment. Deep sigh, undeniable longing. Yet again he's reminded that the price he's paid in this life for being that rare and dangerous combination of genius and perfectionist is incalculable, and worse, normal people just don't understand. Lord knows he knows, he's tried on several occasions to explain it to several Normals, and without fail they miss the point of his precisely chosen words and they never laugh at his jokes. So-called intellectuals are no more sympathetic; invariably their petty jealousies and well-founded insecurities blind them to his needs. Therefore, Joe has turned to very unintelligent women and the criminally insane for companionship. Or, preferably, very unintelligent criminally insane women.

"But keep your guard up, dude."

"Yeah, guard up, no shit."

"No rest for the weary."

"God, I'm stupid sometimes."

Joe's discomfort grows with each tape-recorded syllable. ***"Keep it around 60, avoid attention. You can pick it up again on the other side of Covina."*** Steam is filtering through his shirt and his stringy hair. ***"So prop those eyelids tight but relax those reflexes so…"***

He ejects the tape and chucks it into the back seat, hoping it'll melt back there. He grabs another from a haphazard pile behind the passenger seat and inserts it into the deck without glancing at the label. The speakers produce a familiar warbling sound, but a well placed thump and the guts of the player sync up with the tape and a clear reproduction blasts through the small car. It's a little known recording of Vanna White singing "Blue Suede Shoes." Joe's mood immediately rushes back to the manic; he's always had a weak spot in his heart for really unusual music. He sings along with gusto and disregard. "You can do what you want, but lay off of them blue suede shoes," he croons, badly.

Singing is one area where Joe has no delusions. He's bad, he knows he's bad, and he sings anyhow. It has never failed to annoy a traveling companion, and the fact that Christian hasn't said a word of protest, even just after the first line, is a strong indication that something's Wrong. Joe looks in the passenger direction for the first time in miles, and sees his partner in crime curled up in a fetal position in the passenger seat, his head wedged between the seat and door, his arms hugging his knees close to his skinny chest. His eyes are vacant, his skin clammy and cool; the only indication that he's not stone dead is the incessant quivering of his upper lip, moving fast and furious enough to endanger his ability to breath through his nose. In the plus column, his mouth hangs open, so at least he won't suffer asphyxiation.

Joe immediately is worried, wondering if this life on the run is going to be a little too much for his buddy. Immediately another emotion strikes: shock. He's surprised he feels the least concern about this undeniably annoying person in the seat next to him. Could it be, Joe wonders, that he actually likes Christian? Chris, he means. Chris, can he actually like Chris?

It seems unlikely.

It's far more likely, his thoughts go, that he's just become accustomed to his presence over the years, and this sense of familiarity can often be mistaken for friendship. And, of course, Joe's life is a little on the solitary side, not lonely (of course), but still one does like company, some basic human interaction from time to time. That's got to be it. Certainly is easier to accept than admitting friendship for the geek. In any case, better find out what's going on; he's pretty shitty company in this state.

"Chris?" he asks, and is displeased at the half-heartedness of his voice. He clears his throat and tries again. "Chris? What is it? Sensory overload?" Joe reaches across the car and touches Christian's shoulder, meaning to be reassuring. Christian screams like an Amazon with PMS, causing Joe to immediately recoil. This excess of life force thus spent, Christian returns to lifeless, fetal, uninteresting behavior as Joe maneuvers the car through the long, 50-mph left hand turn ridiculously placed on the Santa Monica Freeway. It's a smooth, unthreatening corner no real driver would dream of slowing down for, and yet there it is, a warning sign with 50 mph in small print underneath. Just dumb dumb dumb. Joe is disgusted, as he always is on this stretch of road. He turns back to Christian. "Look, Chris, it'll be OK as soon as…"

Christian screams again, punctuating the impressively loud sound by pointing straight ahead. Joe follows this particular direction and sees traffic at a complete stand still, all lanes, as far off into the distance as he can see. Immediately both feet go for the brakes, pushing the pedal to the floor. The seat supports none of Joe's weight, his body is a 45-degree angle wedged between the roof and the brake pedal. Christian screams a few more times, pointing, clutching the seat belt around him and hanging on. The Pontiac in their lane is still growing larger by the scream, taking up their entire windshield. The Pinto veers a little left towards the crash wall then rights itself with a staccato little hop back in line. The Nissan behind them has eased off the gas and smiles, anticipating a crash he's not going to have to pay for in cash or pain. Joe and Christian can read the serial number imprinted on the approaching rear bumper, their steed practically kneeling on its front axle when, exhausted, it stops.

There's a quiet moment in Los Angeles, or at least it seems that way to Christian. The Pinto balances on all four tires again, Joe's ass makes contact with the seat again, a solid quarter of an inch separates their bumper from the Pontiac. Its driver is relieved, the driver of the Nissan curses violently in disappointment. The female sensor's voice says, "Car, fore, zero meters" and Joe beats the shit out of it, both fists, his teeth grinding into each other relentlessly. The anger proves cathartic and Joe recovers to his preferred personality almost instantly, his trademark arrogant sneer again on his face. This is too much for Christian, who pounds both his fists into Joe's right shoulder, making occasional contact with his face and ribs.

"Hey! You son of a…stop!" Joe shouts, covering his head with his arms in self-defense. "God, kill me later, right now we gotta think!"

"Think!" Christian hits Joe once more for good measure, square on the shoulder. "You've never in your life, never ever even entertained a thought! Never! You almost killed me, right here and now, almost killed me dead!"

Joe wishes Christian would go back to comatose. "You through?"

"No! Not even…"

"You're through, because we're soon gonna have some very friendly cops sniffing our butts if…"

"Then move! Get over and take the 60! Just don't…"

Joe smiles. "But isn't that just what they'd expect me to do?"

"If they're smart they'd put money on you being dead before dinner!"

Joe ignores the threat, cheering up at the same time. "Yeah. Yeah! They don't think I have the balls to wait it out!"

Christian is steaming. "I don't think you have the balls to wait it out!"

"The hell I don't!"

Christian's expression changes for the worse. "I don't think I have the stomach to wait it out…"

Joe's expression drops as well. "The hell you don't!"

CHAPTER 12—GRIDLOCK

At the source of the traffic obstruction, the Sergeant is learning his life lesson for the day: Making bold, on the spot decisions gets easier the more you make. For instance, he found it quite challenging to decide how to handle the angry crowd. However, once they pulled the guns on him, he found it very easy to decide on a course of action for him and his men: they immediately got back inside their cruisers, where the bullet-proof glass can protect them.

Unfortunately, there are some negative consequences of this action. First off, it ended any dialog that was going to resolve the situation amicably. What exactly that dialog might have been he can't fathom, but it certainly didn't take place. Secondly, a few of his men, the most militant in an admittedly macho profession, looked at him with searing hatred for causing them to act like wimps. He tried to pass on understanding, compassionate yet stern glances towards them, letting them know he feels for them and all but he's still God damn in control so don't try to cross him. Finally, it rather gives the crowd the run of the situation, an unfortunate (but inevitable) by-product.

There are life lessons for each of us each and every day, by the way. Most people miss them; I've missed a vast majority of mine over the years, but am resolvedly convinced there was one out there for me every single midnight to midnight. The fault lies with me, not with nature, a statement I'm certain anyone who's met me will back up with conviction. I believe my lesson back on the day I'm writing about was I should not expect to slip into people's minds at will without occasionally finding myself stuck within their friendly confines for longer than planned. That's what happened, all right; I slipped into Christian's mind and didn't manage to fully extract myself until…

Well, not yet, actually.

Anyhow…

The vigilantes are certainly making the most of the free rein the Sergeant has given them. Organizing quickly they formed eight person teams, one assigned to each car. Initially, they were satisfied to bounce up and down on the vehicles, ruining the springs, maybe do a little key striping or denting, minor vandalism at best. This phase just didn't last, though. Someone, it's difficult to say who, came up with the idea of pushing the cars off the pavement, thereby allowing traffic to continue as normal. The majority quickly agreed this to and they went about their work with gusto. A welder in Pumas was enlisted to cut a decent sized hole in the guardrail, and each team pushed out their cars, one by one. Each occurrence of an automobile skittering down the embankment brought a louder cheer from the masses, and a louder plea for help from the Sergeant.

"I need back up, God damn it! Where the hell are you people?" he screams when his and another are the only cars left standing. He doesn't have a lot of room to work with, being in a car and all, but his body is convinced it's standing and pacing around like an expectant father. His limbs flail at unexpected moments, every muscle taunt and ready for action, should action be required. His partner warily keeps his arms up, protecting his head from the Sergeant's flying elbows and his balls from the kicking legs.

"We're coming, just hang in there," the radio answers, the distant end having picked up the urgency of the situation in his voice.

"Well, were are you? What's your ETA?"

"Uh, hold one," comes the response. The car next to theirs is being ceremoniously escorted off the road. "We're at the 10 and the Harbor, and…"

The Sergeant hits his head on the roof and his shoulder on the driver's window. "And what?"

"And we're stuck in traffic. Looks like pretty bad gridlock, I'd say…"

Several well dressed, tennis shoed members of the city walk towards the Sergeant's car, smiling.

Chapter 13—Polysyllabic

Christian's head hangs out the window, his chin hooked over the ledge of the door like the crook of an umbrella over a ledge, awaiting rain.

"Oh hell, you didn't..." Joe wails, disgusted by the contents of Christian's stomach, concerned what they're doing to the sensors on that side of the car.

"Sorry about the paint there," Christian says, shaking his head from side to side in an attempt to dislodge anything still connected to his chin or lips.

Joe stares at the ceiling of his car. This being a Pinto, it's only a few inches away from his upturned face, but he concentrates on it all the same. "You know, Chris, you really haven't changed an inch, have you?" He waits for contradictions, and gets none. "You're still the same baby boy, cowering in shadows, puking out car windows."

Christian pulls his head back in the car, and wipes his mouth on his sleeve. "I've never puked out a car window before."

"I was speaking symbolically."

"Bullshit!" Christian is at least as surprised to hear this outburst as Joe is. "You were speaking assholically! You've grown up from an obnoxious bully to an egotistical asshole!"

Joe smiles. "A fact of which I am quite proud."

"Now you're just robbing banks instead of stealing milk money!"

"A fine example of personal growth."

Somehow, this conversation just isn't going as Christian had intended. Joe, instead of feeling remorse and learning from Christian's wisdom, is grinning like the Cheshire Cat who ate the Cheshire Canary. Now, to the old Christian, that would've been reason to stop this idea entirely and try something different, but not now. He reminds himself that the new Christian doesn't back down from challenges. He breathes heavily, forcing oxygen into his brain. Certainly a single verbal victory won't change much, but it'll change something. Christian continues on, undaunted. "You are the most obvious waste of sperm ever to crawl across this planet!"

Joe grins even more. He's always enjoyed the challenge of the Put Down Contest, and is confident of his chances for success. "Characteristic of my commitment to excellence."

"Characteristic of your need to be committed!" Christian retorts, only vaguely concerned that he isn't making too much sense. Joe just smiles, being of the opinion he can maintain a sufficient level of annoyance without having to say a word.

He's right, of course.

"I hate you!" Christian screams at the top of his lungs. "Pure, fine uncut hate!"

"Hey, don't hold anything back, Chris, I can..."

"Christian!" His voice cracks with the intensity of emotion he's gathered and packed into this one word.

"No, born again Moonie." Joe has an expectant grin on his face, waiting for Christian to get his little joke.

He waits for a moment longer, the grin fading away. The car is silent, and Joe assumes Christian didn't hear him.

"My name," Christian says evenly, "is Christian. Traffic's moving."

They inch forward with the general flow of steel and rubber along the choked freeway. Christian stares straight at the car in front of them, reminding himself to take deep breaths. Joe glances around, trying to figure out how to get past this stupid little problem the two of them have so he will never, ever have to deal with it ever again. When he speaks, he speaks as gently as he can manage. "Look, I just can't deal with polysyllabic names. Ya got a middle name?"

Christian doesn't look over. "Bradley."

"Brad?"

"No, Bradley."

Joe stops himself from saying anything further for a few minutes. He's starting to realize why he usually doesn't give a shit about what he says to people; this self-censorship is exhausting. He wonders why he cares in the least what Christian thinks of him. Was there some occurrence in their collective past that makes him seek Christian's approval? None that he can recall, but he knows his mind doesn't always remember everything it should. He looks out his window at the graffiti stained retaining wall keeping their stream of automotive hardware from flowing over into on coming traffic and exhales slowly.

"Oh boy. How about C. B.?"

Christian turns slowly towards Joe. "Christian."

"No, born again Moonie." Joe becomes convinced that Christian had actually heard him the first time, because he doesn't laugh with even greater intensity this time around. Joe stops looking over and stares at the traffic ahead, every car picking up the pace and starting to resemble people actually getting to their destinations. Christian looks out his own window, tired of this situation and unclear how he'll ever again be free of it. Just after they pass, two uniformed police officers venture out of their vehicles and stand at the side on the shoulder. The first is the Sergeant, trying to figure out a good way to spin this situation when presenting it to Captain Smith. The other is a rookie, his eyes wild with adrenaline and excitement. "Gol, Vern!" he squeals with delight, "This is a lot more orgasmic than workin' in Modesto!"

The Sergeant doesn't attempt a reply.

CHAPTER 14—SUFFERING WITH FOOLS

"…so, Sir," the Sergeant's voice crackles over the radio, "We didn't stop soggy shit. I've no idea if they came this way, and I need a fucking vacation. Over."

He doesn't need this sort of abuse, he really doesn't, Captain Smith reminds himself. Hasn't he suffered enough in this life, working with morons morning, noon and night? And, he hasn't even killed any of them, though they all deserved it, each and every one of them. His sort of self-control should be reason for celebration and reward; perhaps they could name a trophy after him, the Captain Smith Suffering of Fools Cup. He remembers what he learned at his last stress management class: when you feel this way, like your head is going to explode and you are going to empty your service revolver into the next torso that presents itself attached to an airhead with low pressure, take a deep breath, count to ten and look at the situation with a fresh perspective.

Inhale. Exhale.

One….Two…Thr…

Fuck that.

"Sergeant!" he bellows at his assistant, who is too afraid to move.

"Yes?" his shaky voice ambles back across the room. A paperweight from a recent charity fund-raiser crashes into the wall behind the

Sergeant's head shortly after leaving the Captain's trained hand. "Yes, sir?" he corrects himself.

"Do you think you can find a phone?"

"Yes, sir!"

Captain Smith sits down and opens a fresh pack of Marlboros. "Then get me the National Guard on the line."

Chapter 15—Insults

The restaurant is exclusive and expensive enough you can accurately estimate the price of the Lobster Tails just by feeling the heft of the atmosphere when you walk through the door. The clientele all have expensive suits/dresses, long necks and legs and broad shoulders. There should be advertisers with camera crews waiting for them when they step out of the restaurant to climb into their Lexus or Infinity or Mercedes for the elegant cruise home. The waiters all have short jackets and immaculate hair cuts, and have never, ever spilled a drop of wine or said, "Would you like fries with that?" The lights are low and the romance is high, particularly at the table for two next to the aquarium where Christian and Marilyn sit. The music is campy yet complex, a simple melody backed by a warbling staccato bass line which is hard to resist or forget. The lyrics are of the boy-meet-girl variety, sweet yet sticky.

Christian. Marilyn. They are saying very little, with words anyhow. But their eyes are speaking expansively, staring deep into each other in a nearly obscene way. Their meals are decimated on their plates, the gargantuan bill has been carted off, and the Perrier is almost gone. Christian reaches across the table and takes both of her hands in his, firmly yet tenderly. The music swells, a gritty baritone backed ably by a driving bass and a screaming guitar·: "I hold… your hand. I whisper…"

The singer and Christian shout together, "I love you!" Christian gets up from the table, knocks his chair halfway across the floor and starts to dance like a marionette out of control. His feet are on a hot plate, each jumping back into the air as soon as it touches the ground. Marilyn stares at him with admiration and unbridled lust; the other patrons appear not to notice.

The song, by the way, is called "Gimme Some Gimme," by High and Outside, an L. A. bar band that never quite made it. What a heartless shame.

Anyhow, suddenly Christian and Marilyn are transported to her apartment. Their shoes are off, and a nearly empty 2-liter bottle of Sprite and two wine glasses sit ignored on the coffee table. Christian is leaning over to Marilyn and kissing her passionately, their lips inseparable, their tongues intertwined. The music continues, the notes played furiously and the tune carried on mercilessly, the two on the couch getting carried away in their passion. The singer gets to the chorus, screaming, "Gimme some Gimme!" Christian disengages from Marilyn's embrace and again does his awkward yet earnest dance around the elegant living room, his feet light on the champagne white shag carpet...

"Yo, cool! Tower Records!" Joe exclaims, startling Christian from his dreamy sleep.

One of the problems with modern society is that fantasizing is no longer a sweet, simplistic pastime. Instead, it's become linked to the genre most often seen, the music video. It's difficult to keep the mood consistent, what with all the interruptions of choruses and bridges, and all the wacky camera angles and visual effects. And it's bloody difficult to consummate the experience; the images are all the heavy tease of writhing bodies and fresh skin with absolutely no climax allowed. Christian looks completely disoriented, taking nearly a minute to realize he's still in Joe's car, on the 10, headed east, and that his imagined activities with Marilyn were, alas, imagined. He looks over towards Joe with apprehension. “Hey, Chris, welcome back,” Joe says with a smile. “Where ya been?”

“Christian,” he mutters under his breath.

Joe glances very deliberately at Christian’s lap. “I hope that’s not for me.”

It’s at this point that Christian realizes that the uncomfortable feeling he’s experiencing is due to his erect penis stressing the material of both his boxer shorts and Armani slacks. He quickly crosses his legs, turns red, and tries to think unpleasant thoughts.

“Aw, c’mon, Chris, who was she?” Joe persists. “Anyone I know?”

“No.”

“I bet it was! Who? Christie Brinkley? Kathleen Turner? You know, she’s got the greatest eyes… huge, blue. I bet she wears Paul Newman’s contacts.”

“Just give it a rest, OK?” Christian asks, even though he knows the approximate odds of that happening.

“No no no! How about Katherine Hepburn? A bit of a long shot, I’ll admit, but she’s got those mannerisms that tell ya she’d be all business when it counted.”

“Stop it! Stop it!” Christian continues his and Joe’s only method of interaction: annoying the other into explosive contempt. “I don’t share your pathetically childish view of sexuality! I didn’t back in your ***Playboy***’s in 7-11 days, and I don’t now, so shut up!”

“Pathetic?” Joe asks, with emphasis. “Childish? My friend, those are words of a man who hasn’t had any since Truman screwed Korea!”

“Wait, is that an insult?” Christian launches into a prepared speech, which he’s used before. “Are you suggesting that I’m just not the man that you are if I don’t father as many bastard children? God, there’s more to life than sex!”

Joe nods his head. “Yeah, I know, but I try not to dwell on it.”

“Don’t you use your mind for anything?” Christian demands.

"Oh, is that supposed to be an insult?" Joe responds mockingly. "Are you claiming that since your cerebrum is more wrinkled than mine I'm a lower life form, is that it?"

"Yes, yes! I sure as hell am!" Christian's heart is beating like a rabbit on speed. He can feel his pulse in his ears and the heat off his flushed face is steaming up his glasses.

"I wish you'd watch your language, Chris," Joe says sternly.

"Really?" Christian responds abashedly.

"And, I'll have you know, I use my mind. I'm presently working on a philosophical treatise of great import!"

Christian wrinkles his nose. "Sure you are."

"I am!" Joe insists.

"Joe, you couldn't make me believe you."

"Look, you haven't seen me in how long? How many years?" Joe turns perhaps a little too much of his attention away from driving his car and stares at Christian for long stretches of his argument. "Well, things have changed with me, man. I happen to do very important papers on metaphysics, when I'm not teaching at USC."

"USC?"

"Yes! In the Philosophy Department."

Christian is falling behind in this conversation. There's one piece of information that just isn't getting through. "The University of…"

"Southern California! Yes!" Joe's eyes are shining. His joy in sharing this side of himself is obvious, even to Christian.

"So you're really…"

"Dr. Bridgers, yes! Graduated Cum Laude from Harvard, where I learned from the great Immanuel Kant! You've heard of him, haven't you?"

"Yeah…he's at Harvard?"

"Yeah!" Joe is really starting to enjoy this, in a foul and rather twisted way. "And that paper I'm telling you about? Well, it's a sensitive synthesis of the ideas of two great thinkers, Sigmund Freud and René

Descartes." Joe forgets about the road entirely and stares at Christian for the big moment: "I call it, 'I fuck, therefore I am.'"

Joe starts to laugh, like a river breaking free of its banks and flooding all of creation. Nothing has ever brought him greater joy than going fishing, hooking the guppy on some smelly bait and playing him for all he's worth. Christian looks away, annoyed, angry, and embarrassed. He never thought he'd have to remind himself of this again, but obviously he does: never believe a goddamned word Joe says. Ever.

"'I fuck, therefore I am,'" Joe repeats, giggling. "I love that one."

"Shut up," Christian mutters to himself.

"That story works on girls too, by the way."

"Shut up," he repeats, a little louder.

"I had you going there, didn't I?" Joe suddenly looks like a normal person, vulnerable, wanting approval and vindication. Christian can't stand to look at him so doesn't. "For just a minute, didn't I?"

"No."

"Oh come ***on***. Be man enough to admit it."

"No!"

"OK, fine." They are passing over the hill that leads into the valley consisting of Pomona, Azusa, and more airborne particulates than is healthy for any animal, from biped upright mammals to Bantas from the Ice Planet Hoth. Forest Lawn Mortuary, the Disneyland of Burial Plots, ambles by in all its greenery on their right. Joe turns back to Christian, the thrill and need gone from his face. "If I were a philosophy professor at USC, why would I rob a bank in Santa Monica with an AK-47?" Christian doesn't respond verbally, but his face does darken up a hue. "You claim to be a man of the mind, Chris, so use it! I've used mine to plan this quite successful operation, thank you very much, and I've had spare neurons to pull your leg with!"

"You didn't fool me." He still can't look at Joe when he says it, though.

"Yeah, OK, fine. But, if you're going to keep on this trail with me, ya better start employing a little logic or cognition or something, OK? OK."

Christian stares at Joe without much affection. "Fine."

Joe shakes his head. "Not using your mind or body; how fucking sad." They cruise past the 57 interchange, choosing not to visit Orange County or other points of interest further south.

CHAPTER 16—AN EXCLUSIVE

The following was spotted while channel surfing, the details having been filled in a posteriori.

The camera starts running, but Doug can't see a damn thing. It's dark, too dark; his mind rapidly surmises that something's wrong. It takes another few seconds to work out that the lens cap is probably still on his video camera. He removes the cap and continues on with his job.

Lynn James appears in his viewfinder. Doug notes her lovely breasts are centered between the crosshairs, picture perfect and camera ready. She is holding a microphone and a full ration of ego-induced hostility. She is speaking into her microphone (under its subtle lavender windscreen) in a singsong of a voice. "Hello? Hello-oh, teasing 1-2-5, hello? We rolling, Doug?"

That's what the little red light means, dear, he thinks to himself. But it's a bad idea to say that sort of thing to the talent; he's been around long enough to figure that out anyhow. "Yeah, let's get it."

"OK, on three," Lynn commands, tossing her head like a proud tigress. She inhales deeply, and doesn't allow her body the luxury of coughing the smog back out. As a tough, cynical yet incredibly beautiful journalist, she doesn't let the outside world influence her behavior. "Is my hair OK?"

"Yeah, fine, beautiful, salon fresh."

"Yeah, thanx," she replies, believing him. If there's one thing Lynn knows, it's hair maintenance. Lynn turns to the bank teller she's ferreted out for this interview and completely fails to find her. A moment of panic strikes; did one of these other crews swipe my exclusive with the actual teller who'd handed over the cash? "Where'd she go now?" she asks Doug with concern lacing her words; Doug points reassuringly toward the front of the bank. Lynn sees the teller sitting on the steps leading to the front entrance. Somehow, this woman doesn't seem quite...right. Lynn's keen instincts had picked up on that right away. But then again, she has just been through a vaguely violent robbery, so it's not too surprising she isn't at her best. Lynn could tell you some stories about people not at their best; that's when she and her camera crews meet people, when they are having a rough go of it.

It's part of the job. Or, maybe, it is the job, Lynn isn't immediately sure.

She walks a couple paces from her carefully selected and staked out Interview Spot (which emphasizes the bank's confident facade), glancing back territorially from time to time. "Excuse me, Miss Green? Could I? Could you..." and Marilyn Green rises and walks over to the Interview Spot. "Oh, thank you," Lynn continues to coo in an overly reassuring manner. "Oh yes, right here, this won't take a second..."

Lynn makes sure Marilyn is in the right place, and then goes through her interview checklist: spine straight, eyes glimmering, hair carefully tousled, shoulders back, damn microphone not obscuring her face. She closes her eyes. "On three, Doug...deep breath, positive visualization, good vibrations, and one two three..." She snaps her eyes open and focuses directly into the camera. "Good evening, I'm Lynn James at the scene of today's robbery in Santa Monica. With me is Ms. Marilyn Green, the teller who dealt directly with the robber. Ms. Green, what can you tell us about this man?"

Marilyn considers this carefully and a bit too long for Lynn's taste; she'd gonna have to edit this tape when she gets back to the station, and there isn't that much time before the evening news. These damn interviewees always make her life a living hell. Finally, seemingly just before they run out of tape, she answers with a hint of surprise in her voice, as if she just heard the question. "Oh, the police asked me not to give out details but... well, they were both white Caucasians between the ages of 18 and 47, and under 8 feet tall."

Lynn does a double take, and quickly checks her notes. "Wait, you said 'they.' There were two thieves?"

"Yes." Lynn stares at her expectantly, so Marilyn continues, "It seems the original reports of the robbery weren't exaggerated enough."

Lynn does not appreciate this sort of surprise during an interview. As a matter of fact, she is quite upset with Ms. Marilyn Green but does her best to hide it behind her finely chiseled features and expensive suit. She merely continues on, professionally, with her next prepared question. "What, exactly, happened this afternoon?"

"Morning, " Marilyn corrects.

"Morning," Lynn repeats, unthankfully.

"No, wait, you're right, it was this afternoon," Marilyn concedes.

"Afternoon," Lynn repeats. Thank God for the editing room.

"Well," Marilyn begins, then pauses again, deep in her thoughts, "without devealing anything key to the investigation, I think I can tell you that we were robbed by two men, white Caucasian, between..."

Before you start to wonder, let me explain: "Devealing," as near I can tell, is short hand for "Revealing" plus "Divulging," but I could be wrong. I'm not a mind reader. OK, I am a mind reader, but I didn't read this conversation in real time.

Lynn cuts her off. "And about when did this occur?"

"Oh, shortly before my break." Lynn glares at her with undisguised malice. Marilyn eventually figures out what the problem is. "About three fifteen, Pacific Standard Time."

Lynn soldiers on. "Ms Green, I've been told you did not throw yourself to the floor when the robbers entered."

"Yes, I did not."

"Could you share with our viewers where that sort of courage came from?"

Marilyn shrugs. "To quote, sometimes a cigar is just a cigar."

At this point, Lynn decides she's asked just about enough questions.

"Thank you, Ms. Green, for being so helpful." Most viewers this evening agree Lynn just is not one of those people who looks better when they're angry. "This is…"

"Oh, thank you!" Marilyn chimes in.

Lynn looks at her like she's gone mad; Marilyn, that is, had gone mad, not Lynn, though it's often difficult in life to differentiate between the two looks. "You're welcome…"

"It's such an honor to be interviewed by ***the*** Lynn James…"

Lynn tries to ignore this. "This is Lynn James, reporting."

"***The*** Lynn James," Marilyn corrects.

Lynn just can't take this anymore, and pretends she can't hear Marilyn at all. "What'd ya think, Doug?"

"Beautiful, moving, gripping, Pulitzer material."

"Shut up," Lynn suggests. Doug's smile at finally over-stroking Lynn's ego is, luckily for him, hidden by the bulk of the camera. For her part, Lynn figures this interview will never get on the air. Her miscalculation is due to the fact her producer will run anything with an attractive woman in it. "Cut this thing, will you?"

Marilyn glances back and forth between Lynn and Doug. "Are we done?"

Lynn stares evilly at Marilyn and shouts, "Cut!"

Mere moments after I saw this report on the tele, the phone started to ring. "Hello?" I said. He identified himself as Captain Smith of the LAPD. "You wanna talk about a bank robbery?" I asked. He said he damn well does. "Normal rates?" I asked. Damn straight, he replies. "I'll be right there," I said even though it wasn't true; I actually hung out in my dark apartment for nearly an hour after I hang up, letting my mind flow about the city, giving it its own head to search for whatever it will. I had been amused by Marilyn's manner with **the** *Lynn James, about the two Caucasians under eight feet tall, and enjoyed reliving the moment, but I was mainly trying to arrive late. Captain Smith is much more fun to work with when I arrive late.*

I fell asleep for a few joyful minutes, woke with a start, and headed out into the gathering night. But I fear I may be upsetting those of you who cling helplessly to linear time, so I'll quit for now, until you get to the point in the story where I appear in Captain Smith's office. See you there.

Chapter 17—Off the Freeway

The sun is going down just a bit behind them, heading out to sea over the Pacific. Joe and Christian don't notice it, though. They are, surprisingly enough, having a disagreement.

"Now, you're being a bit unreasonable, don't you think?" Joe asks as calmly as possible.

"No!" Christian responds, without any obvious claims to reasonableness.

"Now I told you no, and please try to follow this bit, OK? I mean no."

"No!"

"Yes!" Joe doesn't know where the argument's gotten to, but the contrary position seems to be a safe enough one to stick with.

Christian explains himself. "I want out of this car."

"I can't let you out."

"You can, you just won't."

Joe shakes his head. "I can't. You'll call the fucking fuzz on me."

Christian shakes his head. "No, I won't."

"'Fucking fuzz,'" Joe repeats. "Interesting phrase."

Christian attempts to persevere through Joe's lack of focus. "I told you, I won't go to the police."

"Oh yeah, and why exactly should I believe you?"

"Because I'm a man of my word."

“Well, man-of-your-word, you also told me you would go to the police, not much more than an hour ago.”

Christian considers this. He, unfortunately, remembers that moment of his life and doesn’t particularly regret it, since that turn of phrase is the only thing that’s thus far kept him out of jail. He was just hoping Joe had forgotten about it. Alas, no such luck; the thick twit had picked this one thing to recall, damn the luck. “Look, an hour was a long time ago, considering what we’ve been through. I was young and foolish then…”

Joe smiles, feeling he’s got the momentum on his side again. “You’re still foolish, but your hair doesn’t say you’re all that young.”

Joe exits the freeway on Central Avenue, in lovely downtown Montclair. They fall down the off ramp, one of an avalanche of vehicles that just couldn’t take the open road even one more mile. They decelerate smoothly; Joe is very conscious of not drawing attention to themselves, not when they’ve made it this far into the dense overgrowth of people that is the Inland Empire; they’re about as far off the beaten path as Dr. Livingston ever managed to get. The signal lets them turn left onto Central, joining the late afternoon gathering gridlock.

“Look,” Christian squeaks, turning to his audience, “just give me half and then get the hell away from me. I won’t say a word, I swear on my mother’s grave.”

“And what makes you imagine that I wouldn’t call and tell ’em where I let you out? Your guilt is as established as mine by this time.”

Christian shakes his head. “Oh, well, my mother isn’t dead anyhow.”

They continue north for a few more blocks, making slow work of this short distance. Joe knows the question is coming; Christian won’t be able to stop himself forever. Finally, minutes later, Christian asks, “Where are we headed?”

“Mountains.” Joe changes lanes to avoid a plumber’s truck with an attitude. “This car is too hot, gotta go cool our heals for awhile.” He’s been looking forward to this part of the conversation. “And keep each other awake.”

Christian again is miles behind Joe's conversational track. He has never gotten used to the feeling of never being on the same lap as the leader; he doesn't like it, though he's felt it all his life and doesn't have any idea how to catch up. Christian pilots his life like someone driving a car without ever having seen a car being driven: it's not obvious to him which is the accelerator and which the brake, let alone figuring out how to steer.

It's not that Christian is stupid, far from it. He's bright enough, but for him there are just a large number of steps from the beginning of an idea to the end, many more than the normal average intelligent person has to take. He has to re-read books several times to really get what's being said, he plays phone messages over and over, and don't even get me started on his over-use of the rewind when watching films on his VCR.

Despite himself, he asks, "Awake?"

Joe is smiling again. It's the little victories in life that make the day worth getting out of bed for. "If you fall asleep, my friend, I won't be there when you wake up."

As usual, once he hears it, the idea seems preposterously obvious. Did he miss the day in school when he was supposed to learn this common sense thing? He frowns at his limitations. "You wouldn't be, would ya?"

Joe shakes his head. "Not a chance I'd take, if I were you."

The traffic is clearing up a little, north of the mall. "So where does that leave us?"

That's what Joe wanted to hear. He should be ashamed of himself, getting such a giggle from these little power trips, but he hasn't gotten around to that particular emotion yet. "I've got a possible solution to this little poser… but I don't think you're gonna like it."

Chapter 18—The Toy Box

Of the moments one remembers in life, that first instance of having a pair of handcuffs clamped on your wrist has to be high on the list. Christian is immediately convinced he will never forget a single nauseating detail of this moment. These details include, though are not limited to, the following.

First, the cuffs are lined with a comfortable fake fur; the tag proudly proclaims, "No animals were killed to manufacture this product. We at Artie's Titillations are proud of our environmental sensitivity and earth-friendly policies."

Second, a large sweaty gentleman named Bubba in a leather vest laced together by black rawhide straps was applying the cuffs to Christian's left wrist — and Joe's right.

Finally, there is a crowd of half a dozen regular patrons of the Toy Box watching the proceedings with a mixture of amusement and malice.

"OK, now, Bubba, we want you to hold onto these keys until we come back for 'em, got it?" Joe says to the man behind the counter while testing the strange sensation of lifting Christian's left arm when gesturing with his right. There is the slightest twinge of a threat behind his words.

Bubba doesn't usually respond well to threats. He's no more than five and a half feet tall, but weighs over 300 pounds. There's a solidness to a man, which only this sort of stature can provide. His hairy arms are covered in tattoos and his chest is poured into the leather vest like an overfull beer. In response to this insinuation of danger, Bubba yawns. "Sure shit, dude. I'm here for ya; ain't I always here for ya?"

"Sure, Bubba, now…"

"When you needed those eight inflatable Barbara Bush's for your election party, who found 'em for ya?" Bubba inquires. His voice is like a double bass fiddle piped through a Dixie cup.

Joe nods. "You did, man, but…"

Bubba interrupts him again. "And who's going to keep his mouth shut now that you're re-evaluating your sexual preference?"

Joe grabs Bubba by the throat with his cuffed hand. Christian, surprised, has just enough time to ball up his hand into a fist before it smashes into Bubba's chin. Lacking experience in these things, he tucks his thumb inside his fingers and nearly breaks the appendage when it impacts Bubba's jawbone. Though Christian's hand is throbbing, Bubba barely appears to have noticed he's been hit. Joe wants to pick Bubba up off the floor and give him a good talking to, but clearly does not have the leverage or strength to do so. So he decides he'd better just start talking. "Bubba, I'm going to ask you one question. Can we go now?"

Bubba is not used to being treated this way; this is his shop, his castle, after all, and he feels he deserves a great deal more respect than is being afforded him. "No," he says calmly. Joe tightens his grip a little, and the other little dude handcuffed to him has his fist pushing unpleasantly into his Adam's Apple. "No!" he repeats. Joe lets go, giving up any hope of intimidation. Joe couldn't do any real damage to Bubba anyway or anyhow. Joe knows it. Bubba knows it. Bubba straightens his leather vest with his short pudgy fingers. "Hey, man, relax. We here at the Toy Box will always be here for ya." He offers his slab-like hand to Joe. "I'll take care of ya, dude."

They shake, flopping Christian's left hand about like a frightened mackerel.

"I know you will, my man." Joe gives a cheap smile away. "Thanx."

The other customers in the shop this afternoon, stocking up for the weekend, start to laugh in unison. In difference to Bubba, they had given him the first chance to do some insulting. Since he appears to have refused the opportunity, they now feel it's their turn. There is nothing quite so gratifying as finding out your particular perversions are much less severe than those of your fellow man, and this group is feeling down right superior at this point. One of them, there to pick up some crotch-less panties for his mistress, shouts out, "Gonna be a long weekend, eh, boys?"

Joe and Christian turn towards the group, but since they aren't used to coordinated movement, it takes awhile to execute this 10-point maneuver. Joe doesn't like how this is sorting out, so tries to laugh it off and get moving. "Yeah, yeah, long long weekend. Ha!" Then, under his breath to Christian, "Let's go."

Christian has been ready to leave for a while now.

Joe moves determinedly towards the door, pulling Christian awkwardly (and a bit painfully) along in his wake. Christian responds with a muffled yelp. One of the others in the store looks up from the movie bins. "Oh, come now, be gentle with him."

Joe calls over his shoulder, "We're just going to mind our own business, OK?"

"Sure," the first guy replies with a smile, "Sure, that's OK. After all, fags need love, too…"

This is good for a laugh from his mates and stops Christian in his tracks. He turns and pulls Joe back into the room a few steps. "I'm not gay!" Christian volunteers.

"Yeah, right," the first guy snorts. Christian's cheeks are flaming red, his forehead burning up. "Tell us another one."

"Let's just go, Chris," Joe pleads, trying to get his feet back underneath him to pull Christian out of the shop.

But Christian will not be moved. His spine is straight and he's got something to say. Years of not expressing his opinions fall away as the

New Christian starts talking. "I want each and every one of you to know I wish to hell I was gay, 'cause I want nothing in common with a gaggle of straight assholes such as yourselves."

Oh boy, here we go, Joe thinks to himself. The tension in the room definitely thickens, and Joe is still falling backwards. He sprints in front of Christian and attempts to turn him around. While facing the now angry faces of the other patrons, he coos soothingly, "He didn't really mean that; we're leaving."

Christian keeps them spinning till he's facing the crowd again. "I sure as shit did mean it, you backwater homophobes! You make me retch!"

Joe spins back towards them again, pushing Christian a few feet closer to the door. The other patrons have frozen in their tracks, amused by the floor show, unsure if they're going to get a decent fight going or not. Joe and Christian are spinning round and round like beginning ice dancers, where they'll stop nobody knows. "I'm sure he meant that last part figuratively," Joe reassures them.

Christian goes on the offensive again, but Joe is ready for him. Christian does manage to face the crowd, but Joe picks him up by the armpits and carries him to the edge of the shop; Joe opens the front door with his forehead. "Figuratively my ass! I'll…" he sticks his finger down his throat and makes very unconvincing vomiting sounds. Joe has to try not to laugh; he's never seen Christian try to act and he's suddenly convinced there are no Academy Awards in his foreseeable future.

"Academy Awards" is a trademark of the Motion Picture Academy of Arts and Sciences, all rights reserved. Don't tell anyone I wrote this part, OK?

Joe pops the door open and spins Christian out onto the front step. "Bye, now!" He calls and then steps out himself. They nearly fall in a heap on top of one another, but Joe grabs the rail to avoid falling down the three steps to a high impact landing. As Christian regains his balance, he attempts to go back into the store. Joe grabs his shoulder with his unshackled hand. "Where the hell are you going?"

"I've got a couple more things to say to those…"

"Christ! We're supposed to be laying low and you're trying to start a rumble!"

Christian considers this and allows himself to be pulled off, away from the Toy Box, towards the car. "Hey, you're the dude with the revolving line of credit here. Where'd you find this place?"

"I was drawn to this place, just as I am now inexplicably drawn to you."

"By fur-lined handcuffs?" Christian asks incredulously.

Joe doesn't appreciate this. They get to the Pinto and try to go to their respective sides of the car and fail miserably. Joe drags Christian over to the driver's side, opens the door, and pushes him over to the passenger seat. He climbs in, fires it up, and pulls out into traffic, to the inspiring view of Bubba and his mates in a 7-fingered, middle digit salute.

Chapter 19—The Captain and Me

In the late afternoon at a police station in Los Angeles, there is a mad rush of people (the good, the bad, the ugly) in every corner of the decaying building. This sometimes goes for days before a brief respite will occur. Then, out of nowhere, there is silence in the hall. Deafening, overbearing silence, smothering to those used to an encompassing whirlwind of sound and sensation. It'll last for a few awkward moments before someone drops a cup of coffee, or screams an expletive, or fires a spare round from their service revolver. This climatic moment restores order to this place in an instant of noise and calamity.

I am bumping into a wide variety of human detritus as I fight my way into the main entrance. I know where I'm going, I've been here before, but find the actual going quite challenging, fighting my way through prostitutes and pushers and police of all shapes and sizes. Lives in the balance, in one way or the other.

(In case you were waiting for it, I'm not going to tell you what I look like, and sound like, and what my favorite colors are. That's for my characters, not for me. I want to be able to walk the streets anonymously after this book hits the shelves, after the glowing reviews pour in, after the weeks on the best seller lists, and after the royalty checks start stuffing my mailbox unstoppably.)

The light in the station seems dim, though it could just be the great number of people leaving the photons precious little space to hang out and vibrate. I recognize a few of the officers every now and again; they don't say hello, and neither do I. They don't like me around here, and consequently I don't think too much of them, either. Their Captain doesn't like me, either, but he needs me, which can sometimes work out to being almost the same thing. I keep my head down and weave my way towards his office. The traffic magically clears when I get near his door; no one wants to walk too close to Captain Smith. They either end up fired, with shitty assignments, or (if they're lucky) yelled at to within an inch of their lives. There's a magic bubble of empty space surrounding his doorway.

Also, he's not there.

I go to the nearest desk to ask if the Captain will be gone long. The Sergeant sitting there doesn't immediately notice I'm there. His focus is miles and miles away, far off into the gloomy corners of the room. I tap him on the shoulder and he jumps like a nervous cat, spinning in mid-flight to face me. "I'm sorry!" he screams defensively.

"Sorry? Don't be sorry, I was just wondering…"

Slowly, creeping up on him stealthily, something occurs to the Sergeant: I am not Captain Smith. He therefore comes down off his tiptoes and out of full alertness, and begins to breath again. In this relaxed state, his mind starts up enough to recognize me, and the contempt with which I'm treated in this place returns to his expression and demeanor. "He'll be back in a few minutes," he sneers. He has a further idea almost immediately. "Why don't you wait in his office?"

"Sure, thanx," I reply. I immediately walk in and take a seat. Please understand, the Sergeant is not trying to be nice to me, he's trying to get me killed. No one waits in the Captain's Office without the Captain; it's just not done around here. But I figure I am special enough to get away with anything in this station.

And that's probably even true. But, what the hell, you've got to find out what the limits are somehow, and this is a pretty good way to go about it.

I've also found being arrogant can bluff you through a great many difficult situations. It doesn't get you as far as the movies sometimes make it appear, but it does get you a ways. I close my eyes so I'll look asleep when he gets here, the perfect, "You don't scare me" sort of behavior.

Being a bit tired, I go ahead and fall asleep. The next thing I remember is Smith shoving me about half out of my chair after his return. "What the hell are you doing in here?" he asks me, wishing my feet were up on his desk so he could knock them off.

I rub a little of the sleep out of my eyes, blinking at the bright lights. "Waiting for you. I was summoned, wasn't I?" That's an excellent tone to start with, I think; it's obnoxious, but not too offensive. Perfect.

"Don't ever come into my office again without my permission, got it?"

"Sure; I didn't mean to offend."

He storms around to his side of the desk, enjoying the sensation of being in control. "So, you have heard about the bank robbery this afternoon?"

I nod. "Saw an interview of some teller this afternoon, right before you called."

"Do you know where the robbers are?" he snarls.

I smile and calmly pick up a paper clip off his desk. This annoys him, also. "Now, Captain Smith, it doesn't work that way. I need to search for them out there in the gathering darkness, and there are an awful lot of brains to go through." I bend the paper clip completely out of shape; this really annoys him. "Of course, if you can tell me anything about the perps it'll help immensely."

He hesitates, trying to decide if he's going to use me or not. Smith doesn't really believe me when I say these things take time, and for good reason: they don't take very much at all. I always take much longer to provide him with information than I really need to, and Smith is just psychic enough to know it. On the other hand, he really needs the help and I do always come through for him, eventually. He decides to let me screw him over again, so says, "We know a few things."

"And you'll pay me $100 an hour, plus an extra thousand if I help you get 'em?" These are our standard terms, but I figure it should be said to avoid any misunderstandings later.

"Yeah."

I nod. "Give me what you know and a place to work." I say it not as a request but a demand. The veins on his neck stand out and throb visibly as ever nerve he has wants to pounce on me and punish me physically. As an act of self preservation I tune into his mind at this moment and repeat his thoughts to him: "You're right, my asshole is larger than any known black holes, but I get you results don't I?"

This is enough to get him to put up with me again. He tosses the folders across his desk and bellows for the Sergeant to show me to a quiet room. When we get there, I find a single hard-backed wooden chair, a small wooden table (both with scuff marks and graffiti) and a small amount of stagnant air. The Sergeant closes the door, leaving me alone and all but imprisoned in here, segregated from more respectable police professionals.

That suits me fine. I sit down and get to work.

OK. I fall asleep for another hour or so, and then I get to work.

Chapter 20—Galileo Magnifico

They turn north as soon as practical and head up onto Mount Baldy. It is starting to get serious about getting dark; the shadow stretches from their car onto the fences surrounding the semi-enclosed communities to every side. Neither of them says a thing; any spare attention they have beyond replaying the last few hours of their life stories in their beleaguered minds is dedicated to getting used to the annoying sensation of their hands hanging knuckle to knuckle. Every time Joe shifts, Christian reacts by tightening the muscles in his arm in discomfort. They stare straight up the road, unwilling to glance aside since they are getting plenty of exposure to one another through physical proximity.

Joe turns on the headlights. The road angles steeply up beyond the foothills, into a no-man's land between the beautiful, expensive houses in the low hills and the expensive, rustic vacation homes along the dirt roads off this minor highway to nowhere. Nowhere except an abandoned ski area anyhow, and that's pretty close to nowhere in my book. For these brief dozen miles, a Californian can actually drive along a scenic part of the state where nobody lives. It's an experience one doesn't get very often anymore, not in this city.

Christian wonders how he'll ever get untangled from this web he finds himself struggling in. He woke up determined to change his life;

well, he'd rarely had a day so completely live up to expectations. Instead of a respected businessman with a dull yet secure future and an addiction to asking a stupid question about Butch Cassidy, he's now a wanted criminal handcuffed to a raving lunatic riding in a Pinto deep into the darkness of the Southern California Mountains. And, if that weren't enough to mess with his mind, he'd also met The One he's been looking for, and he's being dragged further and further away from her with each click of the odometer. Even if he did, say, know her full name, or her phone number, or her erogenous zones, he can't contact her because of the other changes his life has undergone recently.

Damn.

It's a relief and a pisser, all at the same time. He finally gives up on trying to find her, and then he finds her. Now he's the prisoner of feelings he never even considered. Once he'd met The One, he always assumed he'd be able to sit down with him or her and figure out why the hell he'd been looking for her or him all these years. Instead, he meets her, hits the floor due to automatic gunfire, and then makes a get away with the worst driver this side of Boston. And, strictly physically speaking, he wants her more than he's ever wanted a woman before, or ever hopes to in the future. And… and this all isn't exactly what he'd had in mind when he said he'd wanted a change in his life.

What is the deal here, anyhow? He's turned his back on fate, and it's stabbing him in between the shoulder blades. The implications of all this are almost too much to grapple with right now, his mind just can't concentrate on the problem, can't grasp it and hold it. So he decides to take little looks around the edges instead, nibbling on part of the concern here, another part there. He attempts to break it down into component pieces in hopes of gaining some perspective, and it goes like this:

He met her.

He can't go anywhere near her.

He's in a car with Joe.

He's a wanted felon.

He's wearing fur-lined handcuffs purchased in an adults-only store and he's never felt so sexually frustrated in his life. He's constantly mentally erect, seeing female forms in glorious states of undress in every shadow, every tree, every blink of the eye…

Christian shakes his head, but it does little to clear his mind. All this, it's all interconnected in some hideous, ridiculous way, obviously, because it's all happening to him. He suddenly fears that means it's his fault. Are weird things happening to him, or is he creating weird things for himself? He's no longer sure of himself at all; that at least he has in common with the old Christian. At least he thinks the old Christian acted this way, it's all getting so hazy now. He's lost the clear vision he had when driving back to his house from the prostitute's side, or even from his well-appointed office earlier this afternoon. It's all a murky fog where he can't tell where he is, or where he's going, or perhaps even where he's been.

Joe is pissed off he's missing M*A*S*H reruns on the local Fox affiliate.

In addition, his head is drooping slowly towards the steering wheel. He awakes with a jolt and jerks the car back into its proper lane. He looks at Christian, embarrassed, but his passenger is too deep in thought to even have noticed. Joe figures he'd better do something to keep himself awake; the log in the next seat certainly isn't going to be much help. Joe gets a very familiar feeling of self-reliance; after all, he's obviously going it alone in life with no one to help him out or even pretend to. He sings out the words which accurately reflect his sense of isolation: "I'm just a poor boy, nobody loves me."

Christian ignores the hell out of him, though he is a Queen fan and immediately recognizes the tune: "Bohemian Rhapsody," from the album ***A Night at the Opera***.

Ya know, when Joe stops to consider it, Christian is looking pretty damn alone over there as well. As they say, you're never as alone as when handcuffed to someone. The next line in the song seems appropriate: "He's just a poor boy from a poor family, spare him his life from this monstrosity."

Christian tries to stop himself from falling into another of Joe's petty amusements, but the next line is just too darned appropriate. "Easy come, easy go, ***will you let me go***?" he croons, emphasizing the last phrase.

Joe jumps in with gusto. "He will not, no! Will not let you go."

Christian hits the high notes: "Let me go!"

"He will not, no! Will not let you go."

"Let me go!"

"He will not let you go."

"Let me go!"

"He will not let you go."

"Let me go!"

Their words start overlapping, Joe feeling each syllable in, "He will not let you go, no…."

Christian is shouting, "Let me go go go go."

Joe: "No no no no no no!"

And the car lapses back into silence. Neither shows any reaction to their preceding exchange. Christian is paging through his memory trying to recall lyrics that will make his point equally well. He settles on a little known song by The Knack: "Let me out, come and get me out, 'cause I've been stuck in for too long."

Joe is ready for his come back, again relying on Freddie Mercury and the boys: "Joe walks warily down the street, his brim pulled way down low. There ain't no sound but the sound of his feet, ***machine gun*** ready to go."

Christian comes back with REM immediately: "Time I spent some time alone."

And then Genesis, Joe challenging his limited vocal range by attacking the words, "They say I must be crazy, 'cause I don't care who I hit, who I hit!"

They both would be really enjoying themselves except they're too busy trying to think of new lyrics to top the other's offerings. Christian remembers a line from the Beatles that works pretty well: "and, when I awoke, I was alone, this bird had flown."

Joe's voice cracks when he sings, "Oh no, this means no beer, steer clear!"

Christian stares at him as if he's speaking a foreign language. "What the hell does that mean?"

Joe shrugs. "Nothing. It's just a cool song, man…"

Christian is stuttering, his hands clamping together while imagining he is placing them around Joe's neck and crushing his windpipe. This means that three of their four hands are more or less fondling the gear shift, with only Joe's left hand left alone, steering the car. Metaphorical steam rises from Christian's ears. "The first even partially intelligible conversation we've ***ever*** had, and you screw it up! I…"

Joe shakes his head. "You shouldn't be allowed outside by yourself, Chris. You take this fucking life too damn serious."

"-ly." Christian corrects.

Joe smiles. He accepts, momentarily at least, that Chris is a putz, this one time Joe decides to try to be tolerant and not spoil the moment. "C'mon, let's sing one together, shall we?" Christian shakes his head, still pissed and starting to pout. "Geez, Chris, you did quote that song first, after all, that's why I was thinking of it." Though this is true (both lines coming from "It's the End of the World as We Know It") it doesn't cause any conversation to emanate from Christian. Joe figures he can bring him around with a little effort, so starts in on a U2 classic. "I have climbed highest mountains, I have run through the fields, only to be with you, only to be with you…"

It's a good thing Bono doesn't have to listen to him; it would be sad to see a grown rock star cry.

Christian tries to hang onto his anger. "Yeah, right. Shut up."

Joe is undaunted and off-key. "I have run, I have crawled, I've scaled these city walls, only to be with you…"

Christian hates himself for it, but he's starting to like Joe again. It'll pass, he's sure, but it's happening. "Come on, Joe, you're giving me a headache."

Joe increases his projection for the big finish. "But I still, haven't found, what I'm looking for…"

Christian sings softly, almost to himself, "I have…"

Joe turns toward him. "How was that?"

Christian immediately retreats. "Uh, Jimi Hendrix, 'Are You Experienced,' sorta."

Joe doesn't fall for it. "No, no, I said, 'I still haven't found what I'm looking for" and you said, 'I have.'"

Christian thinks about this one for a second. He sure as hell doesn't want to let Joe inside his head. Maybe he can change the subject. "Where did you say we were going?"

"Chris!"

"Just because I said it doesn't mean that I meant it. And I don't." He turns and looks out the window again, the lights of the valley becoming less distinct from distance and smog. They turn a corner and head through a short tunnel hewn out of the rock.

Joe shakes his head. "You're a secretive little nit, ain't ya?"

"I can neither confirm nor deny…"

Joe laughs with him, and even clasps Christian on the shoulder. This causes Christian's hand to darned near hit himself in the face, but it doesn't take away from the camaraderie of the moment. Christian still feels the subject is a little too close to him, so continues, "So where are we going, Joe?"

"North!" Joe responds heartily. "Straight due north! Right off the flipping map!"

Christian gets immediately tired of Joe's response. Though I may have mentioned this previously, it's worth repeating: Joe is the type that's a pain in the ass to be around when he's depressed and even worse when he's joyful. When joyful, he insists that everyone else be just as jolly as he is at the moment, and it's not always easy to comply. Christian suspects he won't like the answer, but asks all the same, "And then?"

"Then, we'll find a nice little vacation place that is not presently occupied, crash, and regroup."

Something nags at Christian's mind about this plan. "Unoccupied… what if it looks unoccupied and they're just asleep?"

"God, it's only 7:30! I bet even you stay up till nine — 9:30 on Thursday's for ***Seinfeld***," Joe snorts

"OK, fine, they're not asleep. What if they've just popped out for supper and come back later? Or if they get a late start from the city and…"

"And they arrive with pizza and beer to screw in the clear mountain air?" Joe interrupts. "Or maybe they've gone down into their fallout shelter for fear of World War III but risk their lives to come back to the main house for a Mr. Pibb and some fried pork rinds? Or they have the ability to make themselves invisible and suddenly reappear just as we start to make ourselves comfortable?" Joe laughs with feeling; Christian begins to feel sheepish, again. "You'd make a damn fine Rolaids® Poster Child, you know that? If we have some time and a hot tub, I'll make it my sacred mission to teach you how to relax."

After a few more turns in the dark road, Joe continues, "Did you notice that I even out paranoid you back there?" He grins, making Christian feel a little smaller and angrier. He feels like his extraneous emotions are being drained off to leave his hate behind, concentrated and boiling. "My examples were both more likely, or wittier, or both at the same time. Just thought I should point that out, for honesty's sake."

Christian, his face burning, nods. "I would think paranoia could be a definite asset in your profession."

Joe shrugs. "Hey, man, this is only a hobby."

"Really?" Christian doesn't know what to believe, or when to believe it.

Joe, feeling wonderful, continues. "And besides, who's going to come up to a vacation cottage this early in the season on a Thursday?"

"Friday."

It takes them both a long, long second to grasp what's just happened. Joe turns full face to Christian. "Really?"

"Yes, it is god damned Friday!" Christian can't decide if he should be angry or exultant. He settles for pissed off with a wicked smirk. It's a look that sticks with Joe, though he tries not to notice it.

Joe stares at the lifeless watch on his wrist. "No…is it?"

"Friday!" Christian is picking up momentum and confidence with each word. "God damned Friday! The day before the weekend, the prime night for scooting off to vacation cottages in the mountains!"

"Well, I guess it could be Friday…"

Christian shouts a single syllable that says it all. "Ha!"

"Oh well, doesn't change…"

"I can't believe the master planner doesn't even know it's Friday!" Christian realizes he should reign himself in here, but is enjoying the moment too much. It's a moment he's waited for and he finds it impossible to stop the flood of feeling he's packing into each utterance. "Doesn't that great mind of yours have a calendar built in?"

Joe refuses to look over. "Hey, there's a lot of days, man…"

"Seven! As in wonders of the world!"

Joe sees a chance to change the subject. "Yeah, and how many of those do you remember?"

Christian refuses to take the bait. "None, but I'm not counting on a god-damned hanging garden to save my ass."

Joe looks out his window. "Shut up."

It's good advice, and Christian would love to take it, but he just can't back down from this one. "Me, shut up?" His voice has a razor sharp edge of indignation. "You're taking us to the bungalow of some weekender with a shotgun and an attitude!"

"Shut," Joe says, very very distinctly, "up."

"You shut up! You're trying to get us killed!"

Christian is staring at Joe, desperate to see the defeat in his face, the admission of a mistake. When Joe does swivel his head slowly back towards his companion, defeat is not in his presentation. His eyes have seemingly grown closer together. His forehead hangs over the rest of his face. There is no laughter, no doubt when he says, "There are easier ways to die."

Christian breaks the gaze almost immediately, shocked by the response he's getting. Therefore, he notices what Joe apparently was referring to: the logging truck just up the road, approaching the narrow tunnel they are a few hundred meters shy of. Without taking his eyes off Christian, Joe eases the car into the lane the truck is allowed by law to use. Christian glances back at Joe; the bastard must be kidding, right? Sane people don't do this sort of thing.

Christian remembers it is Joe who's driving. Joe doesn't appear to be hampered by the things sane people don't do.

This is one too many terrifying turns for Christian. He can't think of a single thing that would possibly help at this point. The headlights of the truck are looming dramatically, and Christian is like a deer caught in their snare. He can't turn away, can't move, can't do anything at all. He is going to die, and that's all there is to it. The letters MACK are clearly visible, and the sound of the truck's air horn shatters the silence and continues to echo in their ears.

Joe continues to stare at Christian. Like many humans, chicken is the game that Joe is genetically well suited for because he's more than willing to give up his life to prove he's Right and someone, anyone else is Wrong. He doesn't want to die if he doesn't have to, though, and so watches Christian intently and the road ahead covertly. The beads of sweat spontaneously generating on Christian's forehead are the first sign. The doe eyes, helpless and the size of serving platters, tell Joe he's won. He doesn't feel joy in victory, just relief and a sense of appropriateness. He has to win, after all; he always has, and sees no reason to admit defeat just because he happens to be wrong. Christian's whole face starts to quiver, every muscle spasmodically firing, and Joe realizes the truck must be getting quite close. He glances forward and sees the same look of fatalistic fear in the eyes of the truck driver, hovering high above them like an angel.

Well, perhaps more like an angel who has just soiled his holy vestments.

Joe yanks the wheel sharply to the right. The truck hits the Pinto's left rear fender, ripping off the rusted metal and shooting a ray of sparks into the night. The Pinto is thus spun back at the wheels of the logging trailer, the huge trees leaning toward them already since the hard-braking truck is jack-knifing slightly in their direction. Of more immediate concern to Joe are the trailer's large wheels which could easily smash the car and continue on little worse for wear. He ignores decades of advice on how to deal with such situations and turns away from the direction of the skid and hits the accelerator. The wheels catch and pull the frightened car away from the truck as if stung by a bee.

So far so good, but now the car is headed directly into the wall of the tunnel. Joe tries reversing his previous maneuver but the rubber he left on the road in executing the last one leaves his tires unwilling to accomplish any more panic plans. The Pinto smashes into the tunnel's guardrail at a slight angle and ricochets back towards the truck. Joe is getting a little tired of this whole out of control business, and Christian's eyes have mercifully closed so he doesn't have to watch the whole affair. Luckily, the truck has passed by the time the car gets to the other lane and Joe gets his machine to run even to the left hand wall by blowing out the left side tires with a jerk of the steering wheel. So they merely glance off this wall gently, slowing and smoking. The momentum of the moment is gone now, and the car nestles into the left hand ditch just outside the tunnel, its nose settling comfortably into the new spring weeds.

Joe exhales the breath he's been holding onto during the last minute or so. He reaches up to turn off the car, dragging Christian's hand with him and accidentally commanding Christian's attention. When he opens his eyes, Christian realizes he is still alive, and takes little comfort from it. He looks at Joe, helplessly, and for that moment Joe does pity him. Christian just wasn't cut out for this type of life, and Joe would like to release him from it, if he could. But, hey, you can't always do what you want, either. Joe shakes his head. "You shouldn't push, Chris; not unless you know where the edge is."

Christian says nothing, making no response at all. His eyes lock up with Joe's in resignation, a fighter willing to admit defeat from the depths of the canvas.

They pull themselves awkwardly from the car's passenger side, Joe having to push Christian most of the way out the door. Joe brings the briefcase with them and they continue along their original course on foot. The truck is long gone. Joe figures the driver is too damn scared to stop or worry about the fate of the occupants. Christian moves stiffly at first, but quickly accepts his new lot in life; now he's climbing mountains in the dark. It can't be too much more dangerous than the rest of the day has been, so he doesn't complain. In fact, at this point, he wouldn't say a word if Joe led him to the edge and pushed them both over. Christian is in no condition to question Joe at all, on anything.

Just before they turn a corner which would obscure the car from view, Joe takes a remote control out of his pocket. It is the model from his 13" Sony back in his apartment. He hits the power switch, 1-2-3, and ENTER. The night is torn open by the force of the car exploding behind them, the sky briefly illuminated like mid-day in the desert. A small fireball rises dozens of feet into the air. Behind them the wreckage of one more Pinto and everything near it is burning to the nub. Christian jumps, surprised. Joe does not.

Chapter 21—Adolescent Eskimos

Christian and Joe walk on, ever upwards, silently. Somewhere between a forced march and a weekend hike, they continue to place their trailing feet in front of their leading shoes through sheer stubbornness. The quiet night seems alive to their overtaxed minds, every sound jumping out at them threateningly, unfamiliarly. Joe blocks these sounds out and concentrates on the pavement directly in his path. Christian can't stop listening, and is too tired to spin his head about like a gyroscope to try to keep track of them all. Instead, his mind grasps and cherishes every sound and brings him back to the last time he felt this out of control.

Darkness had fallen hours before their basketball game had finished; in winter, darkness usually hits before anything is finished. After a 27 point defeat at the hands of some very poor sportsmen, the team had listened to their coaches' admonishments and showered. Through the unaffected zeal that being in the seventh grade can cause, the loss is pretty much forgotten by the time they get to the bus.

The team climbs in and takes over the back two thirds of the vehicle, as always. The front few seats are reserved for the cheerleaders, with coaches and other teachers forming the buffer zone in between. Everyone knows this, it's the rule the junior high has lived with for years. Christian sits in the front-most basketball-player seat by himself, still a bit preoccupied with the two free throws he'd missed in the third quarter; Joe sits a seat back, on the other side. Even Christian notices when the cheerleaders walk in a few moments later, resplendent in their trendy street clothes after changing out of their traditional uniforms. They march onto the bus and sit in the rows of seats right in front of the players. What is this? A mummer of amazement and testosterone circulates among the only very slightly post-pubescent players. The girls look as nonchalant as possible, sitting very demurely, facing forward, not saying a word; they hope to go unnoticed.

And then, a miracle occurs. The coaches and teachers along for the trip climb on the bus and sit in the front seats, as if that's where they always sit. The doors close and the lights inside the bus are extinguished as it starts to roll along the street in front of the school. A few of the boys gasp or giggle, to the exasperation of Cindy, the head cheerleader who has planned and executed this unprecedented maneuver. A warm glow is growing inside her, the thrill of a successful conspiracy adding to the anticipation of here-to-fore hidden delights until she is positively flushed. But, if these damned boys don't keep it quiet, they'll ruin the whole plan; Miss West will turn around and realize there's something wrong with this whole set up and rearrange them back to normal. Cindy holds her breath as the bus turns through the various intersections of this small town leading them back to the highway, when it'll be darker, and the bus engine will be loud enough to cover up any unusual noises.

Joe is grinning like a hyena and staring directly at Cindy's long, straight hair. He echoes Cindy's thoughts on timing and prepares a place for a companion, as the boys most prepared when darkness falls on them will get first choice of a very limited resource. He wills the bus onwards and out of town, never taking his eyes off of the dark mass of over-grown follicles a few feet in front of him. They pass the sign telling them they're leaving this community and the bus settles into a steady, straight course through dark fields on a moonless night.

Cindy feels the glares of all her fellow cheerleaders; they're willing to follow her anywhere, but aren't making any moves on their own. She enjoys this sense of power, and waits a few minutes to build their anxiety and make sure she has the boys' undivided attention. It occurs to her she doesn't have to make a move at all, if she just stays in this seat the whole way home each boy in this bus will suffer through temptation and frustration for 60 miles, all because of her. They wouldn't dare come up this far in the bus, with Miss West only a seat or two in front, it's all up to her to make any move that's going to be made; the entire under-aged population of the bus awaits her decision. The headlights of a car pass in the opposite direction, showing that the teachers are all facing resolutely forward.

She rises from her seat and walks quietly back towards the team. She passes Christian, who is staring straight ahead, as if he hasn't even seen her. A few more steps and there's an arm in the aisle, blocking her path; it belongs to Joe, with a lecherous, crude, and slightly dangerous smile dripping off his lips. She sits down next to him and is tantalized by the feeling of his lips searching all over her face for hers. Their lips meet, and cling to each other enduringly.

Christian watches them all walk past, one after the other, every cheerleader heading back for a rendezvous with a different boy. He doesn't move his head, of course, and gives the impression of being a statue more than a kid. One after one they walk past, and the giggling and gasping become quite noticeable behind him. Once in a while, he can hear a girl get up from one seat and move to another, changing partners in a lusciously dangerous abandonment of social convention. He refuses to turn around; Christian isn't a moralist, he's just a scared shitless. He's torn between the want for one of the cheerleaders to come back to him and the fear it might actually happen. He has no idea how to react in this situation; can't even come up with a decent guess, to be honest, and so adopts the stare-straight-ahead-and-pretend-it-isn't-happening philosophy, but he can't stop his mind from thinking about the thrill of it all. Christian (a ridiculously late bloomer, he fears) is still years from Puberty Proper, and can't imagine what may be happening back there. Beyond kissing, that is; he's pretty sure there's kissing happening. Groping has occurred to him, but he isn't at all sure what to grope and he doesn't want to try to figure it out on the fly.

Well, there are breasts, he figures, but is sure, is absolutely *certain* he would get slapped if he touched one. So it's the lips he imagines, coming at him, gasping and wet and huge, big enough to devour him whole and then move on to the next boy. He imagines he's in his basketball uniform, dribbling down the court when a pair of bright red lips eats him in one nibble and then devastates the rest of the team. The lips then start on the coaches, then the spectators. All in all, as fantasies go, this one is a little on the conflicted side.

By now Joe has traced ever inch of Cindy he can reach, kissing constantly. He fears he may have sprained his upper lip somewhere along the way, and she still keeps at him, lips in full pucker. He's getting a little bored with the whole situation, to be honest; Joe is so cool he's already bored with kissing as a seventh grader and ready for more dangerous pursuits. So he disengages himself from Cindy's gaping, carnivorous mouth. "Cindy," he whispers.

"Yeah?" she whispers back, gasping for air.

"Cindy, do you want to have some fun?"

Cindy thought they were, and is a little concerned where this line of questioning is going. She's heard stories of what happens after this, and doesn't think it's the sort of thing to experience on a bus. Still, she's cool, and doesn't want to back down now, so coos, "Sure," and moves back towards him to find out what he has in mind.

Joe leans away from her. "Why don't you go up there to Chris?"

"Chris?"

"Yeah, the tall, skinny kid up there."

Cindy looks at the back of Christian's head. She wonders if he can hear them talking about him; she can't see it from that distance, but he has started to shake involuntarily.

"I know who he is, but…"

Joe kisses her quickly, full on the lips. "He's never kissed a girl, you know."

For some reason, this is a line that instantly gets the attention of a teen-aged girl. Please, I beg you, don't ask me why. Cindy smiles and slides over towards the aisle. What is it that makes an un-kissed boy an attractive target? Is it the thrill of getting there first, going where no girl has gone before? Cindy stands and moves unsteadily the few steps forward, the bus rolling about on its springs. Is it the fact that you're safe with an inexperienced boy, and he'll gratefully stop whenever and wherever you choose?

She sits next to Christian. He tries to make no sign of noticing her arrival, though he does shake a little bit more perceptibly. Cindy sneaks a glance forward as she slides closer to Christian; Miss West is still staring straight ahead at the bleak roadway. Christian also is completely immobile.

"Hi, Chris," Cindy whispers in his ear.

He doesn't respond.

"Chris?" she tries again.

"Christian," he stutters, and gasps for his next breath.

"Christian," she whispers, her lips practically pressed to his ear. "Do you want to kiss me?"

This is a difficult question to answer. Of course, Christian has tried to imagine what kissing must be like, with little success. It looks interesting enough, admittedly, but he can't figure out what exactly one does during the time that four lips are locked together in mortal combat. Do they move? The movies he's seen suggest they do, but is there such a thing as too much and too little movement? He remembers a *Cheers* episode where a character talks about his lips being too dry when kissing; is one supposed to wet the lips before engaging? That would imply there's probably such a thing as too wet also, another thing to be concerned about. And what the hell is supposed to happen once the lips are pressed together, where do the noses go, how do you breath? He doesn't know, and he doesn't want to know, though he longs to find out. All totaled, Christian has pretty much decided it's too damned complicated to be concerned with right now, and until now there didn't seem to be any immediate danger of having to kiss anyone, so he'd pretty much pushed all concern with it well out of his mind. And then, suddenly, there's a girl sitting practically on him, asking him if he wants to kiss her. His lips are too dry to even move, his throat is constricted, and breathing is something he's forgotten he might need to do eventually. He shakes his head in a negative manner.

Cindy is not one to be detoured easily from her chosen course. She blows lightly in Christian's ear, cooing, "Come on, it'll be fun. Just a little kiss?"

Christian feels his face flushing. Violent, distracting sensations are being broadcast from his groin. He shakes his head again.

"How about if I just kiss you? On the cheek? Just a little peck?"

He shakes his head again, wondering how long it'll be till they got home or one of the teachers came back to break up the party. If he could just hold on a little longer, this would all be over, and he could go home and work out in his mind what exactly happened.

Cindy leans forward in the seat, and sees the fear in Christian's eyes. She is thrilled by the challenge of it. She'd never expected anyone to turn down an offer of affection, not because she thinks so highly of herself but because boys are supposed to always be ready for this sort of thing. That's what Mom always said, anyhow. She reaches out and touches his shoulder, and he recoils like a frightened snake. His whole body is shaking. She is scaring him badly, probably to the point of wetting himself, and she finds something else surprising out: mixed in with the pity she feels for him, she kind of likes the fact that it's her closeness that is having such a dramatic effect on him. "Christian, it's OK, we don't have to do anything. We can just Eskimo kiss, you know, rub noses. Would you like that?"

He takes a few seconds to ponder this one. She *is* making some concessions to his wants and needs, and there isn't anything you can do wrong when rubbing noses, is there? Not that he could think of, but he realizes he probably isn't the most rational thinker available at this moment or anything. Then he thinks of something which could go wrong: what if you have a cold and your nose is all runny? That doesn't sound very appealing, and he did hear Cindy sneeze about a week earlier. He remembers this because he tried to take the opportunity to strike up a mini-conversation by saying "Gesundheit" to her, but hadn't the nerve.

In any case, it seems safest to just say no to this as well; he shakes his head no.

Cindy is beginning to lose the thrill of this game. She decides to take a little initiative and leans in, intending to rub her nose against his shaking appendage. The closer she leans, the further back he leans until his body is practically flat, his feet providing the leverage he needs to brace his shoulder blades against the back of the seat. Joe, who's been watching and listening, shouts out, "Kiss her, you idiot!"

Every temporary coupling on the bus halts in mid-smooch. Every kid realizes the game is up, the teachers are going to turn around and catch them red lipped, there's no chance of getting the girls back where they belong in time. The sit like a bus load of hot and bothered deer, watching the headlights coming closer and closer…

Miss West shouts to them, without turning around, "Keep it quiet back there, if you don't want me to come back and separate you all." The teachers continue to stare forward at approaching headlights, like small-mouth bass caught in a camera flash.

I don't know about you, but I was getting tired of the deer metaphor.

Not another kiss is exchanged on that bus that night. They were all set to get caught doing something illicit and exciting, and were told that it was practically a school sanctioned activity. Quickly, one by one the cheerleaders return to their seats and begin comparing notes. The guys sit still in the silent darkness, wondering how the hell they'd just gotten so lucky, how they could get it to happen again, and when their erections will die down. Christian starts breathing again, slowly, deeply, relieved and disappointed all at once. It's a horrendous curse, to be able to feel so many emotions at one time.

Chapter 22—The Artistic Temperament

The night is starless, the smog being a door closed and locked on the heavens. No other vehicles are there to see the two shackled figures trudging implacably ever higher into the tree-covered mountain. Christian has begun singing TV jingles in his mind to suppress the unwanted memories that have recently plagued him. Amid the sounds of "It's the real thing" and "Plop plop, fizz fizz, oh what a relief it is," he is keenly aware that Joe's steps have developed a careless, undisciplined lope. He wonders what visions are infiltrating his accomplice's mind in this dark and strange moment. He figures it's probably something much more positive than he had just recalled, and feels angry and jealous at the same time.

Joe stops the lift and opens the safety door, nineteen years old and on top of the world, wearing minuscule round spectacles and a sharpened goatee. He leads the way into the loft his parents are financing, though truth be told they think he's sharing a two bedroom place right off campus with this nerd named Kent. Joe's companion follows him into the drafty space, clutching the lapels of her coat together with both hands.

Seventeen and nervous, she walks the perimeter of the room looking at the brick walls across the street from each window, barely visible through years of smog precipitate. She wonders why she agreed to come here, with him. Wonders what the hell she was doing in this part of town in the first place. Searching for a little adventure in life doesn't have to be lethal, right? She'll be walking out of here (in one piece) in an hour or so, right? She wonders what his invitation really meant.

Only 30 minutes ago, she'd been walking back to the bus station after discovering this part of LA wasn't really the place to walk off a three-hour layover. In her six minutes of walking, she'd seen thirteen homeless people, a couple of drug dealers, and more garbage than her hometown had produced in the last year. And suddenly there he was, tilting back in his chair in front of a charmless bar with a broken BUD sign in the window, a beer in hand. Put a beret on him and change the beer to wine and he'd look ready for any café on the Champs-Élysées; as is, he looked ridiculous. She looked an instant too long and he caught her gaze, and smiled. "Good morning," he cooed. She walked past, keeping on her way, embarrassed, but he persisted. "Excuse me, can I trouble you for just a moment of your time?"

She was startled when her feet stopped and turned her towards his unflinching stare. He settled his chair on the cracked sidewalk and placed his feet on the ground, slowly and deliberately, without letting his eyes wander from hers. "You are just," he paused, looking for the appropriate word. His expression blossoms into a smile when he says, "perfect. Would you like to sit down?"

She couldn't hold his eyes any longer, and dropped hers to the ground. "No."

He put his beer down on the ground and stands, moving a little too close to her. "I know this is a bit forward, and perhaps unexpected, but — would you care to model for me?"

She immediately knew the answer was yes, whatever he is implying with the possibly suggestive remark and laughing eyes. Something inside of her wouldn't let her say yes immediately, so she instead tried, "I've changed my mind. I would like to sit down."

He sauntered inside very calmly and emerged with another chair. One beer and several philosophically questionable treatises later and they walked the block and a half to this warehouse containing his loft.

Joe stands in the middle of the space, watching her pace like a big muscular cat testing the boundaries of its new cage. He acts as if he's unaware she's considering changing her mind and sets about the simple task of arranging the room for the session. In the center of the hard wood floor is a patch of relatively pure light. There he places his lone chair, an orange vinyl kitchen monstrosity that had been abandoned in this place by a previous owner. About five paces away he places a stool his parents had intended to throw out but he'd gotten to first. He sits on the stool, crosses his legs, and clears his throat.

She jumps, just a little, and turns to him.

"That's your chair," he says, his voice dripping with confidence. "I'll sit here the whole time."

She nods and swallows with difficulty.

"I'm just about ready, if you are."

Her head nods itself, quickly, a little too curtly to let her convince herself she's comfortable here. She thinks, "As least he hasn't asked me to undress."

"You can disrobe behind that screen, there." Joe points towards the curtain over a clothesline, near his futon. He smiles again; "disrobe" is the perfect word for this situation, and (as congratulations are in order for using it) he congratulates himself. "Come out whenever you're ready."

"OK." She doesn't move. Joe takes a pocketknife out and begins sharpening a pencil he'd picked up from the kitchen counter. She is nervous, certainly, as nervous as she'd ever imagined possible. Her courage is partially reinforced by his businesslike, undisturbable manner, by the careless spread of pencil shavings he's leaving on the bare floor.

Her feet carry her behind the screen, followed by a deep breath or two and it's happening. Her hands remove the overcoat, unbutton the blouse, and unzip the jeans. She neatly folds each item and stacks them on the floor at least a meter away from his mountain of dirty socks, underwear and T-shirts. Working with the bra and underwear are a little trickier, her hands losing the momentum that had carried them this far. Eventually, unable to unhook the bra she removes it over her head still connected. She unfastens it before adding it to the stack. Her panties refuse to slide easily to the floor, getting caught on every inch of her legs on their way down. She steps out of them at last, and puts them on the pile. Her coat goes back on, the cold material sensitizing her skin and causing a moment's panic; what the hell am I doing here? Have I lost my mind? Am I showing self-esteem or self-loathing? And, strictly practically speaking, am I going to freeze my butt off in this place and end up with a nasty cold? She savors the thrill she's felt just coming this far; is it enough? Is she ready to return to sanity?

Not quite.

She starts to walk out, and then on a sudden impulse picks up her panties and puts them in the pocket of her coat. Somehow, she feels safer knowing they're nearby. She walks out to the main room and directly to her chair, pretending she's alone in this strange, cold place.

Once she sits down, she looks at him and sees a decent representation of The Artist. He looks straight back, earnestly, dispassionately, confidently. Her startlingly large hazel eyes blink first. She looks away, dropping some of her long loose brown hair over her eyes in the process. Her left hand gathers the unruly locks and tosses the whole mass over her right shoulder. With only one hand gathering her coat protectively around her, she feels a rush of cool air against her breastbone and thighs. For some reason, which she really can't guess, the remaining hand lets go, allowing the coat to hang open, her face turned away. The cold plastic-like material is hanging precariously on her breasts; that fact and her crossed legs are the only things retaining her modesty.

Joe exhales deeply. He picks up his green spiral notebook and his poorly sharpened pencil and speaks as he writes. "Her coat hung open, mysterious shadows playing enticingly on her alabaster skin. Her silken tresses hang over her shoulders, framing her oval face in a chocolate waterfall. Every muscle is tight and firing, the corner of her full, delicious mouth quivering slightly against her chiseled cheekbones."

This writing gag is great! he reminds himself as he pauses for dramatic effect. Suddenly he feels like a fisherman, playing a difficult catch. If he gives her enough line, maybe this lovely young woman from rural Arizona will take the bait. The silence stretches, seven, eight seconds. She won't look at him at all, Joe notices, but she's not immune to his game either. After a dozen seconds, her left shoulder shrugs, unsuccessfully trying to remove the coat.

Unable to budge the coat with one shoulder, she uses both and is incredibly surprised to find the garment deposited lifeless over the back of the chair. Her breasts rush out into the cold air, and her nipples sharpen up much quicker than Joe's pencil had. Every inch of her skin is screaming in arctic vulnerableness, and she desperately wants to put the coat and the rest of her clothes back on. But she doesn't. She wills herself still, and begins to warm up through the excitement of her exhibitionism and Joe's voyeurism.

Joe again puts lead to paper. "She removes her coat to stay awhile. Her hair now waves as an unfurled banner behind her, her symbol of pride, her claim to the land of the living. The line of her torso is smooth yet sharp, running past her breasts through her tape measure waist to connect to her inclined hips. Nothing can compare to the gentle slope of her breasts, almost perfectly round and yet shaped undeniably, intricately, sublimely. Their nipples are full of life and apparently looking at a point on the wall behind me. In the shade of these immaculate providers of life hides the perfectly formed, flat abdomen, too alluring to be a stomach and too sensual to be gnarled or muscled." He has to pause to take a deep breath, and fights the urge to wipe the beads of sweat forming on his brow. "And, below the synched waist, nirvana itself, the starched pitch black hairs intertwined, guarding the gate to all that is sacred, all that is good and right and sweet and holy in this life or any other. Her strong, sculpted legs uncross..."

Joe waits, and slowly the left calf rises over the right knee and continues along a tenuous arc until both of her feet are on the floor. Joe wants to smile, and does when he realizes she doesn't dare look at him. "...And her breathing becomes more shallow, expectant, demanding." His mind has hit its zone now, and the thoughts are coming in too quickly for his pencil to keep up. He therefore stops writing them down. "She's intimately aware of every inch of her skin, of every nerve screaming for attention. She tilts her head back, her lips part and the tongue travels the trip from one corner of her mouth to the other, and every so slowly back again."

His model is keeping pace with the plot he's devising, no longer surprised at her willingness, no longer reluctant or resistant. She can't keep her arms at her side, inanimate and uninvolved, any longer, so Joe incorporates them into the story. "Her hands trace the long lines of her body, along the belly, in slow spirals around the heft of the breasts, lingering on the throbbing nipples. Her left fingers trace her neck, over the chin, along the lips. The right ventures downward, over the feelers impatiently awaiting its arrival to the small button hidden just within, the doorbell at this entry way, and there it stops." Joe can't believe how well this is working. "Clockwise, then counterclockwise. And then the fingers move rhythmically, asking an unknown force to come hither, quickly, urgently. Faster and faster over this sacred ground, begging, incessant, pleasing to release..."

"Joe?" she shouts, surprising both of them.

"Yes?"

She clears her throat nervously. "Do you..."

"Yes?"

She turns to look into his eyes with the intensity to burn straight through them. "Do you have any condoms?"

Joe smiles and puts down his notebook. "Phyllis, my dear, I thought you'd never ask."

CHAPTER 23—ARRIVAL

The night presses in on them, making them feel trapped and confined beneath the wide-open sky. Darkness surrounds them, but occasionally shows signs of letting up. Upon turning corners as they climb still higher there are brief patches of a certain glow in the sky, hinting at either the approach of civilization or the invasion of aliens. Dark and mysterious melodies swirl in their minds thanx to years of suspense-thrillers on the television and big screen. The effect is not lost on Joe, and nearly causes Christian to be lost altogether. Another corner beyond and there is no mistaking it: streetlights and neon signs await their arrival expectantly, impatiently. Joe drags both of them into the trees on the downhill side of the road.

They've reached the point on the main road on Mount Baldy where architects and developers felt it's high enough to be considered "away from the city," and therefore had moved in the heavy equipment and built cabins along side roads leading off in both directions. This led to the creation of gas stations and restaurants along the main road, and thus an economy was born. Joe isn't particularly concerned with the socio-political ramifications of it all, he'd just prefer to find a place to hide out without having to stroll through town, announcing his presence to anyone sober enough to pay attention. He and Christian struggle along the wooded trek for about 50 meters before they hit the first side road. They turn along it and begin checking each house as they pass. You may not believe it, but the guitar solo from "Stairway to Heaven" by Led Zeppelin is rising in both their minds. It's just the perfect song for this moment, dark and mysterious, full of foreboding and portent.

Plus it really wails.

The cabins each sit on about a half-acre of land, their plots butted up against one another as regularly as city blocks. To give the illusion of country separation, some of the homes face the street at an angle, allowing a short gravel drive to stand as a dramatic facade to their simple estates. Each house they look at shows signs of life: lights on, cars in the drive, the sound of people's voices carrying out into the wilderness. Christian tries to get Joe to turn around with only a few cabins left on the street, but Joe persists. The next to the last one, on the left, looks promising. No lights, no sounds, one vehicle in the garage, but it's an elderly Volvo which apparently made it up Mt. Baldy Road once but doesn't look like it'd make it ever again. They walk up to the side of the house and see nothing to discourage them from exploring further. Once around and it still looks perfect; the owner must still be working in the city, or maybe is off to Vegas for the weekend. They walk towards the front door, stopping briefly as Joe fiddles with something along the finished wooden wall. They climb the few steps onto the porch and Joe picks the lock with an expert's precision. Their audio soundtrack tails off to Robert Plant's plaintive, "And she's buying a stairway... to heaven..."

The door swings open silently, and their shadows fall into the living room. There is nothing too surprising about the place: it looks comfortable and simple at the same glance. The furniture is sparse and a bit faded. The drapes are heavy and dusty, making the interior a small shade brighter than absolutely dark when Joe closes the front door behind them. Christian's mind replays the room he'd glimpsed upon entering, and he exhales deeply: they're safe, at last. They can relax.

Joe doesn't immediately share his opinion. His ears think they hear something now that the door is closed on the sounds of the night. He can't make out the individual sounds, but there's a barely audible rumble, which seems very familiar. Another cautious step into the room and he notices there is a crack of light visible underneath the door at the back corner of the main room. He immediately reaches for the gun tucked into his belt, and then pauses. He leaves the gun where it is and drags Christian towards the room. Christian resists, but just a little; if Joe really thinks there's someone in here, he'd prefer to just get the hell out of here and look for another home away from home. Unfortunately, he can't think of a quiet way to make that point at this juncture. He follows Joe instead, letting his fears coalesce in the pit of his stomach.

After a slow, silent traverse of the room, Joe leans against the door. He can now clearly hear the sounds he thought he recognized upon entering, and he smiles. Motioning Christian back a step, he settles himself and throws the door open into the room.

In the light of dozens of small scented candles surrounding the bed are a suddenly still man and a woman, she on top. He (somewhat older) is lying with his head off the foot of the bed, so their faces both look at the doorway as one, like a reflection on a mountain lake. They say nothing, and make no effort to cover themselves, waiting for an explanation. Joe says simply, "Hi there." There is no response, so he continues, "We were looking for a place to stay, do you…"

The man answers, "Oh, fine, help yourselves to the fridge. I'll see ya in the morning."

Joe smiles and closes the door again. The familiar, rhythmic sound of the bedsprings starts again immediately. Joe leads the speechless Christian to the refrigerator, grabs a beer, and returns to the couch. Christian sits next to him, his jaw hanging open.

Joe smiles. "Isn't that a pleasant sound?" He opens his beer and takes a long, slow drink. "Music to my ears."

"So what do we do now?" Christian asks.

"Well, after I finish my beer, I think we should catch some sleep."

"Right. Some sleep."

Joe drinks again, savoring the sour taste as a spoil of war. "But first I gotta take a leak."

Christian shudders. "Oh great."

"Do you want to go first?"

"No, I may never go again, if we stay handcuffed together for too long."

Joe shrugs his shoulders. "Suit yourself." He rises, and Christian follows. "Just don't wet the bed."

I was there. Just after they had left the main road to rumble through the trees, I was there listening to Christian's thoughts. The Led Zeppelin bit was mine, they didn't think of it, though given time they may well have. I, personally, found it added the right air to the moment.

I could have immediately gone to Captain Smith and reported, had patrol cars there in half an hour. I could have, but didn't. The reason was simple: the longer I stretched this out, the more money I would make. I never, ever told Smith I'd found his people right away; I got to know them first. If they're bastards, I collect a few extra hours salary and send in the hounds. If they're decent folk (which is roughly equivalent to asking the question, "Do I like them?"), and I don't need the money too badly, I lead Smith close, but not close enough, to his prey.

Does this behavior bother you? It might; it bothered me, once, until I realized I knew the answer to the following question: Who has the right to play God with his fellow men?

Answer: Anyone who can.

I'd only been on the clock a few hours, I didn't know these goons from a pair of mis-matched Adams, and my rent was a month overdue; I was going to play this one like a Stradivarius.

Day 2: Saturday

Chapter 24—Waking Up

I've had sex before, he reminds himself, because he'd definitely forgotten. He'd had calm, caressing, sweet sex with several girls and young women who had seemed precious and priceless as a Ming Dynasty vase or an aging fresco. Those solemn, delicious moments seemed to be as closely related to this experience as mango is to a large pizza with everything. The woman he finds himself current atop is constantly fighting with rages from deep within her, each movement of their joined flesh sends her into throes of a passion he'd read about but never imagined he'd see. Her mouth seeks his out ravenously, teeth and tongues and lips all flung together in a cataclysm of sensual overload. She rolls them over and is sitting high above him, her face a mask of pleasure and concentration and determination.

He'd had sex before, sure, but never with Marilyn. The music is loud in his ears, angry, the beat driving it his brain, a song called "Estrus" by the now defunct L.A. bar band named High and Outside: "My girl is in Estrus; my favorite time of the year."

"Say my name," Marilyn demands, between the breaths she has to fight to grasp.

"Marilyn," he whispers, air escaping between his teeth like a slow leak in his bike tire. "Marilyn."

"Louder!"

"Marilyn?" he tries, a little louder. No response. "Marilyn?" louder still. She reaches behind her and finds his testicles, pulling them none too gently upward until they, too, are penetrating her. "Marilyn!"

"Oh, Christian!" she cries, looking heavenward. "Christian, oh yes, Christian!"

This, he thinks, is not bad. A little loud, perhaps, who knows who's listening, but…forget that, he tells himself forcefully. This is great sex, who cares who hears.

Marilyn bites her lip, moving a little faster, a shade more intensely. Is she coming again? he wonders. Again? This woman is amazing! Or, maybe he's the one who's amazing? Maybe, just maybe, she's never had an orgasm before, and it's only with him, this time, together, that she's….

Yeah, right.

Still, it's a sight to see, in the soft light of an overtly Victorian bedroom, with the four-post bed and canopy, ruffles and frills oozing out of every corner. Marilyn, sitting erectly on him, suddenly stops moving, her mouth open but not making a sound, her face starting to contort in the ecstatic anguish of her latest orgasm. Her body falls against his but she's not done yet, she's begging him to move faster, to move for both of them, to extend the sensation as long as he can. And he's doing his best to comply, reaching further and further inside of her with each movement, suddenly realizing that this is it, he's going past the point of no return. Will she be disappointed? Have I been OK? He thinks, but quickly, because he hears the soundtrack for this magic moment fading to silence and the very last of the blood that's supposed to be in his brain heading south and…

…He wakes up in a bright, strange room he and Joe had fallen asleep in the night before, feeling his body contracting one last time, the issue meant for Marilyn instead finding its sticky and slimy way into his underwear. "No! No no no!" He yells, though (afterward) he wonders what exactly he had hoped to accomplish. His penis had never taken orders from him before in his life, why did he think it would start here and now, especially at a time like that? "Oh, hell," he mutters in the aftermath, sweaty and frustrated, and extremely lonely.

At least Joe's still asleep, he figures. Things could be worse. He looks around him, and sees that the heavy curtains are open so he has an unobstructed view of the gentle slope of Mt. Baldy in front of him. There isn't a cloud in the sky, the birds are singing sweetly, and the air has the strangest sensation about it. It takes him a long moment to realize what's odd about this picture: the air is clear. For the time being, at least, they are living above the smog.

There's a knock on the door.

Christian wonders what would be the most appropriate course of action at this time: say come in? Wake Joe? Pretend to be asleep? He would have spent several minutes working this one out, except the door opens a few seconds later ushering in the smiling face of their host. Christian hadn't really gotten a good look at him last night but he assumes this is the gentleman who was busy when they arrived. His hair is thinning but still covers his head in a chestnut gray mix. He stands nearly six feet tall, thin, wearing a cardigan. He reminds Christian of Mr. Rogers more than anything else; he wouldn't have been too surprised to hear this gentleman ask, "Won't you be my neighbor?" But he doesn't ask that. His eyes are sparkling, and his smile seems sincere. "Good morning!" he chimes. "Breakfast is ready and the coffee is hot, so… do the two of you need anything? I left some fresh underwear and socks in the bathroom, so feel free to take whatever you need, and…I didn't catch your names last night."

"Christian," he manages, pointing at himself. He lifts up their handcuffed hands, and then quickly hides them below the sheet again. He motions with his head. "Joe."

"Well, I am Tony, quite pleased to meet you, Christian." His smile brightens dramatically, and Christian is appropriately dazzled by it. "So, breakfast is ready for you whenever you're ready for it." Tony closes the door behind him, leaving Christian with Joe and in a panic.

"Joe!" he hisses, shaking his bedmate mercilessly, "Wake up! I think he called the cops!"

Joe rolls over, away from his alarm call. "I think I should call the cops."

"No, really, wake up! He says he's got breakfast!"

Joe opens his eyes and rolls onto his back. "What, pancakes?"

"I don't know, but..."

"I hope so. Extra syrup."

Christian is exasperated. "No! I bet he's got the cops in the kitchen, waiting for us!"

"Instead of letting them wake us up, how sweet. Well, disengage that imagination; he's got no phone. I disconnected it last night."

Christian, to himself anyhow, admits this changes things somewhat. "Well, maybe..."

"He jogged out and got 'em. Or, maybe he made us breakfast. Maybe, hopefully, pancakes." Joe throws back the covers and swings his feet onto the floor.

"But what if he's got a cell phone?"

Joe shakes his head. "Chris, you just have to learn to take a few chances in life. Let's go." He sniffs the air and recognizes the familiar odor coming from Christian's nether regions. He smiles playfully at the abashed Christian when he says, "You wash first."

Chapter 25—Breakfast

Joe stands outside the bathroom door, his hand inside the commode with Christian. Tony walks over to him, bringing a cup of coffee. As he approaches, he says, "Hi. Tony."

Joe shakes his outstretched hand with his left hand, awkwardly. "Bob," he says, referring to himself, then with a shrug towards the mostly closed door, "Doug."

"Douglas," Tony corrects him.

"Really?" Joe asks, accepting the cup of coffee.

Tony nods. "We met. Sleeping you were."

"Oh," he intones, while slurping the coffee. "I heard some rumor about breakfast?"

His host takes a sip of his coffee, nodding. "Yup, French toast. My mother's recipe."

Joe doesn't attempt to hide his disappointment. "I was hoping for pancakes."

Tony shrugs. "You can't always get what you want."

Joe smiles. "The Rolling Stones?"

"Oh course." Tony starts to head back to the kitchen, Joe calls after him. "Um, where's your friend?"

"Who, Diane?"

"I guess."

"She had to go back to civilization for the day. Won't be back up till tomorrow."

This is not exactly the news Joe had hoped for, and he feels torn between two courses of action. Tony continues, as helpfully as possible, "If she'd talked to anyone, wouldn't they be here by now? Better just to relax and enjoy your breakfast."

Joe can't come up with a good argument for this one. "Where was her car? Last night?"

"In the shop. She had to walk over to get it this morning."

Joe chuckles to himself. "The old car in the shop trip; oldest trick in the book. What about the Volvo? You drive that thing up here all the time?"

"Yes."

Joe shakes his head. "Brave man." Tony heads back to the kitchen, smiling. Joe shouts through the door, "Hey, Chris, ya drown yet?"

Christian mumbles from within, "Do you have any idea how difficult it is to pull up your pants with one hand?" Joe laughs hard enough to spill coffee on his available hand.

Soon they have managed to change their skivvies and socks and make it to the table. Every time Joe puts his right hand (and Christian's left) on the table, Christian puts it back under the tablecloth and indeed sometimes under the table itself. After a few rounds of this Joe takes their hands and puts them firmly on the table, accompanied by a firm stare in Christian's direction. Then, he focuses on the French toast. "This is great, Tony," he sputters with his mouth full.

Tony smiles his award-winning smile again. "I'll tell my mother you said so. She takes great pride in her cookery."

They take a few minutes to eat. Christian glances around the small kitchen/dining room, noting that everything is in its place and neat, but there seems to be an over abundance of stuff. Utensils line the walls and live in different vases like bunches of metallic and plastic flowers. There are pots hanging high from the rafters and overflowing from the drawers.

The refrigerator door is tiled with magnets, some with cute sayings, some fuzzy animal creatures of random varieties, and all fifty states appropriately arranged on the freezer. Even the small table the three of them sit at has three centerpieces, one left over from Christmas some five months ago, leaving barely enough room for their plates, coffee cups, and the maple syrup. The main room, Christian now notes, is completely austere and nearly unadorned. Hard wood floors, a simple sofa facing the fireplace, and a small bookcase with worn paperbacks neatly stacked.

Strange.

But the main puzzle is their host himself. He is not eating with them, but just sits drinking his coffee and looking… happy. Content. Like a man without a care in the world. Christian can't remember ever feeling that sensation, and here's someone who gives the impression he can't remember ever feeling any other. Christian finds this unnatural calm disheartening and yet inspiring. Exasperated, he decides to concentrate on his French toast, at least for the time being.

Joe is thinking about the French toast and the excellent coffee, and is almost to the point of forgetting all about pancakes. Still, the silence gets to him eventually and he tries to make a little conversation. "What do you do, Tony?"

He smiles. That is to say, his nearly perpetual smile cranks up a notch. "My job description says I teach courses in ethics, metaphysics and epistemology. What I actually do is try to keep my students awake."

Joe's eyes light up like a sparkler on the fourth of July.

"Does it work?" Christian asks.

"Occasionally." He pauses to drink his coffee. "Of course, sometimes I try to put them all to sleep, just for the variety of it."

Joe has regained his breath. "You're a philosopher?"

Tony looks at him with a touch of suspicion, his smile dropping a step back down the scale towards normalcy. "I've been called that, but I don't think it really suits me. I just like to study people, what people think, what they do…" He shrugs his shoulders non-committally. "I suppose it's more accurate to say I get paid merely for living and then talking about it."

Christian swallows a mouthful of toast. "Sounds like a good job…"

Joe doesn't appear to have heard the last line. "You're a philosopher?"

Tony nods. "Yes, I am."

Joe slaps himself on the forehead with his right hand, jerking Christian around. He doesn't notice he's causing an inconvenience, however. "I've always wanted to be a philosopher!"

"Then do it," Tony states flatly, then returns his attention to his coffee.

Joe shakes his handcuffs a bit, like a horse would with sleigh bells. "Well, I'm rather tied up in another profession right now, as you may have noticed."

Tony shakes his head, putting down his cup. "I'm not talking about professions; what you do to make money often has little to do with who you really are." The smile is gone, and his face is tightened in an intensity they haven't seen. He is speaking steadily and harshly, letting them know he means every word. "You want to be a philosopher? Just call yourself one and be."

There is a long silence of eating and drinking. Joe won't look at Tony; Christian can't take his eyes away.

"Look, it's not that easy," Joe replies, still working on the French toast.

As if the spell is broken, Tony is again all smiles and compassion. "OK."

"I mean," Joe continues with a half snort, half laugh, "if I started calling myself a sexual powerhouse, that wouldn't immediately mean it's true."

Tony stares at him, but gently. "Have you ever tried it?"

Joe's eyes bulge just a bit and his head bobs like a toy dolls. "Yes, actually."

"Maybe you just never believed it."

Joe sets down his fork, considering this possibility. "I thought I did."

Tony again becomes serious and intense. "Did you ever fully believe in your potency, and read up on positions and anatomy and techniques and become an expert in the art of massage? Did you begin to dress and act the part, feeling your power with every ounce of you soul, so that none could doubt your destiny, your motivation, your energy?"

Joe leans back a little in his chair, an unconscious reaction to put a little safety space between himself and Tony. Christian notices that Joe does not have the upper hand in a conversation; it's the first time he's ever seen it happen. He decides, then there and forever, he likes Tony. "No, I just…"

"You just said it." Nice Tony, with the smile that goes to eleven, is back again. "That's not enough. Stating your decisions is fine, but living them is much more," he stops, looking skyward, searching for just the right word. He selects, "impressive."

Christian is staring at him with a look he'd previously reserved for God, if he believed in the old Geezer, which he doesn't even though he keeps wandering around asking His question. He says in quiet awe, "Has this technique worked for you?"

Tony shrugs again. "Well, I left out a couple of important points. I've been studying with a wonderful woman for the last few months. She's taught me about patience and finesse and communication; basically, how not to be an asshole, if you'll pardon the phrase. The sum of this information and my induced self confidence have proved to be…effective." A less confident speaker would ask if his listeners know what he means; Tony is convinced they do. "More coffee?"

He stands to retrieve the pot from Mr. Coffee. Christian takes this opportunity to try to hide the handcuffs under the table. Joe jerks their hands back into sight, adding, "I think he's seen them, Christian."

"And whose fault is that? I swear, you…"

"Mellow out, OK?" Joe holds his cup out for more coffee. "You're starting to be a bit draining."

Christian also accepts a refill in silence, allowing himself a small smile at Joe's expense. He realizes Tony's way of talking is causing a certain imbalance in Joe, and wonders if Joe will survive. Even this joy can't stop him from adding, when Tony is again a few feet away, "Well, we can be discrete."

"Yeah, we could not tell him our real names," Joe hisses. Christian realizes his mistake and looks so self-loathing Joe immediately wishes he could unsay his words. Instead, he tries a more polite tone with, "Look, he knows we're handcuffed together; he's just being polite."

As Tony returns to his seat with his mug, Christian stares at him placidly. He is trusting him more and more each second, but tells himself he should be discrete, be ready to move on at a moment's notice. And then he hears himself asking, "Don't you wonder why we're wearing handcuffs?"

Tony nods but says, "I'm not a slave to my curiosity."

Christian turns to Joe. "I think we should tell him."

Joe doesn't stop eating. "So tell him."

Christian turns back to Tony. "Tony, we're on the run."

Tony looks neither surprised nor like he's expected it. "Really?" he answers flatly.

"Yes, from the law," Christian continues.

He shakes his head a little. "That's too bad."

"And we'd completely understand if you feel it's your duty to turn us in, right now."

Christian glances at Joe, expecting a sudden, angry reaction, but gets none for his trouble. Joe keeps on eating, as if he hadn't even been listening. Tony, however, has been listening. "I strongly suspect Bob and his gun feel differently about that."

Joe nods, but gives no other input to the discussion. Christian glances back and forth between them. "Bob?" he asks, rightly confused.

Tony adds, "I also suspect he checked for phone wires last night and cut them."

Joe smiles a little broader, nods a little stronger. Christian asks anyone who'll answer, "Who's Bob?"

Joe answers without looking up, "Don't be so silly, Doug."

"Douglas," Tony corrects.

"Who's Douglas?" Christian asks.

"Oh all right, Douglas." Joe puts down his fork and turns to Christian, hoping his glare will stop his partner's questions. Not that it really matters, of course, but he finds it more enjoyable to play a little cloak and dagger from time to time. "My name is, has always been, and will remain to be Bob, OK?"

Christian turns to Tony. "His name isn't Bob."

"I know."

This catches Christian a good deal off balance. "Then why'd you call him…"

"He said that's what he prefers," Tony interrupts. "I call you Christian for the same reason. "

Christian can't wade through anymore of this and shouts out, "But his name's Joe!"

"Mine's Antonio Vladimir Green, but you can call me Tony."

Joe has finished breakfast and wipes his mouth. "Chris here has problems with any deviations from his perception of reality."

Tony nods. "He balks at changes."

"Damn simple way of saying it," Joe notes, disappointed.

"Exactly." Tony does the simple act of drinking his coffee in a most dramatically impressive manner, to Christian anyhow. The economy of effort, the dramatic purposefulness of it all fills him with awe. Christian realizes he was incorrect when he thought to himself he likes Tony; truth is, he's falling in love again. For the second time in two days, love has come to town. Amazing

Their conversation stalls. Tony is predictably placid about it, Joe tells himself he doesn't care, and Christian can't think of a damn thing to say. Tony looks at him, his eyes sharp and almost piercing. "Christian, if you respond to your curiosity occasionally, it doesn't necessarily make you a slave to it."

"Really?"

Joe perks up. "No, one doesn't follow the other logically. You see, if you ask questions, you can either be a slave to your curiosity, or you may be responding to it for the first time in years."

"Thank you, Joe, that's..."

"Tony won't be able to judge immediately which it is, it could really go either way."

Tony puts a hand on Joe's shoulder. "Very well put." His voice implies the rest: don't put it any more. He turns to Christian. "You can speak freely, I don't mind."

It suddenly occurs to Christian he does have some questions to ask. He usually doesn't believe people when they make general statements like Tony just did, but he's far too enamored not to believe him now. "How can you let us in your house, sight unseen, without any idea what we've done, what we're doing?"

"It's the ultimate learning experience, isn't it?" Tony asks.

Christian can't fathom an answer.

"If you only spend your life talking to people that you know everything about, you're not going to have a wide variety of experience, are you? And, as I've said, I like to think I get paid for living and then talking about it; this is the living part."

"Besides," Joe chimes in, "I might have to shoot him if he isn't hospitable." Tony nods. "Not that I would, mind you."

"Of course you would," Tony says. "I don't like deluding myself about these things; my options were contact the cops while you were asleep, which wouldn't have been difficult, or live with you until you decide to leave. I chose to live."

"That's crazy!" Christian cries, and he means it. It's completely turned around from the safe, comfortable life he's always lived...till yesterday. "Well, maybe not crazy, but..."

"But not advisable, I know. I don't encourage anyone to live as I do, except myself."

"Kids," Joe jumps in, "don't try this at home."

Tony's face lights up again. "Well said." And then, to Christian, "Anything else on your mind?"

"Yeah, but it's all in a spin cycle. Can't catch up with much of it."

"That's OK, we've time." He rises and collects the dishes.

"Wait!" Christian adds; Tony sits, waiting. "I want to apologize for walking in on you and…"

"Diane? Don't be silly. We weren't offended or embarrassed."

"Or even particularly interrupted," Joe adds.

"True." Tony's expression becomes one of pride, for having won the love (or at least the affection) of a good woman. "She's a wonderful woman; works at a funeral home, a mortician; she says she'll give me the best and most prompt funeral humanly possible, when the time comes."

"How sweet," Joe responds sarcastically.

Tony refuses to rise to the bait. He simple says, "In a way, yes." He rises with the dishes again. "Anyhow, you're both welcome to stay as long as you like, but I should warn my sister is going to be stopping by tomorrow night."

Christian rises to help him, but Joe refuses to budge, forcing Christian to stand there helplessly and try to hand things to Tony with his free hand. "Oh, we'll be long gone by then, I'm sure."

Tony and Joe answer at the same instant: "I'm not."

Chapter 26—Her

Captain Smith is nervous. In his 23 years with the force, he'd never met any of the Chiefs. Never. He'd seen each of them, of course, giving speeches or opening shopping malls or attending games at Chavez Ravine. But never in person, never close enough for them to tell if he has bad breath or to count his nose hairs or anything. And now, not only is he on his way to meet The Chief but he's been ordered to meet Her at Her gym. On a Saturday.

Relax, he tells himself with little effect. After all, there are several things working in his favor here. First off, the lackey who'd been assigned to fetch him had found him at work, seven albuquerque meridian on this Saturday morning, and that sort of dedication should count for something. Secondly, there's his unblemished service record, and the fact he'd made captain the second most rapidly of anyone on the force, ever. The fact that She holds the record time shouldn't diminish his accomplishment at all, he hopes. Thirdly, they are reputed to have the same leadership style: whip 'em early and often, and keep the troops out of trouble and in line through fear. He suddenly realizes this is not necessarily good news for him in this particular situation, but common interests can't hurt. And, lastly, he doesn't even know why she wants to see him. Maybe it's something good! Maybe She's heard how he's been handling this whole bank robbery affair and wants to give him a well-deserved pat on the back...

He wonders how often she calls for people on Her time to give them pats on the back, and concludes it probably doesn't happen very often. On the other hand, She has a well earned reputation for kicking butt punctually when she feels it's needed and deserved, and his seems to be the next on the old kicking tee.

He parks on the street and attaches The Club to his plain jane police cruiser. He hurries up the steps and into the lobby; at least he can point out he isn't wasting any excess of Her time, if called upon to make such a case in his defense. He makes a beeline to the young man sitting on a high stool, dressed in an expensive looking workout suit which has never, ever been sweated in, wearing an expression of competence and willingness to serve. Captain Smith wonders if it's appropriate to flash his credentials at this young punk.

Before Smith can say a word the attendant says, "The Chief is expecting you. Go right on in." And he indicates to continue straight down the corridor. Captain Smith is rushing past a barrage of doors leading to lockers, saunas and racquetball courts before it becomes clear he's no clue where the Chief is and therefore where he's going. He turns to go back to the desk for directions and notices the attendant is striding down the hall, coming to his aid. They meet in the middle, and the attendant holds open a door for him. Smith reads the legend as he enters: Women's Locker Room.

"Are you insane?" Smith inquires, spinning on his heels. "Are you trying to get me killed?"

The attendant continues to hold the door open. "All I know is She said She wanted to see you as soon as possible. If you want to explain that you've been waiting outside this door for ten minutes ten minutes from now, be my guest. I'm standing here telling you where She is, that's all." He smiles, glad to be setting up the moral dilemma instead of being trapped in it. "What you do with the information is entirely up to you."

This requires a few minutes thought, Smith reckons. He remembers reading once that indecision is the worst trait a leader can have; a bad decision is most always preferable to no decision at all. In this case, though, he wonders if that advice is wise. He is damned if he does, damned if he doesn't. Only the overwhelming stench of fatalism hurries him onward; he straightens his tie and marches into the locker room, head high, looking neither left nor right.

The room looks like something the Dodgers have at home for the players to lounge about in before the game and give interviews in afterwards. There is a bath mat before each locker, long and shaggy. The lockers themselves are huge, enough room for every suit Smith owns, with multiple hooks and shelves and little bags for toiletries and dirty clothes. There are no doors on the lockers; expensive clothing and watches are hanging there, in the open, their owners secure in the fact that every member of this club is rich enough to buy whatever they want. At each juncture he reaches, he stops, turns sharply and loudly, and looks down the row of lockers. Each row is deserted till the last, where the Chief stands at the last locker on the right, dictating orders to her young, male, body-builder of an assistant.

For those keeping score, that makes two men and one woman in the room. Only the woman is unclad. Well, not completely so, Smith realizes suddenly to at least some small measure of relief. She still wears white underwear, silk, with a delicate lace border framing her bottom. As he walks on bravely, making each step as loud as possible, she pulls a jogging bra over her head and into place, adjusting the elastic carefully so as not to pinch what he can only assume are her breasts on the far side of her body. Smith, he realizes, had never thought about it but now sees the Chief is a very well built lady, a very eye-pleasing hour glass from the hips through the shoulders without an extra ounce of baggage in-between. His mind stops proceeding predictably at this point, though: his appreciation of her form is merely aesthetic, sterile and pure. She's the Chief, after all. He could never aspire to sex with someone of her stature.

Not yet, anyhow.

"I hear you, Smith, you can stop stomping now," she calls and then returns her attention to passing out assignments to her assistant. "I want you to call up Sheen and tell him to keep the noise down or we'll call the Times and let them investigate the situation, you understand?" Her assistant nods, giving the impression he's never had the courage to speak in response, letting his half of this relationship be non-verbal. "Good, now get out of here while I talk to Smith."

The assistant turns and goes. The Chief pulls on a pair of gray gym shorts and ties a knot in the waist. She pulls a T-shirt for an ancient 10K over her head, enlarging the rip in the collar to about half an inch. She doesn't look at Smith; he stands as far back as he figures he can get away with, back straight, knees buckling. She sits and takes her shoes and socks with little pompoms on them out of her designer gym bag. "Smith," she says, her attention still focused on the shoes, "I am getting ready to play racquetball with the Mayor. Of Los Angeles," she adds for clarity, putting her left foot down and starting to lace up the right. "He is going to ask me a question, and I need your help to answer it. Are you ready to help me?"

"Yes, Ma'am," he snaps. Some reservoir of bravado adds, "Of course."

She looks up at him with a look that could emasculate. "He's going to ask me why a member of my department has the California National Guard on full alert, waiting to help apprehend two bank robbers. He's going to ask me because the Governor has asked him. Both these esteemed gentleman, as well as myself, would like an answer to this question." She stops, plants both feet firmly beneath her, and rises to her full height. She waits a long second; Smith looks straight ahead, trying to focus at a spot somewhere well past and slightly over her head. When the word comes, it's with a force he simply hadn't prepared himself appropriately for. "Well!?" she demands, the word echoing off the tiled walls and ringing in his ears.

"I called them, Ma'am." He says it simply and honestly, just like he'd been practicing it in the car on the way over.

"I know you did, you stupid son of a bitch! I want to know why! I want to know why I shouldn't fire you right here, right on the spot!"

That is a darned good question, Smith suddenly sees. He attempts to pick a course of action again, and again fatalism is the only philosophy that seems to offer any advice: once you've crashed and burned anyhow, you may as well go out in as brilliant a fireball as possible. Besides, during the aforementioned drive over, he'd prepared a defense; he just wasn't all that convinced it was going to work. But, any port in a storm, and any plan in a massacre. "I was just following your direction, Chief."

This gets her attention, just in case he hadn't had it before. She closes the space between them slowly and deliberately until she is standing right in front of him. As he's a few inches taller (especially when she's in her gym shoes) she is shouting directly into his neck. "Say that again, I dare you to say that again."

"I was following your direction on apprehending criminals who…"

"What the hell did you construe to mean we should mobilize the National Guard?"

"Your direction to spare no resource to catch third time offenders."

She backs off a few steps, unprepared for this new wrinkle. She wants to keep yelling at him, certain he deserves it, but waits a moment to let this idea sink in. "They're third time offenders?"

"Yes Ma'am. Well, one of them, anyway," he concedes, hoping not to lose any appreciable momentum. "The other has no criminal record that we can find. But the ringleader has a conviction for forgery and another for felony fraud. When we nail him this time, we can put him away for good."

"Good God, Smith, I meant any resources we have, not those of the entire state!" She still hasn't found complete control of Herself, but the anger is gone from her voice. This is more of a token reprimand. He feels confident enough to take the next step along his verbal tightrope, and punctuates it with an authentic step towards her.

"I just figured this would be a great chance for you, the Mayor and the Governor to make a joint statement about how serious you are on crime." Captain Smith lowers his voice to deeply conspiratorial tones. "And this guy will be the perfect example, Ma'am. His crimes are bad enough to strike the public as punishable, but not so horrendous as to put them off their lunch. And he's charismatic, arrogant, and flashy. The trial will be the highest rated non-celebrity moment ever to hit CourtTV." The Chief is listening intently and beginning to like the idea a little, just a little. "Besides, those Guardsman have to train somewhere, right? Why not a little live action?"

This is a new experience for both of them. Smith had never imagined himself politically savvy; the Chief had never lost control of a good ass chewing. But, accidents do happen; She smiles broadly, and picks up her racquet and goggles. She taps Smith on the shoulder with the catgut on her way by. "Interesting, Smith." She walks away a few more steps; he decides not to follow Her, to make his stand right there while hoping She'll turn around. Turn around, he thinks loudly. Turn around!

As a matter of fact, he thinks it so loudly it causes my brain to ring.

Just as She gets to the end of the row of lockers, She turns around. "You'll never do anything batshit like this again, will you?"

"No, Ma'am!" he sings, knowing full well he's going to be rewarded handsomely for this inspired bending of the rules.

She smiles, and Smith is feeling so damned proud of himself he can actually feel the first vague tinglings of an erection between his legs at being alone with her in a locker room, at having seen her bare back and silk-encased bottom. Before turning to go, leaving him standing straight and tall and alone, she nearly whispers, "I'll talk to the Mayor."

Smith smiles. He stands still for a long while, making sure she's gone. He might have stood their in a pleased stupor forever if an octogenarian with an attitude hadn't arrived a few minutes later and chased him out so she could change for her step aerobic class.

Chapter 27—Where the Plan Leads

Breakfast, the event, the meal, the social gathering, is over. Tony is doing the dishes in his kitchen, Christian having offered help which his handcuffed state really didn't allow him to give. In any case, Joe had declined any sort of domestic servitude, and led them to the living room. The coffee table offers an array of magazines, including ***Smithsonian***, ***Popular Science***, ***The New Yorker***, and ***Playboy***. To the last of these Joe turns his attention, propping one leg over the other and slouching until his butt hangs off the couch. The ease at which he seems to take over his surroundings annoys Christian immediately, both because it's so impressive a feat of ego and it's a sign Joe is getting back to normal again. Christian was beginning to have just the slightest warm feelings towards the defeated Joe. In any case, this is no time for idle fleshy browsing; Christian has something he wants to discuss.

"Look, Joe," he begins, completely failing to draw Joe's attention away from Miss May. "Are you listening to me?"

"Unfortunately."

"Look, he's a damn nice guy and all," Christian is hissing, trying to ensure their host can't hear their literally behind-his-back words. "Damn nice, but we've got to get moving!"

Joe looks up. "Why?" Christian doesn't immediately answer, pondering what answer he could give beyond the fact they robbed a bank yesterday and are currently shackled together in steel and fur. The obvious questions are always more difficult to answer than the tough ones. "Where to?" Joe continues.

That's a tough one. Christian doesn't know how to answer it, either. He eventually settles on, "Well, to wherever your plan was leading."

"Ah," Joe says, nodding. "Excellent." He returns to his magazine. "You know, I've often wondered if the backgrounds and hobbies of these women are any more authentic than their tits."

"Breasts," Christian says, automatically.

"OK, whatever. Those fleshy things hanging off their torsos, often silicon enhanced." Joe turns the page and fans out the centerfold.

Christian doesn't want to ask, he puts it off as long as he can, but eventually hears himself saying, "Joe? Where is your plan leading?"

Joe doesn't bother looking up. "I'm sure this'll piss you off, but…"

The long pause is all the worse because Christian knows what's coming next. He tells himself he doesn't, he tries desperately to believe he's not going to hear what's about to be said, but it doesn't work. He knows what Joe's going to say, and he's already unhappy about it.

Joe looks at him again. "This is it." He spreads his hands, indicating the room, a possessional gesture a few steps along the evolutionary chain from marking one's territory by urinating at its boundaries. "The plan goes no further than sitting in some deserted condo and waiting it out."

Christian was right, of course: he did know what was coming, and he didn't want to hear it. "Wait for how long?" he asks, yearning for at least a loose, sweaty grasp on his rapidly regressing life.

"How long, oh Lord, how long?" Joe cries far too loudly for Christian's taste, since he wants to maintain the impression of a private conversation. "As long as it takes, till the end of time, till the dawn of time. Till I have a good reason to move." He fixes Christian with what he hopes is a conversation ending glare and resumes his anatomical studies.

Christian doesn't even notice the look, let alone take the hint. His mind is shutting down extraneous pieces again, attempting to focus all its thoughts on the problem at hand, which it is stating as: we are going to jail. "That's it?" he asks, surprised at the sudden volume in his voice. Then, quieter, "End of plan?"

"Yup." Joe turns to the party jokes page, hoping to improve his suddenly dampening mood. "I can play the end of the tape for ya, if you don't believe me."

"You blew up the tape," Christian reminds him.

Joe shrugs his shoulders. "Take my word for it."

"Whose word, yours or Bob's?"

A brief gust of anger rushes through Joe. "And just what the hell was your plan after walking out of the bank?" he wants to shout, turning the tables on the little ingrate where they belong. But some little used part of his mind stops him, censoring his thoughts before they're offered to the public. Admitting Christian made him angry is tantamount to admitting Christian has any effect on him whatsoever. Not that almost killing both of them last night wasn't a bit of a give away; it was, but seemed necessary to get himself firmly back in control. Instead of any emotional response, he shrugs again. "I just don't see any real reason to rush off. Tony there is willing to feed us and offer safe haven; what more could we want at this point?"

"I wanna go home," Christian answers, surprised at how appropriate the mother-needing implications of the baby-talk feel to him. He wants his mother, not like Oedipus wanted his, but more traditionally. Of course, he doesn't have a home; he sold it last week, closed escrow yesterday morning. So he settles on the idea of wanting to get a home and then going there.

Joe steps back into the conversation. "You can't always get what you want."

"Didn't Tony say that?"

"No, the Rolling Stones."

"I know that, but I meant..."

"I'm not stealing it from him," Joe explains. "I'm stealing it from the Stones, just like he did. The fact he's here, though I'll admit not part of my original vision for this part of the operation, is working out very well."

Christian suddenly sees what's been bothering him. He is completely in love with Tony, the feelings hit him less than 5 minutes into their conversation, and he feels unworthy of that love. He is here, offering himself as a common criminal not a fellow intellectual. He is endangering his object of affection through his presence. That, more than any fear for his own freedom and safety, is tugging at his consciousness and demanding their flight from this sacred place. This is one aspect of the lawless life he hadn't planned on: the change in self-perception. He couldn't quite find a fully formed guilty conscience, since the bank is insured and Mr. Goldstone will be completely compensated for his cash. The thing that has changed is how Christian looks at himself. It had become second nature to sneer at the shadier, less reputable characters in reality, literature and the visual arts. "Me, the bad guy?" he thinks, comparing his despicable form to that of Darth Vader or Alan Rickman and finding he just doesn't fit that particular mold very well. But, he's no longer the innocent, never-having-sinned boy he woke up as a couple days ago. Now he's found someone he has always wanted to be worthy of knowing, finds he doesn't feel worthy and wants to flee that sensation immediately. He would have exactly the same problem if Marilyn were here right now, but his mind compassionately doesn't bring this point up to him.

Joe, though, doesn't seem as concerned with the moral or philosophical implications of their actions. He's much more concerned with the moral and philosophical nature of the carefully posed and airbrushed women before him. Once more into the flail goes Christian. "What if the trucker saw us crash and called the cops?"

This gets him to put down the magazine anyhow. "Have you ever escaped from certain death without a scratch?"

"About three times yesterday."

"Then you know you don't have a lot of excess energy for looking in rearview mirrors. Wouldn't want to waste that sort of luck on pointless observations, either. Even if he did report the incident, I doubt he could've told them much what with the natural and overwhelming focus on just being alive." Joe glares at his mate, daring him to try his next ploy.

Despite a decreasing sense of purposefulness, Christian continues with the next objection his mind can grab hold of and form into a sentence. "Someone's found the car by now."

"Not much of it. I blew it, as you know, and the jug of sulfuric acid in the trunk should've taken care of most of the remaining big pieces." Joe smiles his omnipotent grin.

"Acid." Christian hears a car drive up to the cabin and is about to saying something when he realizes that Joe hasn't heard it yet.

"Damn clever, huh?" Joe continues to smile without limits.

Christian has to fight the urge to smile a sly grin of his own. "Damn."

Joe moves to summation. "It's possible, but unlikely, that we'll ever be found here."

There's a knock on the door, and Christian involuntarily erupts in a short burst of self-satisfied giggles. Joe stands and drags Christian back to their bedroom. Joe stares at Tony while walking silently, sending a loud yet silent message: get rid of whoever it is. Tony wipes his hands on a dishtowel and waits till their door is closed to just a crack before opening the front entrance.

In the bright, sunshiny room Christian and Joe wait silently, breathing as little and as quietly as possible. Christian's thrill of victory has been replaced by the reality that Joe's demise, even if he predicts it, is also his own. Joe keeps one hand on the doorknob and the other on his pistol tucked inside his pants.

"Phil!" Tony's voice calls, natural, lyrical. "How ya been!"

"Oh surviving, surviving," the other says. His voice is old and a little gnarled, either through too many cigarettes or too much shouting over the years. "And yourself?"

"'Bout the same, I must admit. What brings ya by?"

Joe draws his gun and tightens his grip on the doorknob. Christian is attached to the gun hand, and isn't thrilled about the idea of being powder burned while killing a couple of people in a cabin on Mount Baldy. His stomach is fluttering dangerously, and he feels like either his breakfast or his bladder may give way at any moment.

This visitor switches into a business mode. "Well, the wire gave us the word of two bank robbers who mighta been headed this way, so I was out early this morning checking for a car matching the description and found the damnedest thing. A wreck, well, an explosion but the metal of the frame had pretty much been eaten away, too. I've never seen anything like it…"

"Uh, Phil," Tony gently interrupts, "I have some stuff in the oven, so…"

"Oh, sorry Tony. I'm just wondering if you saw anything unusual last night or this morning."

There is a pause, Tony thinking about the question presumably. Joe holds his breath, leaning backwards slightly to better rush through the door shooting, if necessary. After an eternal silence, Tony's voice rings clear and true: "Well, no. Last night was just about as typical a night as I can remember."

"Glad to hear it," Phil gushes, his mental notebook snapping shut, being done with this witness. "Take care, then, Tony.'

"You too. Stop by one of these days, we'll have some coffee."

"Love to. Bye."

"Bye, Phil."

And the door closes. Joe doesn't move, wondering if there are still two men in the other room, one of whom is ready, willing, and even paid to shoot him. The sound of a car driving away, scattering a fine spray of gravel over the drive, relaxes him just a bit. A string of obscenities floods his mind, chastising him for assuming the obvious. Tony could have driven away, leaving Phil there with his gun drawn and jaw set. Or…well, that's about he only option he can think of. There's no way to know what's happening on the other side of this door, he insists to himself. Keep yourself alive. He gets Christian's attention and motions towards the door. He raises one finger, then another. At the count of three he bursts into the room, dragging the nearly immobile Christian, to find Tony standing in front of the door, hands in the air.

"He's gone," Tony informs them, in as reassuring voice as he can muster.

Slowly all three of them relax. Joe puts his gun back in its storage space between his gut and groin, Tony lowers his hands quasi-statically, and Christian exhales the breath he's been holding since the last time he was in this room. Joe glances around them, laughing. "You had us a little worried there, mate."

Tony nods. "Understandably."

Joe's nose senses something is wrong. He turns to Christian, shaking his head. "Maybe Tony's got some more clean briefs."

Chapter 28—Making One's Parents Proud

The news waits for no man; in fact, it rarely waits for any actual events anymore, it just goes ahead and keeps reporting and the story will be created in its wake. During the early morning hours, before Christian woke to his rather pleasant dream, I starting soul surfing to the other people involved in this whole torrid affair, and tapped into the following interview:

"Good morning, Los Angeles. This is Lynn James, reporting from the house of the parents of suspected bank robber Christian Whitney. As you can see behind me, Mr. and Mrs. Whitney have refused to talk to me on camera; the solidly closed door behind me will, in all likelihood, remain closed throughout this interview. But I owe it to you, my viewing public, to give it one more try, no matter the risk to my personal safety."

She turns profile (so the camera doesn't have to shoot her butt directly, she doesn't consider it her good side) and knocks loudly on the door. "Excuse me, Mr. and Mrs. Whitney? I'm sorry to disturb you again, but…"

A woman's thin, exasperated voice can barely be heard through the closed door. "Go away!"

"Yes, Ma'am, I understand you are reluctant to speak to us, but…"

"Get off the steps! Are you deaf?"

"No, no I'm not, but…"

"Go go go go go!" Mrs. Whitney screams at Lynn, still through the door.

"Calm down, honey, you're going to give yourself an aneurysm," a male voice (presumably Mr. Whitney) joins in the conversation.

"Calm down! How can I calm down with crazy television crews barracking at the gates?"

"Barracking at the gates?" he repeats incredulously. "That does it, no more PBS for you…"

Lynn turns and stares into the camera, somewhat incredulously. "Excusing me, Mr. and Mrs. Whitney, but if I could just ask you a few questions…"

"Who?" the male voice asks.

"Mr. And Mrs. Whitney," Lynn answers.

There is a long pause. Then, the man yells with all his might, "Who the hell are Mr. And Mrs. Whitney?"

"I don't know, but she keeps asking for them, and I keep telling her to go away."

Lynn looks a little nervous. "This isn't the Whitney house?"

"No!" the couple answers in unison.

Lynn smiles very weakly. "Cut."

I wonder why I never saw that interview on the air?

Chapter 29—The Truth Will Set You Free

Even back in the bathroom, Christian has something to say.

"But why did you lie to him?" he demands of Tony, who is standing next to Joe in the main room. Joe is, of course, standing immediately next to the bathroom door and being occasionally jerked about by Christian's unseen actions.

"Why shouldn't have I?" Tony counters.

"Yeah, why not?" Joe chimes in.

"I thought all you philosophers searched for truth," Christian bleats.

"Oh please," Joe moans.

"Here, it's very simple," Tony says. "I told him what he wanted to hear, 'cause if I'd told him you two were hiding in the bedroom Bob would have rushed out and shot twice, turning Phil and me into a St. Peter joke."

"The truth will set you six feet under free," Joe says. He's growing a little tired of this line of questioning.

"Instead, I hit him with a white lie and he lives to see another day."

"Be true to your school," Joe says.

Christian isn't satisfied with this answer. "Whatever happened to dying for your principles?"

"It was ruining life insurance companies. They had it outlawed,' Joe speculates.

"You only get to fall on that sword once, Christian," Tony answers earnestly. "You've got to pick the best time, and this just didn't seem like the one to me."

"So, you consider it a white lie?" asks Christian through solid oak.

"Sure, very white."

"Like telling someone you like his tie when it looks like a Jackson Pollock print." Joe smiles, feeling it's a reference the undereducated wouldn't hit upon. The only positive feedback he receives is an unenthusiastic "Good example," from Tony.

Predictably, the unenthusiastic response annoys Joe. "Did you really want him to take the moral high ground, Chris?"

Tony corrects him. "Christian."

This pretty much completes Joe's mood swing. "You two have a one track mind."

Tony shrugs. "It happens."

"Would you quit shrugging your shoulders?"

"I've been trying."

"For how long?"

"About 45 years."

Joe shakes his head. His arm is going numb from lack of blood flow, Christian pulling the cuffs tight in his efforts to clean and dress himself. He's tired of standing up. He hasn't completely recovered from the total lack of pancakes in his life. He's starting to get the impression he's wandered into a situation where it's two opinions against his one, and he's already tired of that. He needs to just ***be***, for a few minutes (preferably alone) but if the aloneness can't be arranged he'll settle for no whinging for a half an hour. He leans heavily against the wall. "Besides, Christian, we're just bank robbers! We'll probably end up in a relatively nice level of hell."

Tony cocks his head slightly to one side. "You know, my sister works in a bank."

"Really?" Joe intones, heavy in a syrup of sarcasm. "Maybe we've met her, then."

Christian opens the door, his soiled undergarment wadded into a ball in his free hand. In an effort to make pleasant conversation he asks, "What's your sister's name?"

CHAPTER 30—POUGHKEEPSIE!

When he comes to, Christian is lying on Tony's couch with his head aching and his mind reeling. Joe sits next to him, of course, looking very put out by this whole fainting ordeal. He stares at his left (or free) hand, balled over into a half fist with the nails facing him, though whether he's contemplating his manicure or in the first stage of punching someone isn't clear. Tony is standing over Christian, placing a cool cloth on his forehead. Christian's vision is a bit on the unfocused side, so he shakes his head to try to bring in a better picture. He hears a voice saying, "Marilyn. I believe that the gentleman said Marilyn..." and eventually figures out it's his own.

Tony takes the cloth off and soaks it before replacing it. "It'll be all right, Christian. Whatever the hell you're saying, it's OK..."

Wistfully, Christian exhales, "And they call the wind Marilyn..."

Joe shakes his head, wondering how this will ever be over. Not just the immediate crisis of Christian losing it, but this whole situation of being shackled to his partner and staying with a philosopher. Ridiculous. "Chris ain't never been too stable, almost any word can snap his mind in two like a twig." He thinks about this for a second. "Hey! Maybe some other word can snap him out of it!"

"Oh Marilyn, my Marilyn..." Christian continues to rave. He rolls a little from side to side, rocking himself for the comfort of it.

Joe leans over Christian and shouts in his face, "Poughkeepsie!"

Tony pushes him back. "Stop that."

"Why?" Joe demands.

"It's pointless."

Christian rolls his eyes. "Life could be a dream…"

"Christian, I want you to listen to me, are you listening?" Tony asks.

"I heard it through the grapevine," he responds, nodding.

"OK, good. Now, let's try something. When I count to three and snap…"

Joe leans in again. "Guacamolé!"

"Shut up!" Tony turns to Joe with a flash of anger more intense than Joe had expected. Joe leans back, pouting, leaving the two of them relatively alone. "Christian, when I snap my fingers, you will wake up, calm and relaxed, OK?"

"Relax, don't do it…" Christian answers.

"One…two…" and Tony snaps his fingers, loudly, near Christian's ear.

"Hey!" Joe shouts out automatically, but is silenced with a look from Tony.

Christian sits up a little, shaking his head again. Tony helps him prop his head on the arm of the couch. "It's OK, Christian. You're OK, you're safe," Tony tells him.

"Did you say Marilyn?" Christian asks him.

"You only counted to two; you don't go on three, you count to three and then go," Joe mopes, but is ignored by the others.

"Christian, if I say yes, will you be out again?"

He considers this. "No, of course not." He tries to sit up again, but Tony firmly encourages him to stay down. "I was just a little surprised, that's all. I just happen to know someone who happens to work in a bank who happens to be called…" He stops, deciding if now's a good time for this question. He decides it isn't, but asks anyhow, "Where does your sister, your Marilyn, work?"

Joe and Tony answer in unison, "The First Federal in Santa Monica."

CHAPTER 31—LUCK

In darkness again, Christian hears voices, seeming both nearby and echoing, as if from a great distance. The first one seems to be saying, "I just want to know how you knew my sister works in Santa Monica." A reasonable question, Christian thinks, and one that strikes some chord in him though at this point he can't quite remember how that chord goes. Another voice answers, 'Hey, it was a lucky guess man. Don't you believe in luck?"

"No," the first answers.

"Besides, it fits in perfectly with the shitty way this entire operation has been going," the second explains.

Christian remembers where he is and how he got to this pseudo-conscious state. He tries to think about Marilyn, literally the woman of his dreams, or better still the woman of his destiny, but feels himself slipping back into an uncontrollable mental state. He eases off, thinking instead of what a truly lucky bastard he is. This is, he feels, because of his chancing upon the brother of the woman he feared he would never see again, so it's kind of thinking of Marilyn, but only peripherally, like out of the corner of his mind. So, his consciousness can bask in her glow but doesn't overload and reject all further input. He wonders at the random set of strange occurrences which have lead him to this place, this couch in this cabin, waiting for his love to come and find him. Wonderful. The voices outside his head are getting angrier and louder; he doesn't want to hear them, so doesn't even try to distinguish the words. He does feel a need to interrupt the emotions, though.

He slowly opens his eyes, to find Tony and Joe glaring angrily at each other, their lips moving frantically.

"Why the hell does my sister's name have such an effect on Christian?" Tony demands, keeping himself from pointing a finger in Joe's chest through great will power.

"Why don't you ask him?" Joe says, noting Christian's increase in consciousness.

Tony turn his attention away from Joe gratefully. "Christian, are you OK?"

"He won't tell me a damn thing, anyhow," Joe mutters, shutting himself off from the world again.

"Why do you keep asking me that?" Christian asks Tony.

"Well, are you?" Tony persists.

"I doubt it," Christian admits.

Tony smiles. "Well, just relax for right now, OK?"

Christian props himself up on an elbow. "It's just that I've always been looking for someone…" He stops, wondering exactly where to go from here.

"Looking?" Tony prompts.

"And that someone I've been looking for is named Marilyn and she handed Joe my money yesterday…"

"At the first Federal in Santa Monica," Tony finishes.

Christian nods. Tony nods, understanding exactly how Joe made such a lucky guess now. Joe doesn't nod.

"It's just all so strange…" Christian begins, and then stops again, as if that says it all.

Tony asks, "Would you like to talk about it?"

"Hold it, hold it, and stop." Joe interrupts. "This sounds like a damn long story, and the Dodgers are playing the Cardinals. Ya got a TV in this place?"

"Aren't there better ways to kill your brain cells?" Tony inquires.

"So what's your point?" Joe retorts.

"So…" Tony looks down at his immaculate hardwood floor. "So, there's a Watchman in the bedroom.

"Cool!"

Joe jumps to his feet and starts off in that direction, until he is reminded by a sharp tugging at his wrist that he's still attached to Christian. Tony shakes his head and rises to fetch the Sony. Joe watches him all the way to the bedroom; he turns to Christian as soon as Tony is out of sight. "Are you OK, Chris? Christian?"

Christian almost can't answer. After all the shocks of the last few minutes, this one is mild but still significant. Joe, using his proper name, actually seems concerned about his well being? He mutters a quick, "Yeah, thanx," with some difficulty. Then Joe turns on a warm, friendly smile that Christian immediately suspects doesn't get out much. Tony returns with the television; Joe grabs it hungrily, switching it on and positioning the earphone in its place. The room has the faint sound of crowd noise and a golden baritone calling the play by play. Tony sits down next to Christian again, who shakes his head stubbornly. "I sound like I'm insane."

Tony shrugs his shoulders. "Don't we all?"

CHAPTER 32—YOUR HOLY GRAIL

Christian takes another deep breath. He is starting to feel a little self conscious, just sitting here not talking when he'd made it so clear he desperately needs to talk. Tony sits cross-legged on the couch next to him, settled in for however long the wait may last, keeping a mask of earnestness, peace and understanding glued onto his features. Joe is watching his beloved Dodgers on the tiny screen, but only one of his ears is tuned into the play-by-play via the earphone; the other is waiting for Christian's words as well, though Joe is far too cool and casual to let on.

"When I was eight," he starts, "I received…" and suddenly he has no idea what the next word was going to be. He tries a different direction. "I was…" but again the succeeding ideas fail him. It's the introductory words that are getting in the way, he tells himself, so decides to start in the middle. "God appeared to me and told me I've got a mission in life."

Tony's face hasn't changed at all. It's still the concerned, caring mask. "And did He tell you what that mission is?"

"He gave me a question and an answer, and I was to keep asking the question until I found a certain someone who could answer it for me."

The mask cracks just a little. "Really?" Tony asks, with the slightest hint of incredulity.

"I've been asking around ever since."

Tony looks pleased, yet surprised. “So very few have their destiny spelled out so plainly for them; so many fewer believe it when they hear it. Like Martin Luther said.”

Christian nods for a moment before he realizes he has no idea what he’s nodding about. “Martin Luther King, Junior?”

“No, the original Martin Luther. I don’t remember exactly how it goes, but in a sermon on of the miracle of the Immaculate Conception, Luther said there were actually two miracles that night. One was Mary becoming pregnant without original sin, and being visited by the angel who tells her all about it. The second is that when she told Joseph about it, he believed.”

“Um, Tony?”

“Yes?”

“I, uh, don’t believe in the Immaculate Conception,” Christian says, with a fearful look. “I don’t believe in any religious treatises I’ve ever heard, actually.”

“That’s fine,” Tony says calmly. “Just because you don’t believe it happened doesn’t change the fact it’s a great story. And, whether you like the story or not is also irrelevant, because the real issue is it inspired a profoundly valid philosophical comment from Dr. Luther some fifteen hundred years later, completely independently from whether or not the original story was True.”

“Really?” Christian asks, timidly.

“Well, it’s valid to me. And, that’s really all I can judge, now isn’t it?”

“I suppose so.”

“No, no you don’t,” Tony responds with a stern current carrying his words. “Either you agree with me, or you don’t, or you haven’t decided yet. I’m asking you now, never just take what I say for granted, and don’t let me believe you agree with me just to avoid confrontation.” He pauses for a breath, and his natural smile returns. “Life’s too short for that, don’t you think?”

Christian considers this for a long moment, turning it over in his mind. It's a refreshing experience, taking a pause in the middle of a conversation to think. Christian is much more used to analyzing and criticizing his conversations when replaying them in his head hours, days or even weeks later. Instead he stops, breathes and thinks: Life is not all that short, or at least it doesn't usually seem that way. After all, it's the entirety of his consciousness, everything he knows, remembers or understands is an infinitesimal building block in his life, each stacking one atop the other building up to himself. That seems large enough, significant to him certainly, no matter how many discussions of the infinite and unending expanses of space and time you may throw at him. Perhaps he's being too literal; isn't Tony really suggesting that social pleasantries aren't worth any time at all in a life, no matter how much time there is to work with? Or, conversely, it's important to live each moment to its fullest and that will never be accomplished when contemplating such trivial and unimportant excrement. In any case, it's difficult to disagree with Tony's hypothesis. He opens his eyes to see Tony's patient facade. He answers, firmly, "Yes. I agree."

"Good. So, you have a mission in life?"

"Yes. Yes, I do." He catches himself in mid thought. "I mean, I did."

"You did?"

"I gave it up."

Tony again looks very perplexed. "You had a crisis of faith?"

Christian nods himself dizzy. "Definitely. A nasty, unforgiving crisis of a battered faith. But I already explained all that to the hooker."

Christian looks for the surprise he felt was his due, but sees none of it in Tony's expression. After all, hadn't he gone out of his way to make an unusual, shocking, off the wall choice? Doesn't he deserve some validation? But Tony is unwilling to go in for any of that. He levelly asks, "Why?"

"Cheaper than a psychiatrist...and less pushy."

Joe mutters under his breath, "And probably much more Freudian." He listens for any sign that he's given away his stealthy advantage, but hears none. Their conversation continues on without hindrance; or, as Joe put it to himself at the time, "Good, Chris is spouting the same uncut nonsense as before; he's a complete loon," and several other similar thoughts.

Christian is continuing. "Two days ago, I had had it. I abandoned all hope and fled from my job at the investment firm, trying to take all of some miser's money with me to Rio."

"Which firm," Tony asks.

"Does it matter?" Christian shoots back. "They're all the same, each and every carbon-copy one of them. I could have worked for a dozen firms within a three block radius and felt every bit as fulfilled and loved and appreciated, could have had the same corner office after six years of paying my dues in a cubicle, could have had the same secretary to type up the same memos. It just doesn't matter, they are the same damn organizations."

"Fair enough."

"Unfortunately, before I could get out of the bank, two things happened. Joe here interrupted with his automatic weapon barrage."

"I can see where that would create a need for flexibility," Tony nods.

"But even before that I was a sitting duck because I had asked Marilyn, your sister, the question one more time, for old time's sake…"

Tony's interest is peaked. He's leaning forward in his chair, and isn't breathing. He asks, "And?"

Christian smiles. "And she nailed it. She didn't even think about it, just spat down the answer."

"Amazing," Tony concedes.

"Amazing indeed. I hadn't heard those words since He'd first told them to me. It had gotten to the point where I didn't believe the words even existed anymore. I was completely shocked; a less likely occurrence, I could not fathom."

"And then there she was, your Holy Grail, your pot of gold."
"Yup," Christian nods, smiling painfully. "There she was."

Chapter 33—Power

"And then, almost as quickly, she was gone," Christian continues. "Gone, lost forever it seemed, in a blaze of gunfire and police sirens."

"What was the question?" Tony asks impulsively.

Christian shakes his head. "I said I wouldn't ask anymore."

"You've already found who you're looking for," Tony points out.

Christian smiles, noticing for the first time a change in his partner's demeanor. Tony is now sitting on the edge of his chair as if it's a warming frying pan. His eyes are wide open, and his breathing is as irregular as flights to Dubuque. "I thought you weren't always a slave to your curiosity."

"I'm not. Always."

"Fair enough."

"So, are you going to tell me?" Tony demands.

"I'm not sure," Christian demurs.

"You like this feeling, don't you?" Tony asks him.

"What feeling?"

"This rush of power my curiosity gives you."

"How do you know?" Christian asks, genuinely surprised.

"Do you really think you're any more difficult to read than I am?" Tony asks.

"I'd thought so, yes. For no good reason, obviously, but I had thought so."

"Sorry, mate, you're as human as the next man. Maybe more so, if that's possible."

"How could I be more human than the next man?" Christian wonders aloud.

"Some people have the capability to control their emotions, urges and desires at least occasionally. Their lives can be a little tougher to interpret by the casual observer. I haven't seen any of that in you, not yet anyhow."

"Really?"

"Do you feel I've done a poor job of analysis?" Tony asks, again genuinely curious.

Christian contemplates. He tries to remember any point in his life where he didn't immediately act on whatever impulse flooded his mind. One fine example jumps to his mind. "I have often not pursued women I found attractive."

"Really," Tony replies.

"Yes, I'd have to say I have asked out at most one in ever ten women who got my attention. I have always prided myself on the fact that every woman should be able to live her life without being propositioned by every man she meets, and therefore take it upon myself to not preposition them."

"Except for every tenth one."

Christian feels he's been snared in a trap. "Well, approximately every tenth, yes."

"Why them, then?" Tony is doing it again, Christian thinks. He is pursuing a tangential topic which Christian has given pretty obvious indication he has no interest in discussing further. But like a terrier attached to a sock, he won't let it go. He just keeps on steering the conversation in whichever direction seems to attract his fancy at that instant in time. And Christian doesn't even see him turning the wheel until it's done and they're cruising along in a different direction. Right turns, left turns, U-turns, Christian doesn't see any of them coming. He wonders if he can do the same thing.

"Did you know that some people call U-turns 'flipping a bitch'?" Christian asks.

"No, I didn't," Tony replies immediately, undaunted by this shift.

"Yes, a friend of mine used the term exclusively, anytime she felt the need to reverse course." Christian stops, waiting for Tony to jump in for his turn in this conversation. But all he gets in return is a cool silence. Not even cool, just tepid and intense, his eyes never leaving Christian's face, his lips together but not pressed tight. Calm. Casual. Willing to sit there all day for Christian to continue the conversation in whatever direction he might choose. He can't think of a single further thing to say on the topic of U-turns, at least not a thing he won't feel like an idiot for uttering. He suddenly remembers what he's already said on the topic and sheepishly tries to disappear into the couch. He's having a pleasant, serious, philosophical discussion with a true intellectual and he's talking about urban slang? And coarse urban slang at that. He breaks down and abandons his previous course, falling back into the conversation he'd tried to derail. "I asked out every tenth one because I couldn't help myself. I was afraid to do it, but more afraid not to, afraid I would be missing out on some of the great experiences in life: romance; sex; backrubs; and deeply, intensely meaningful conversations. I was afraid I wouldn't be living if I allowed every woman to pass me by."

"Very good. I'm not all that interested in the one, though. What about the other nine? What made you think they'd be happier not to be hit on by you?"

"It doesn't have all that much to do with me, actually. I just see attractive women around being hit on by every guy they meet, all of them. I feel they deserve a break occasionally, so I was willing to be that break in their lives."

Tony smiles. "I don't believe you."

Christian feels like he's been slapped. "You don't believe me?"

"No."

If his mind had been reeling earlier in this day, the little sucker is definitely spinning around now. He feels like he should sit down for a minute till he realizes he already is. What does he mean he doesn't believe me? I'm me, I have access to my mind, I know what I'm thinking, he has to believe me. "You have to believe me," is all he says.

"I believe that you believe yourself, if that makes you feel any better. I just don't think the reason you gave is the reason you really left a majority of those women alone."

The obvious question tries to rush out of Christian's mouth, but he stops it in mid expression. He is angry, feeling he doesn't deserve to be questioned this way. What the hell does this dude know about me that I don't know about myself? Not a damned thing; I hope. And if he ***does*** know something about me, which I'm unaware of, do I really want to learn something with the potential to change my self-perception? Again, Christian thinks not.

Till he pauses for self-review and realizes what a screwed up state his life is currently wallowing in. He's an unemployed bank robber handcuffed to his harebrained partner in crime. He's in a cabin talking about his destiny and lack of socializing with women with the brother of the woman he achingly needs to see and talk to again. He still has his health, true, but beyond that his life is at about the most confused, muddled and generally lowest point he'd even allowed himself to imagine. What new information about him could make it any worse? "OK," he starts, "why did I…"

Tony interrupts him. "You left those women alone out of fear. No specific fear, not a fear of rejection or embarrassment, just generalized, irrational fear of beautiful women. Don't feel bad about it or anything, I mean, it happens to a lot of us. Beautiful women, truly beautiful women are very intimidating, and scare away much of the attention we all assume they are getting on a regular basis. In my own humble and only slightly informed opinion, you've become comfortable with your sexuality when you don't mind being excited with a partner and you realize they want you, too."

"Really?"

"Actually, I have no idea," Tony surmises, smiling again. "I'm just guessing, working on another wacky, personal theory of mine. Who knows why you left those women alone? And does whatever the reason is have anything to do with being comfortably erect? I haven't a clue. We could simply set the issue aside, assuming fear and unselfish consideration both played a part in your behavior. Fair enough?"

Christian isn't sure if he wants to laugh or cry. "Do you enjoy doing this?"

"What, running conversations that warp other's minds? Yes, I do, actually. I'm pretty sure it amuses my students, also."

"I'm not amused."

Tony stops to consider this. "You're right, I'm behaving badly. I just assume others treat conversations as a joust as well; I forget they are more formal occasions in the minds of many. I hope you can forgive me."

"Sure."

"Do you mean that?"

"I don't know."

"Fair enough." Tony looks away for a second, giving Christian a respite from his intense glaze. "May I ask my question again?"

"Which one was that?"

"What was the question you used to ask people? The one which identified the person you're looking for?"

Christian finds he wants to tell him, which is a little strange since he's really rather pissed off at him right now. "I used to ask people to tell me the more commonly known name of Robert Leroy Parker.'"

Christian never gets to see Tony's reaction to this, since Joe begins laughing like a rabid hyena. He is rolling on the ground, clutching the

Watchman to his chest like a frightened child. His eyes are clenched shut, and yet tears still manage to stream out of them. Christian and Tony watch this show for a minute or so, until Joe is gasping for air. He lies on his back like a beached dolphin, swallowing as much oxygen as he can and giggling. He looks up and realizes he's become the center of attention. "Sorry," he says, then takes a few more gulps of air to recover and continues in broken phrases. "I just… imagined Tommy… Tommy Lasorda in a… in a tutu." There's no reaction from his companions. He finally regains some control and stops snickering. "Hey, it happens, you know?"

Chapter 34—Marilyn and Tony Green

Only a hundred miles out of town, it started. The Green family had gotten up before the sun, packed everything into their canary yellow Chevrolet Impala (the first generation of the once proud steeds to be downsized, but not ***too*** downsized) and hit the road. They are headed over the river and through the woods to Grandmother's House. Or, more accurately, down the freeway and over the toll bridge for about 500 miles, but you get the idea. Tony and Marilyn sit in the back seat; their folks sit up front. No one says much; they are really all about half asleep, including dad at the wheel, but the car knows the way and they're making good time.

Tony, twelve years old and sitting behind his dad, is getting bored. He'd go back to sleep if he could, but he can't. He reads a Nancy Drew book for a little while, but that proves to be boring, too. He's got enough of a sense of the big picture to know they are going to be in this car forever, or awfully damn close to it, and therefore it's not just his immediate boredom which bothers him but the sensation of the hours of boredom to come which makes the whole experience more and more unbearable with each passing mile. He looks out the window; amusement factor very low, it holds his attention for only about 90 seconds. He returns his annoyed gaze to the interior of the car. The back of his dad's head. His mothers profile, staring straight ahead, her hair up in a bun. And then, his sister.

Marilyn sits next to Tony, two years his junior. She is sleepy, her head nodding further and further down before being jerked back to attention by a particularly harsh bump in the road. She's awake and staring at the world for a few minutes, and then the process starts again: nod, nod, nod and then bump. Tony watches this in vague bemusement for a few minutes, but soon can't resist the opportunity to get involved in the process himself, helping his sister, as it were. He holds a finger to her nose as she sleeps, holding her head in place so it doesn't bounce like a rubber ball. This has the additional and intended effect of making her think she has a bug on her nose; in her half-awake state she slaps at it, rubs her nose to get it off. Tony is quicker, and moves his hand just in time to stay out of her reach. She therefore is presented with an everlasting, constantly annoying bug stuck to the end of her nose.

She wakes up, and sees it is Tony who's been messing with her head. He smiles, because he knows what's coming next, anticipates the striking smash of the silence in the passenger cabin. She takes a deep breath, filling her lungs beyond their recommended capacity, before using all that air to wail, "Mom!! He's on my side!"

Tony recalls his hand, absolutely bubbly with self-satisfaction. The trip is now truly, officially underway.

Mom does about a half turn. "Tony, leave your sister alone."

"OK, Mom," he replies, many shades short of being convincing.

"You two just relax back there," Dad adds. "We'll be stopping for gas in another 120 miles."

Which is, of course, about two hours away. Two hours in the life of a child is a long, long time. Hell, it's a fairly long time for me still today, sometimes, depending on what's going on. I spent two hours waiting in my doctor's office the other day, because he was getting backed up by a Ladies Day Tournament and couldn't get off the back nine in time, and all he had to read in the waiting room were health brochures like "Pus: Our Friend Against Infection." Now that was a long two hours.

So, it doesn't take two hours for Tony to find himself in need of entertainment again. In about three minutes his entire world is stagnating in nothingness and desperation. No one experiences anguish as fully as children. The vinyl seat he and Marilyn sit on has a line separating each cushion, so there is a clear demarcation between their sides. He slowly works one lone finger across this Mason-Dixon line and waits, confident the wait won't be long.

He is absolutely correct.

Marilyn fills her lungs again and screeches, "Mom! He's doing it again!"

This provokes at least a three quarters turn. "Tony, stop that!"

"OK, Mom."

And on and on. We get through, "He's touching me!" and "He's looking at me!" and "He's muttering under his breath so you can't hear but I can and saying mean things to me!" within the next 30 miles. Each brings a slightly more annoyed response from the front seat and harsher stares from Marilyn. Tony is not exactly enjoying himself; he's still bored, after all, but at least something is happening. He's on the verge of either getting in big trouble, or getting exactly what he wants: a diversion. In his mind, he's not doing anything wrong; he assumes his sister is as bored as he is, and so doesn't really mind this little game. That's not true, unfortunately, she does mind it quite a lot, but Tony won't find that out for years. No matter what sort of person you turn out to be, at one point in your life you're an annoying sibling.

Or an annoyed one.

Tony decides to go for the goal. It's what he's been working for, where he's been driving as his father has piloted the car. This is a significant risk because this is the thing he's pinned all his hopes to, what he sees as his only chance to avoid death by boredom during this little day of driving: the chance to play Twenty Questions. If the answer is no, he really doesn't know how he'll avoid slipping into insanity before they arrive. Still, he is a risk taker by nature, and he thinks the time is ripe. He's annoyed his sister enough that his parents realize they need to do something to pass the time or else there will be war on their rear flank. Tony takes a deep breath and asks, "How about Twenty Questions?"

No one says a word.

This is, of course, a negative response, but Tony doesn't care. They didn't actively, actually say no, so he can continue on as if they had (actively and actually) said yes. "I'm thinking of a person…" he says, trying to create such a great sense of curiosity within his listeners they just have to start asking him questions. And, if curiosity fails, he doesn't mind eliciting such a sense of pity from them that they will play for a few hours to keep him from going insane. Or to keep him from being annoying in the other, more obvious ways he's been employing. He says it one more time: "I'm thinking of a person…"

"Is it a man or a woman?" his mother asks.

"Man," Tony replies with glee. His sister cringes, and his father swerves, but they are off and playing again.

"Is he alive or dead?" his dad asks.

"Dead," Tony answers. This is no surprise; Tony always picks dead guys or women when playing 20 Questions.

"Has he been dead for more than 100 years?" Mom asks.

"Yes," he replies.

"More than 200?" comes from Dad.

"No." Tony is practically dancing back and forth in his seat. If he can get Marilyn involved, then he's really got something going here. She turns to him, and says with a bit of a lisp, "Was he, by any chance, a philosopher?"

Tony smiles. "Yes."

The family groans.

Thirty-three guesses later (it's family tradition to not keep track of guesses, you can just keep guessing until you get it or give up, whichever comes first) and the family still hadn't come up with John Stuart Mill. So, Tony gets to pick the next mystery person, and he chooses Rene Descartes. This is an easy one, so his father gets it rather quickly and the game keeps moving along. His parents, and very soon his sister, will curse the sixth grade teacher who made learning about different philosophers and philosophies a part of her curriculum; the downside of learning in kids is they want to show it off, and Tony is so enamored with this course of study that he wants to show it off constantly. Even when he's a successful professor of philosophy, his mother, father and sister are not so sure it was all worth it.

But Tony's sure, so that's something.

CHAPTER 35—ROCK, PAPER AND SCISSORS

Tony is not a man who sits still for very long. The opera is a tortuous experience for him, because after each scene he thinks he should go water the lawn of wash the car or otherwise do something involving water. Or maybe work on a macramé plant hanger or weave an Arapaho war blanket or… something. Idle hands and all that. In fact, the fear of idle hands is probably the factor leading to the popularity of the remote control; you feel your hands are doing something when your ass is planted deep into a couch and you're soaking in radiation and punch lines from the television. Active hands and laziness; these two forces in combination are unstoppable.

After Joe's outbreak of hilarity, Tony goes to the kitchen to finishing his dishes. Christian volunteers to dry, wanting to do everything Tony does in an attempt to emulate his life. Joe, tired of his baseball diversion (the Dodgers are three down in the top of the ninth, after all) follows, playing rock paper scissors with himself. Whenever one hand loses, the victor slaps it violently, mercilessly. Since his right hand is still attached to Christian, this occupation becomes a little painful for them both after a time.

"Ow!" Christian intones.

"Sorry."

"So," Tony begins, handing Christian a dripping plate, "now you've found her. What's next? Why were you looking for her?"

Christian shakes his head in time with his hand wiping the dish. "I don't know. He didn't say."

"Aw come on!" Joe exclaims, his hands both showing scissors. "Why do boys with hormone poisoning usually go looking for attractive young bank tellers?"

"That's not it," Christian protests.

"For a little of the old give and take! Don't have to be a genius..."

"That's not what this is all about!" Christian exclaims.

Both of Joe's hands show rock. He looks at Christian with his standard shit-spitting grin. "Yeah, go on. Tell me you don't want her."

"I don't!" Christian reacts without thinking about the question. Tony hands him another plate.

"Get on!" Joe shouts.

"I don't!"

The paper in Joe's right hand covers the rock in his left. The swing of the victor carries Christian with it, jerking him into the living room and nearly causing the demise of an innocent plate. "You don't what?" Joe continues.

Christian has to replay the last few lines to figure out what he's being asked. In this time span, he sees the face of Marilyn drift across his consciousness; he feels his pulse begin to pick up speed, blood being pushed into the far reaches of his being and back again with increasing pressure and cadence. "I don't think I can say I don't want her," he admits.

Joe smiles an octave higher. "Right," he says, and waits for the explanation.

"But this whole thing wasn't about sex," Christian protests as Tony hands over a bowl. He thinks the fact he didn't sleep with the hooker he hired might be a good example to use at this juncture, but doesn't really want Joe to know all that much about him. Instead, he says, "I didn't even know I was looking for a woman, till I found her."

Joe nods. "You could be bi-sexual."

"I could be looking for something a little more significant than…"

"That what?" Joe asks, intrigued.

"Than… whatever you're imagining…"

"Your face is as red as a Macintosh…"

"Macintoshes are green," Tony corrects.

"Whatever."

Christian is tiring quickly in this conversation. His mind isn't made for endurance, it can, at best, occasionally put together a decent sprint but it'll never be one to think with over the long haul. He dries the dishes handed to him in silence for a few minutes, placing each on the kitchen table to perform the action with one hand. Drying dishes is just one of many things Christian is realizing it's difficult to do with one hand. Tony and Joe delve into the horticulture of apples with intelligence and verve: Tony with intelligence; verve being the domain of Joe, now and forever, amen. Christian thinks of Marilyn; his mind's eye is focused upon her sitting on that high stool behind the window of the bank, her hands flying over their work, her eyes gentle and dazzling. His mind's eye then changes focus slightly, and imagines her sitting naked on that same stool. Christian is starting to wonder about the place of sex in life; could he have diminished its importance all these years mistakenly?

"Maybe it is about sex," Christian says, to his surprise. Joe and Tony stop their other discussion. "It's not only about sex, but I definitely think it's about sex."

"I hear she's not very good," Tony says, washing a skillet with precision and enthusiasm. "Unimaginative, afraid to try new things, tires easily…" His audience is stunned into silence; they can't believe their ears. He looks up at them, and realizes this is another one of those situations he finds himself in nearly constantly: where he's forgotten the things other people are hesitant to talk about. "Oh, sorry."

"Tony, how can you say that?" Christian says, genuinely surprised. "And about your own sister?"

"Which do you mean, say she's not a particularly gifted lover, or to discuss her sexuality in general?"

"Yes."

"It's a part of life, you know. There's no reason it should be a taboo topic, hidden from the world. It can be discussed just like the weather and the Dodgers."

Christian can't come up with a response to this. Joe slaps him on the shoulder. "Rough reviews, dude. Sorry to hear that."

CHAPTER 36—ANOTHER INTERVIEW

Lynn and Doug, together again, and on the move:

"Excuse me, Mr. Kauffman, excuse me," Lynn says, chasing a man in a cheap suit down a dimly lit corridor. She is losing ground, because her heels just don't have the traction for sprinting down polished hallways. Doug, in his loose fitting jeans and Nikes, is practically jogging in place to keep from running her over and continuing on after their target alone. Lynn stops suddenly and cries loudly, "Mr. Kauffman!"

The gentleman in question stops at the very top of a stairway, holding himself up just before his momentum would take him over the precipice and on to the next level. "What?"

"May I have just a few minutes of your time? A few minutes, it's all I ask."

"I'm very sorry, but I'm late for an appointment." He doesn't look very sorry; he looks very perturbed and very much in a hurry to keep on moving.

Not that Lynn gives a rat's posterior if he's in a hurry, or sorry, or whatever the heck his mood may be: she needs him to talk, to tell all, to give her something she can broadcast, because her boss is getting quite annoyed at having to wait for a usable update on the bank robbery. She scuffs her shoes along the corridor and places herself in interview position. "This will just take a second, Mr. Kauffman, I promise."

He smiles the toothy grin of the smart aleck. "It's already taken longer than that, Miss."

She chooses to ignore that one. "You are the parole officer for Mr. Joe Bridgers, is that correct?"

Kauffman crosses his arms in impatience. "Yes."

"Can you tell us anything about Mr. Bridgers, about what he's really like?"

Kauffman shakes his head. "No."

"Nothing?"

Again the head shake. "I'm sorry."

"Well, how about you? Were you surprised to hear he's a prime suspect in the robbery which occurred yesterday?"

"No comment."

"No comment?" Lynn asks, incredulously.

He smiles his wicked smile again. "That's right."

"None what so ever?"

He again shakes his head. This is terrible TV, Lynn realizes. "May I go now?"

Lynn tries one more, if somewhat desperate, ploy. "Well, where are you off to? Have the police contacted you to help tracking down Mr. Bridgers and his accomplice?"

"No; I have a meeting with my agent and publisher to finalize my book deal about Mr. Bridgers. If you'll excuse me…"

And he's gone, taking the stairs three at a time, and body checking a reporter from the *Times* a couple of landings down. Lynn watches him go, annoyed. She then turns her agonized expression towards the camera and sees the red light signaling that Doug is still taping. She switches to her patented half smile/half serious professional Look, which she uses to close non-tragic yet still criminal stories. "That's the scene downtown, as people respond to this heinous crime. This is Lynn Jones reporting."

Doug doesn't wait for anything further, but yells "Cut!" himself.

I don't recall ever seeing that one on the air, either.

Chapter 37—Every Six Seconds

It's been stated that your average adult male has a sexual thought approximately once every six seconds during the day. Let's examine Joe's thoughts during this interlude and see if we can verify these facts.

Next project: change the oil on Tony's elderly Volvo. When Joe had seen it the night before, prior to their entrance, he'd assumed a car this old is just abandoned out here. On further inspection in daylight, however, the car proves to be rather well loved, just not at all new. Tony's rolled himself underneath to loosen the bolt, leaving just his feet out in open air, pointing up to the sky. Christian and Joe stand about, untasked. Joe feels just fine about this; Christian occasionally picks up the odd wrench or spare part, feeling he's joining in the process in some small, hopefully meaningful way. The sun glints off the chrome of the car and shines more gently on the surrounding ground just beginning to feel spring's warm embrace. Joe looks at Tony's upright feet and is reminded of the look of an erection on a horizontal male body.

"I," Christian starts, continuing the earlier conversation, "just don't understand my luck."

Tony grunts, straining to remove the bolt holding the oil in place.

Christian takes this as an invitation to continue. "I mean, check the facts here. I had to leave Marilyn to save my butt…"

"Your welcome," Joe interjects, feeling he deserves the credit for that rescue. He also has rather predictable thoughts concerning the word "butt."

"...After I'd been looking for her for the past 20 years, and I end up here, in her brother's house. Go figure the odds of that sort of thing just occurring."

Apparently, neither of his companions has any desire to do those calculations. The handcuffed ones can hear Tony straining still, adding the occasional epitaph to help the process along. Joe begins to pick at his teeth with a matchbook he carries around for just such occasions, reminded of a line from a Kurt Vonnegut book, "picking pussy hairs out of my teeth."

Hey, don't look at me like that; Kurt Vonnegut said it, not me.

"I'm guessing that I'm using up all the luck I'll ever have right here, right now. Everything is going right for me; maybe I should be buying lottery tickets."

Joe spits out the matchbook, snatching at it wildly as it falls to the dirt below. "Let's review for a second, shall we? Here's your story as I see it: boy meets girl, boy loses girl, boy ends up at girl's brother's house handcuffed to a lunatic and pursued by the police. Now, while I'll admit this is a full bodied plot, and 100% hindbrain at that, I wouldn't go so far as to assert that everything is coming up roses."

Joe becomes slightly distracted over the term "full bodied."

"Hindbrain?" Christian asks.

"Yeah," Joe replies, going into full professorial mode. "The frontal lobes are for cognition, emotion and the like. The hindbrain, however, is concerned with the important stuff: procreation, sustenance, power, that sorta thing."

"So you're claiming not to be a pervert, you merely have an overly developed hindbrain." Christian says, smirking to beat the band.

"Exactly." Joe grins as well; Christian nods in pleasant contemplation. The Volvo parked on his face hides Tony's reaction from them. (I know he is amused by the application of pseudo-science in the world of political correctness, but alas it doesn't really affect the story.)

Joe suddenly realizes the word "Volvo" is strikingly similar to the word "vulva." He's not exactly sure what the vulva is or what it's connected to, but he's completely convinced it's dirty.

Tony succeeds in removing the bolt holding the lifeblood inside his crankcase. Quart after quart follows the call of nature into the waiting pan as Tony rolls back out into the open. "Perhaps, when Christian spoke of being lucky, he was looking more at the big picture, Joe. He's about to have a chance to fulfill his destiny…"

"Here!" Christian jumps in. "At dinner tomorrow night!"

"And he might even get laid in the process!" Joe adds quite unnecessarily. But, of course, it was time for such a thought.

Joe picks up his now useless matchbook as the others look away, unwilling to argue over the coarseness of Joe's language at least partially because he's right. Joe is feeling philosophical. The sort of overwhelming positive thinking Christian is exhibiting is the best and worst of humanity, to his mind. The worst, because it's a completely useless way of approaching the world, about as related to reality as Klingons to unicorns. On the other hand, it breeds a very useful sort of gullibility he's been making the most of in his various professions for years. Which, in point of fact, has been the only force allowing him to remain clothed, feed, and gainfully employed, such as it is. And sexually satisfied, he reminds himself (just over five and a half seconds after his previous thought on the subject). This is, it suddenly flashes to him, the con man's conundrum: the failings of your marks are also the failings of your friends, making the opportunities for respecting and therefore enjoying your fellow man few and far, far between.

Despite his feeling that it's useless, he makes the vain attempt to reground Christian in reality. "I thought you wanted to be long gone by tomorrow."

Christian thinks back, but that section of his memory has been completely isolated from his consciousness. "Why the hell would I ever have said something stupid like that?"

Joe gives up trying to re-ground Christian. It would be more possible to saddle a snake. Instead, he decides to be witty some more, which is always fun. "Heredity?" he guesses in answer to Christian's query, remembering the line from the film ***Tango and Cash***, where one of them claims to have a larger gun than the other due to heredity.

Tony wipes his hands on a rag. "I'll admit, Christian, it's all a little hard to believe."

"It's either that or environment," Joe continues. He remembers that Teri Hatcher was in ***Tango and Cash***, a memory which occupies his thoughts for the next few seconds.

"But," Tony continues, "For a person with such undying faith in fate, it shouldn't be too surprising."

Christian immediately feels the hairs on the back of his neck bristle. "Fate?"

"Yes."

"Fate?"

"Which letter didn't you understand?" Joe inquires.

Christian shakes his head. "I don't believe in fate."

Tony glares at him for a long moment. "You don't believe in fate?"

"No."

"You don't believe the course of your life has been predetermined for you?"

"Nope."

Tony tries a slightly different tack. "You don't believe that God came up with a nice little path for you to follow and was even gracious enough to come down and tell you about it in person? That He took time out of His busy schedule to explain to you in detail about the Question, its Answer, and Who would answer it?"

Christian begins to rethink his position as Joe offers his opinion: "He's got you there." Joe starts to recall some of the places he's gotten it.

Mindless logic, if you can call it that, takes over Christian, his self-preserving need to prove himself Right despite the odds or evidence. "No he doesn't! I made the choice to keep asking the question, to keep searching."

"Actually, you'd made the choice to stop asking the question," Joe reminds him.

"Yeah, and then I decided to start asking it again, didn't I?" Christian's blood pressure is surging and his eyes flare like, well, flares.

"Yes, you did," Tony says in his honey dripping, flame smothering voice. "And why did you ask the question again? What were you searching for?"

"For the one with the answer; for Marilyn!"

"OK, and why were you looking for her?" Tony asks. Joe's answer to that question floods back into his mind again, complete with a smoky saxophone soundtrack.

"Because," Christian starts, but finds he doesn't know what comes next. He doesn't know why he was searching for the one with the Answer, he was searching blindly for this human, because...

"Because He told me to find her. He didn't tell me why."

"And yet," Joe adds, "you don't believe in fate."

"That doesn't matter," Tony jumps in, attempting to defuse the anger starting to build in Christian's contorted face again. "It seems pretty obvious that you are searching for her because with her lies your destiny, for better or worse, richer or poorer." Tony sits down on his rolling shop cot, intending to put the bolt back in its comfortable home. "She's the one you're looking for, and you'll just have to wait to see what sort of meaning, structure or whatever she adds to your life."

"He's got you there," Joe prods, stopping himself from commenting on the sexual parallels involved in disappearing from view into a dark, well lubricated cavern as Tony has just done.

"Christian, there's nothing wrong with a belief in destiny," Tony adds from under his car. "I've never had a clue whom I was waiting to meet, nor understood why I occasionally turned left instead of right. But I've always felt a certain, subtle force. Even though it's not as overt as your experience, I feel a guiding hand even now." He rolls back out into the light rather prematurely, causing Joe to bite his tongue again. "I find it very comforting."

Christian gives in to the little voice telling him to stop fighting. This idea, that an observable destiny can actually be a good thing is novel and very tempting to embrace completely. He expresses his relief and hope in a heartfelt, "Really?"

"Absolutely. Of course, like yourself, I feel this force only when I want to feel it."

"So is it really destiny when you have some control over its path and actions?"

"Absolutely." He plunges the opener into the first quart can of oil (Joe winces) and tips it upright, allowing the contents to pour into the waiting vessel (Joe crosses his legs). "You have some input into the whole process, of course; you just don't have complete control over every aspect of your life."

"I'd never looked at it that way," Christian replies.

"Of course you did," Tony shoots back. "Didn't you stop asking your question, and then start again?"

"Thereby showing my faith in destiny being a part of my life by losing faith in my destiny being a part of my life."

Tony smiles. "Something like that."

"So, have you ever felt like you were waiting to meet someone, Tony?" Christian asks, smiling again.

"Well, as near as I can figure, I've been waiting to meet you two." Christian looks shocked and honored by this idea; Joe is distracted by Tony's actions with the next oilcan. "Don't feel too honored. I say that to most everyone I meet."

Joe smiles. "He's got you…" An icy look from Christian stops Joe's comment in mid utterance. Tony pulls the dipstick from the engine block and, pointing it towards the sky, wipes it clean; Joe smiles.

Chapter 38—Thinking into the Distance

I get up to stretch my legs for a few minutes and suddenly become aware of a loud groaning sound in the room with me. It takes a long moment for me to realize the sound I hear reverberating off the surrounding walls is my empty stomach. Based on my previous experience in these climes, I know there's not a damn thing to eat in the police station except stale mini-donuts from the machine down the hall, and even those are usually gone. Instead, when working here, I tend to abuse my body by fawning to my taste buds and eating these outstanding bratwursts from a local hole in the wall every few hours. Today I was just a little bit preoccupied and didn't stop to eat at all; so now, 18 hours later, it's time.

So it's out the door and down the street to the diner. The night is hazy and dark, not a star in the sky and the moon is merely a vague luminance low on the horizon. The streets are dirty, the air calm, and the streetlights are about half burned out: I love this damn town. I walk in and order three brats and a heavily caffeinated drink. The brats (one more than I usually order) are to make up for a lack of eating, and the caffeine is so I don't drift off and miss anything important in the lives of Chris and Joe. It hadn't occurred to me to write it all down yet; I hadn't envisioned any creative part in this process. I'm still the watcher, and like a great movie or a can't-put-it-down book, I can't live without knowing how it ends.

Of course, I'm not willing to miss anything now, either. Fortunately, Christian and Tony are making dinner, and Joe is getting bored, and they're all talking about mutual funds. I check back in every few minutes and thus far no topic change has occurred or is in sight. Therefore, for all practical purposes, I've put the VCR on pause while I went to the kitchen. So I take my time with the brats: piling on the spicy brown mustard, the generous helping of ketchup, and mounds on relish and onions until the chances of eating even one of these creations without spilling things all over myself rapidly decreases toward zero. Just remember, campers, fashion (or even hygiene) should never ever get in the way of good food.

I walk to a booth with my food and drink. As I lay a paper napkin in my lap, I tune back in to the Chris and Joe Show and am immediately overwhelmed by a strong emotion drifting across the city. Longing and sadness and desperation curve together in a triple helix, increasing in anguish one instant and ebbing away into nothingness in another. I am immediately mesmerized, drifting on the wave of this thought, and I'm sure it's not Christian or Joe or Tony but I can't for the life of me figure out who it is. There is a tingling all along my spine, as if little tiny fists are shaking each vertebra with an iron grip but a velvety touch. I lose all sense of direction and comprehension and become despondent and jubilant in equal measures in concert with the emotions this brain is emitting. There is no more cool, psycho-intrusive detachment: I'm completely involved.

Who the hell is this I'm tapped into here? I can't tell if it's man or woman, which is weird; I mean, I can always tell that at least (sort of ruined **The Crying Game** *for me) but here the emotions are concentrated enough that I can't see a thing past them or near them. Who the hell is this? On the one hand, I'm enjoying the sensation of intensity, but on the other I'm panicked at my lack of control. This mind is driving me crazy, like the one mystery Hercule Perot couldn't solve, or the one woman Don Juan couldn't seduce, the one problem Einstein couldn't figure out.*

Challenges are wonderful, but let me tell you this about getting your butt kicked by one: it sucks.

Deep breath time. Breathe. Relax. I remind myself nothing good ever comes from impatience or oxygen depravation. I take a bite of the first wurst; it is excellent, as always, and I momentarily forget about the ringing inside my head. I try to expand on that: concentrate on the immediate sensation of eating and come back to this brain a little later (you may well note the similarity of this technique to people trying to remember something: stop thinking about it for a few minutes, let the back burner of your brain keep things percolating, and then come back to it). I bite, I sip, I chew; nope, not thinking about it. Not thinking about this thing I'm desperate to think about.

The first sausage is digesting deep down and I suddenly, as if surprised by it, return to the large disturbance in my brain. Yup, still there. I try to sneak around it, see it from different angles, somehow break it down into recognizable pieces, but it's impossible. The instant I get too close I'm immediately just listening and feeling without any shred of analysis continuing. Pointlessly pleasant. So I try a different tact: I don't try anymore, simply enjoying the sensation instead. I eat and drink as I experience this brain for all it's worth. Giving up is sometimes the most effective way to exist.

After another half sausage is swallowed the mind calms down; I found out later, this is something her brain does every night at dinnertime. I realize I had felt a similar sort of twinge in my head every evening for the last few years, but not this loud: it must have been the connection with Christian that caused me to hear it clearly tonight for the first time.

But, let's see things from her point of view for a while. I'll start at the beginning, so you can see the whole cycle in the proper perspective:

Chapter 39—Marilyn Green

She sits very still in an inexpensive, uninteresting, worn-white chair, staring at her cat lying on the rug across the room. The cat, being fairly responsive as the species goes, stares back. Minutes tick by as the day's light goes down step by sidereal step. Marilyn is immobile; she blinks, of course, and breathes but otherwise is statuesque. The cat stares at her for a few minutes and then lays its head sleepily down on its front paws and gets in some well deserved snooze time.

This is how she leaves the day behind. Well, no, that's not quite right; actually, she's leaving the rest of the world behind, withdrawing into herself completely. Except for the cat, of course. It's Saturday, but that doesn't matter, the ritual remains the same as the days meld one into the other. Something you probably don't know about Marilyn yet: Ritual is a good thing for her, something she just can't ever get enough of.

Her body calm and her head clear, she rises and walks to the bathroom. First, it's time to wash her hands. She goes to the bathroom and turns on the light, to see everything in the room there is to see. She stares at her hands for a long time, inspecting them visually by slowly turning them over and over, using one hand to rub at a bit of loose dirt on the other, staring at each slight mark to determine if it's a pimple or a bug bite. Marilyn has more problems with pimples and bugs than any other person on earth. It would be easy to write off her constant finding of new blemishes as paranoia or even a marginal excess of vanity, as people who don't know her do, but that would be unfair and inaccurate. Truthfully, when you look at this woman for any amount of time, you do see more pimples arising and bugs a-biting than on a normal human being.

This leads to a chicken and the egg type discussion: which came first, one's personal hygiene habits or one's skin? Marilyn has incredibly sensitive skin, prone to rash, acne, bruise and bugs; she's also nearly terminally anal-retentive. One would seem to cause the other, but who can say which brought about which.

Marilyn doesn't care, she just accepts what she is and makes the most of it. She starts the water running while examining her left hand (the right already having been visually dissected for the day). Down and down it flows, water molecules released into the basin after making their slow and difficult journey from the snow-encrusted Rocky Mountains into the headwaters of the raging Colorado River, after helping to take a few more micrometers off the Grand Canyon, after dangling between the legs of skinny dippers in Lake Mead, after enjoying the thrill ride down and around Turbine 14 at Hoover Dam, after flowing down riverbanks, canals and pipes into the greater Los Angeles area; after all that, they now flow meaninglessly down the drain, through more pipes and into the Pacific.

Talk about anti-climatic.

And still on the water runs. Water is one of the elements of her life: water and paper make the world go 'round for Marilyn. On and on it flows; one finger tests it to see if the water is the right temperature; finding it a bit too hot, she turns on the cold. Then it's too cold; too hot; too hot still; too cold; then, as the baby bear once said, it's just right. She immerses her hands and lets them enjoy the sparkling lukewarmness splashing all over both sides of them. She strokes one hand with the other lovingly, applying pressure to each knuckle as if testing it, seeing if they're ready for another day. She picks up the scented hand soap and slowly massages a generous portion onto each palm; the palms wash the backs of the hands slowly, carefully, and thoroughly as the water continues on and on. Only when every inch of her hands and a decent section of her lower arms are covered in fragrant suds does she finally allow her skin to again be under the water, tirelessly washing off every trace of soap. She then inspects her hands for complete cleanliness.

The water's still running, of course.

Water and paper, water and paper. Toilet paper, napkins and Kleenex don't stand a chance in her apartment, being used by the handful for a vast variety of applications. Anal-Retentiveness is a way of life as valid as any other, and Marilyn is very happy being herself, practically floating in water and papered in, well, paper.

Freud would be very proud. Her hands are clean, and she turns off the water. The immaculate white towel is used to thoroughly dry each hand, and then is adjusted so the front is just as long as the back over the towel rack.

She walks into the kitchen, turns on the light, and looks around. She's pleased to find there isn't the least bit of disorder anywhere. She stops in the middle of the floor and slowly looks across at the beautiful solid oak dining set sitting there, covered in plastic to protect it from the kitchen's airborne grease. She's owned it for six years now, bought it at a great discount at a snooty furniture store in Beverly Hills. Everyday she looks at it just before creating dinner, knowing it's waiting for that day when someone comes home to share it with her. The pleasure this purchase still brings her every single day and the solid reminder of the fact she doesn't want to use it till she's no longer alone cause a rush of interwoven conflicting emotions.

This is what I heard. Cries from the nadir and zenith of her soul intertwine and reverberate throughout the city, waiting for someone to hear. And I hear her, and am immediately impressed.

But become more impressed immediately afterwards. The agony and ecstasy stops abruptly, and I am surrounded by pleasantly banal, happy, *yet slightly squirrelly thoughts about life and love as she boils some pasta for dinner. It's an experience like no other, being inside her mind. Every basic thought which floats through strikes her as a pleasant surprise. She makes her dinner, walks it to the living room, and sits down to eat while watching M*A*S*H reruns on the tele, not the slightest after-effect from the intense emotional experience of a few minutes before. It's not that she's unhappy with her present life: it's a great experience. She just realizes she wants something else, something which she for the moment can't have, so there's no need to worry about it all the time.*

Once a day is plenty.

She eats her pasta. I eat my bratwurst. We watch the colonel and Hawkeye and B.J. do silly things while being morally unwavering. It's a wonderful evening. Though you've probably heard it said before, let me stress that I really mean it: I'm starting to love Marilyn for her mind.

Chapter 40—Foot on the Clutch

I get so engrossed in Marilyn that I miss the beginning of the following conversation. We now join our regularly scheduled novel, already in progress.

Morning breaks and then night falls in their utterly predictable fashion, another day comes and goes. Darkness is embracing the cabin, making the rest of the world invisible and forgotten. After a cold supper and some Fig Newtons, Christian and Tony have taken to the couch to talk and think and, in theory, await the dawn. Joe is dozing lightly, his head resting on Christian's knee.

Tony gestures with his brandy snifter. "OK, let's try a little thought experiment." Christian nods, the warmth of alcohol radiating from his stomach into every limb and neuron. "Imagine this: we're sitting here, approximately a foot from each other, right?" Christian nods again, though it'd be more accurate to say he hadn't stopped nodding from the previous time and so merely continues. "Now, there isn't another mammal on this planet which I am physically closer to at this moment than you, right?"

"Sure," Christian agrees, still nodding.

"Did I mention we need to be carrying a compass for this thought experiment?"

"Yes, you did," Christian assures him, though he honestly can't remember or care.

"OK, now imagine this. Imagine I'm holding my compass. Now instead of facing towards you, imagine I turn directly away from you. I note this compass heading, and then begin to walk in a straight, straight line. At the point where I start walking, you are the furthest destination I can reach on this planet, following that exact course. So, using this logic, right now you are both the closest and furthest person from me."

Christian, with alcohol added, doesn't grasp this idea immediately. It sneaks up on him, as if from a hidden corner of his mind, and takes in his consciousness in one, quick grab. He sits up a little bit, thinking he's starting to sober up. He's not, of course, but his mind thinks it is.

Tony notices this change in posture and takes it to be a positive response. "OK, stretch your imagination a little further, then. Suppose the universe itself is closed and spherical, so that if you follow any heading long enough, you return to your starting point. Then, you and I can think of ourselves as being separated by a nearly infinite amount of cold, empty space."

"That follows logically," Christian answers, and likes the way the phrase sounds rolling off his tongue and out his mouth. He knows very little about logic, of course, but likes the sensation which pretending to know about logic gives him.

Tony takes a sip of the golden elixir making the rounds at the bottom of his glass. "Now, for one final stretch: Perhaps there is an emotional analog to this physical model. Perhaps the better you know someone the less you really know him or her. Perhaps the happier someone makes you, the more pain they cause. Perhaps, the more you love someone, the more you hate them."

Silence becomes the third member of their conversation. So, there it is, Christian says to himself. A perfectly simple, logical, ghastly idea, staring him right in the face. His mind again thinks it's sobering up, and though it's still not true he is suddenly a very serious drunk. He can't stand the thought of causing pain for Marilyn, not to her, not to the woman he's waited his whole lifetime to meet. And he can't imagine ever feeling indifferent towards her, let alone hating her. The tide in his mind is rushing in and out, back and forth, fighting the periphery of the idea while embracing the heart of it because it feels so right. He instantly understands every relationship he's ever had in his life, with women, with relatives, with friends. The closer he got, the more he needed them, the more anger and hatred was unleashed until the union was doomed. He doesn't like it, though. No one has, luckily, told him he needs to like it. He calls an uneasy truce to these conflicting thoughts by saying, "Perhaps."

Tony turns to look directly at him, apparently forgetting his impassioned plea for decisiveness on this very same couch a few hours before, and continues earnestly. "So, it's your choice, my friend. You can either drift through life at a safe distance from everyone, or have emotional highs as high as your lows are low, good with the bad, for better or worse."

Christian takes a small taste of brandy. "Which path do you follow?"

"Personally, I've always tried to cause as much pain as possible."

"I know," Christian says, nodding again and remembering how good and bad Tony has made him feel in their few hours together.

"Subtlety has never been my strong suit."

"But tell me, Tony, how do you do it?"

"I don't enjoy the pain, Christian. But, I'd gladly relive all the pain I've ever felt and more if it would keep me from inflicting pain on others. I tried for years to love someone without hurting him or her, but I finally realized it's impossible. Impossible!" He adds, punctuating his thoughts with volume. "Love never comes alone, Christian."

"If it comes at all."

It's Tony's turn to nod. "I think that's why I've turned to sex so much as of late. There, pleasure and pain become so intertwined that you don't even care which is which, time slides away to be replaced by other milestones of excitation and action… There is no love, and no hate. Just two people, very close together, finding it very difficult to remember the acres of empty space between them."

"Are you sure?" Christian asks.

Tony takes another drink. "Of course not."

Christian is disappointed. He'd never met someone he considered both a friend and a positive influence, and now that he has he doesn't feel all that much better grounded in reality. A prophet who isn't sure of himself, really isn't much of a prophet at all. One of the requirements for the job is an unwavering self-confidence, or at least if it isn't, it should be.

"I have no clue if my little theories and attitudes reflect reality, whatever the hell that may be. All I can say is I like them, and they seem to have worked for me up to this point in my life. I'm just trying to tell you that, from my perspective, you seem to be poised on the brink of your opportunity to feel your greatest love and deepest hate. When you meet my sister again, you'll suddenly be back in a whirlwind of emotions and ideas. This is the calm before the storm, the eye of the emotional hurricane, and you should use this time to think about what exactly you want, what you need, what you are. You will want to love her, but at times you'll hate her. You want to make her happy, but you'll cut her open as often as you soothe her."

Christian drains his remaining intoxication. "So, I'm damned if I do."

"Or, you can look the other way and just let her walk by, take another path other than the one directly towards and away from her, and never cross her consciousness again."

"Damned if I don't."

"No, no, you're not damned. This is your destiny, your mission! But, as we've both argued forcibly for today, you always have a choice to make." Tony pauses and stares Christian right in the eye. "You have a choice to make. This sort of situation can sometimes be frightening for people because their damned imaginations cause them to think there are distinct turning points in life and you can't ever go back again. If you remember nothing else from this whole experience, please remember these words: whatever choice you make, things will work out." Christian doesn't respond, but looks unconvinced. Tony reaches out and touches his knee in a reassuring way. "Please, for once I ask you, accept this without proof or even evidence and believe me, you'll be happy whichever decision you make."

"Get the fuck outta here," Christian spits out, and then is surprised he said it.

"I know, that's not easy to accept, but I'm convinced it's true."

"Why?" Christian asks.

"I don't know, I really don't. I guess this is faith, and without anything more solid than a little circumstantial evidence I'm as convinced of my words' authenticity in this world as I am of that wall's existence. Things will work out, and as you've probably already noted, I mean they'll work out for the best. Your passion in rebuking me makes me think I'm pretty close to the bone here, Christian. Either you already believe me and don't want to accept it, or you disagree very violently." Tony stops, smiles, and realizes his glass is also dry. "And, as we've just discussed, the two ends of the spectrum are really the same thing."

Christian sits in silence as Tony rises and refills each glass. His mind is spinning in circles, round and around the same path. At least if his brain were spiraling he'd feel like he's getting somewhere. Christian suddenly visualizes the sensations he's feeling: it's like he's revving up his car to six thousand RPM, he's placed it firmly in first gear, but is keeping his foot on the clutch. If he lets go for just an instant, if he eases his hold for just a split second, then the transmission will engage and he'll be careening off at great speed into unknown directions. He trembles at the thought of impending disaster if he lets himself believe any of what Tony has just said. He'll be happy, no matter what he chooses? No matter what happens to him? That's ridiculous. And what does that do to his choices in life; why make any at all, if there's no value enhanced in any direction? If he's going to be happy, why even leave his bed in the morning, or work his ass off in a pointless job, or cut the grass or shine his shoes? He congratulates himself on finally learning something: don't follow any prophet too far. He smiles, enjoying the power of balancing his trembling foot on the clutch, avoiding making an impact on the world.

At least for the time being.

Tony comes back and hands across one of the brandies. His face is again its natural calm and gentle mask, but Christian doesn't take to it in the least. "Are you OK, Christian?"

"Yeah, I think I'm feeling better."

"So, if you don't mind me asking, have you picked your path yet?"

"Tony, how do I know that Marilyn is the one, ***the*** person I've been looking for? There must be millions of people who know Butch Cassidy's real name."

"You found her first," Tony replies simply, with a shoulder shrug.

"Yeah, but…"

"If you are willing to believe that God sent you on a quest armed only with a question and an answer, it isn't much of a leap of fate to believe you found the right person first." He stops and drinks, looking at Christian as gently as possible. He thinks there is something else in Christian's mind, and he suspects he won't have to wait too long to find out what it is.

Luckily, Tony has not yet gotten tired of being right.

"But Tony, what if I reject your theory of life?"

"I'd recommend it," he replies.

Christian sits up, surprised. "Really? Your hypothesis, and assumptions, and…"

"OK. It's all OK."

"I'm sorry, Tony, but I just can't feel the space between us."

"Christian, let it all slide off your back like warm water. I'm a firm believer in only one thing: you must live as you will, and let no one come between you and your way." He smiles again, though he's afraid he's been doing it a little too often lately. Que sera, sera…

Joe, without opening his eyes, interjects, "Great, we're hiding out with Yoda on the Mount." Tony laughs out loud while Christian cuffs Joe across the brow. For the first time in their association, all three of them are cheerful at the same moment.

And then there's a knock on the door.

Chapter 41—Ya Gotta Believe

The rest of the day went pretty much the same for Lynn and Doug. They tore across Los Angeles County, the Valley, Orange County, even out into the dense smog of the Inland Empire and returned home empty handed. No story. Nothing made it on the news at five, or even the late report at eleven. Because they were completely shut out, failing to find one lead which would add any twist to the same old same old, the news simply ran with their report from the day before with Marilyn and some Most Wanted Posters of Christian and Joe. It's approximately 11:25 PM, the sports guy is talking about the Dodger's second game against St. Louis, and Lynn is pouting backstage at the studio. Doug is pouting too, but not for the same reasons. Lynn wanted to get the Story, scoop the opposition, nail the vermin and uphold the First Amendment. She's depressed because all she managed to do was burn gas, run up an expense report and put another few tough miles on her Salvatore Ferraganmos.

Doug is pouting because he couldn't use his tickets for the Dodger's game.

It's time to call it a night, get drunk, dive into carnal pleasures, play Sega: whatever you have readily available to shut out disappointment (that is, reality) for a little while and let the mind rest. Lynn looks at Doug; Doug looks at Lynn; they stand and prepare to go their separate ways.

The phone rings.

This is a little bit unexpected; people usually don't call here in the production studio when the show is in progress. But, hey, it's a day for the unusual, so Lynn answers it. Doug, always the gentleman, stands by, waiting for her. "Hello?" Lynn begins.

"Yeah, Lynn, this is Becky at the switchboard. I've got someone on the line who claims to know one of the bank robbers, and Bob told me to forward them to you. Ya want 'em?"

This is a deceptively difficult question to answer. It takes a genuine few seconds for Lynn the Reporter to be reincarnated within Lynn the Tired and Pissed Off Employee. But when she awakens, she awakens with a vengeance. "Hell yes, Becky, put him on."

"Her," Becky corrects.

"I don't care if it's an it, put 'em on the line."

"You got it." The short period of dead air on the phone is broken by Lynn whispering, sotto voce, to Doug: "We've got a lead!"

"Great," Doug says, though he obviously doesn't mean it.

Lynn doesn't notice. She's reaching out madly for a pad of paper and a pencil. She tries to decide if it's more reporter-like to tuck the pencil behind her ear or chew on it while waiting for the chance to actually use it. She thinks of her orthodontic work she's still paying off in monthly installments and chooses to tuck it behind an ear; this proves difficult thanks to the long locks of hair (her trademark look) covering the ear, so she's stuck with the unprofessional look of holding a pencil in her hand. She tries to poise it immediately over the paper, so at least it looks like she's only an instant from writing down something important. Lynn has never been called by a source before, and wants to get it right.

"Hello?" comes the tired woman's voice over the line.

"Yes, Ma'am, this is Lynn Jones of Channel Eleven News; what can I do for you?"

"I was just watching your news, and saw a picture of someone I met the other day."

"What person is that?"

"Well, I didn't catch his name, but the story was about a bank robbery…"

"Was it the professional looking geek or the more wild-looking, gun totting fellow," Lynn asks, proud of her ability to cut through confusion quickly.

"The geek."

"Ah, Christian Whitney. And how do you know Mr. Whitney?"

"I didn't say I know him; I just said I met him recently."

"How did you meet him?"

There is a pause. "At work."

Lynn is in heaven. She's talking to a source and pulling information out of them quickly and professionally. She's wondering if she can take this phone call live, on air, in a special news bulletin; now that would be cool. "At work, I see. And what do you do?"

Another pause. "I'm a working girl, if you get what I mean."

Lynn's eyes light up. "Christian Whitney went to a prostitute?"

"Now, honey, I ain't thrilled with that word, OK?"

"Sorry, sorry." She is scribbling as fast as she can, and manages to get the word "Prostitute" down before attempting to talk and write at once. "When was this?"

"Thursday night. He's a weird one, that boy. He just wanted to talk."

Lynn's pencil stops in mid scribble. She picks her words carefully. "He paid for, um, your time, and then just wanted to talk to you?"

"Yeah, I said he was weird. Told me about how God had talked to him and wanted him to start a mission, somethin' like that."

Lynn looks at Doug with laughing eyes. "He talked to God and wanted to start a Mission?"

"What can I say but what I say? Am I gonna be on the TV?"

"Well, Ms…"

"White, honey."

"Ms. White, we've got a number of leads to follow, but give your name and number to the switchboard lady and we'll get back to you as soon as possible, OK?"

"But, don't ya…" is all Lynn hears as she lowers the phone from her ear to replace it in its cradle. "God, the weirdoes you meet on this job," she smiles to Doug.

"Yeah," he commiserates. "Let's get outta here."

I can only imagine her reaction when Ms. White appeared on Hard Copy the next week after selling her story for $100,000. Actually, I don't have to imagine it, I lived it and Lynn had a cow. I'd never really understood that phrase before, but when you experience it, believe me, it's appropriate. In any case, it sounds more literary to write, "I can only imagine," so there you go.

Lynn soon thereafter shaved her head and joined an extremely strict convent in Thousand Oaks. Doug is now employed shooting erotic filmed entertainment in the Valley. I'd tell you more about their lives, but this isn't a story on social climbing.

CHAPTER 42—CURIOSITY

In case you forgot, there was a knock on the door to Tony's cabin.

Joe and Christian are immediately ready for a fight, though standing up proves to be quite a dexterity test for the somewhat inebriated Christian. They prop each other up like a rickety tripod, Christian having one leg on the floor and the other still stuck on the couch; it had fallen asleep underneath his other leg. Joe tries to draw his gun, but has the dead weight of Christian making smooth moves difficult. Tony holds up his hands in a pleading, appeasing gesture. "Gentlemen, I think I know who this is, and I also think it is time to go to bed." Slowly, and with some excess of testosterone, Joe and Christian catch on to what their host is saying: the lady of the house has returned. They utter a few words of parting, Joe with a serious smirk, and then go their separate ways.

Tony answers the door. Diane, tender and bright eyed, stands there, a knapsack slung over one shoulder. He reaches out his hand and draws her into his house and into his arms. She kicks the door shut behind them. "Are they still here?" Tony nods into her shoulder, holding her a little tighter. "Is it OK if I…"

"Yes," Tony replies, quietly, gently. He can feel her strong arms pulling him closer, feel their hips clanging against each other. He turns his head and kisses her earlobe, holding it firmly between his lips for a long moment. "Let's go to bed."

They release each other for a brief moment. Diane walks into the bedroom and unties her boots, bending over at the waist. Tony turns off the lights in the main room and checks the fire in the soft light of the glowing remnants. He stirs up the ashes and closes the glass doors, turning in time to see the smooth silhouette of Diane's bottom as she unlaces each foot sensuously. He feels undeniably drawn to the outline of Diane, her long legs stretched taunt, her lyre-like hips defined in the stirrup pants she so perfectly wears. As he closes the door he says, "I'm glad you're here." And he means it.

She straightens up and kicks off each shoe. She takes him by the hand and sits both of them on the bed. "Tony, do you still think they are here to…"

He gently strokes her hair. "Say it; it's not as frightening out loud."

"Do you think they are going to kill you?"

He nods.

"Why?"

"What can I say?" He reaches out to her and begins to unbutton her silk blouse, her concession to feminine trappings in her sensible wardrobe. "There's no logical reason for it; they haven't spent the day torturing me or anything. But, I am convinced it's the case. Call it a hunch."

"A hunch."

He reaches out and eases the blouse off her shoulders. "Yeah."

"Do you have these hunches often?"

"No."

She reaches out and touches his face gently. "Ever?"

"Yeah, I thought I was going to win the lottery once."

She smiles. "You're joking."

He nods. He also reaches around her to unhook her bra. "Wait," she whispers in his ear, and he stops right where he is, leaning towards her, his face against the satin of the garment he's attempting to unfasten. "If you feel this way, then let's go, right now. Let's drive off, in the dark, and come back in a week or two when they'll be long gone. Or better yet, leave and call the police, end all this craziness."

His hand finds the clasp. He releases it and pulls slightly away from her grasp, taking the bra with him.

"Tony, why?"

"Because I need to know if I'm right."

"You'll risk your life to find out?" He nods. "You'll risk my life, also?"

"I asked you not to come back tonight."

"I know."

He shrugs his shoulders. "I'm sorry, Diane, but I've made up my mind. I'll take whatever comes, but I'll take it right here."

She reaches out to him, and starts unbuttoning his very practical flannel shirt. "You know, curiosity is supposed to kill the ***cat***..."

They laugh and undress each other the rest of the way. She is slowly massaging his chest when he whispers, "Diane, I need to ask something of you."

She smiles wickedly, and replies, "I'll do anything you like, you know that."

Tony also smiles. "We'll get to that in a minute. First, I need to ask a favor of you, just in case I'm right"

Chapter 43—Sleep

"Joe."

No answer.

"Joe, you awake?"

No answer.

"Joe, I'm scared man. I'm never going home again, we're going to be handcuffed together forever..."

From the pillow next to him, out of the darkness, Christian hears Joe breathe out the word, "And?"

"And, I have no idea what I'm going to say to her."

Joe rolls over and wraps an arm drowsily around Christian. "Get some sleep."

The sun flashes through the craggy gap between curtains in the room's small window. There are sounds of life coming from beyond the door, sneaking into the consciousness of Joe and Christian. They rest as they had fallen asleep, Christian on his back, Joe on his side with his free arm around his companion. As they slowly rise out of their slumber, both wonder where they are, and who they're with.

Christian looks at Joe, and recalls last night's conversation right before sleep. He smiles. Tony knocks on the door and shouts, "Up and at 'em, boys! We've got a big day planned for ya."

Joe wakes up and withdraws his arm as if from a hot stove. He lies there for a moment, taking in the room, and the state he woke up in. He waits for a few minutes, for his traditional early morning erection to die down, before saying, "Let's get up, then."

"Thank you," Christian says, embarrassed.

They awkwardly climb out of bed, and make their way to take turns at the bathroom.

Day 3: Sunday

Chapter 44—Rembrandt van Rijn

Ask yourself, if you will, what does it take to hide a pair of fur-lined handcuffs in public? Now, this particular question may be a bit novel to ya, but it's closely related to other, more common questions of deception and physical appearance. How can I hide this hickey I got last night? Especially when I have a date with someone else tonight? How can I de-emphasize my nose? How can I walk around town with this throbbing erection? The answers may be slightly different, but they all have one common thread: necessity becomes the mother of invention.

Christian and Joe enter the small general store on Mt. Baldy, a step or two behind Diane and Tony, wearing a sweatshirt draped strategically over their common thread.

Tony and Diane have changed into their biking gear, spandex shorts and loose T-shirts fluttering in the breeze. Diane shows the wide cotton straps of her jogging bra as she moves lithely through the aisles, searching for the raw materials to be processed into lunch when they reach a pleasant picnic spot high up on the mountain. Tony is in charge of the beverages for this outing. For those of you curious about these things, his attire makes it obvious his ass is holding its own even after all these years. Christian and Joe stand awkwardly and silently in a corner, Joe wearing a backpack into which their money has recently been transferred.

"I'm still not exactly thrilled about this," Joe hisses out of the side of his mouth. He feels like he's getting ready to make a drug deal, sunglasses on indoor, standing close to someone else as uncomfortable as he. Christian, barely breathing, doesn't answer.

Tony wanders back to them, six packs in hand. "Oh, come on, you two. We'll find a nice little spot for a picnic, and this time of year there's next to no one on the mountain." He smiles to punctuate his conviction and confidence.

Joe is not impressed. "No one? This is California! The big L. A.! There are people everywhere, every time!" he hisses with feeling.

Tony moves closer to Joe and whispers, "Besides, I'm afraid if we don't get Christian out of the house, his nerves will knot."

Christian exhales the words, "No, I'm all right, really."

This is completely untrue, Joe knows. He can feel his partner shaking through their cuffs, and when they walk he can feel the cool sweat being flung off his hands. Be that as it may, there's still something suspicious about this need to get out of the house, to return to the more dangerous real world. He trusts himself as a judge of character, and his close examination of Tony's eyes doesn't reveal anything to cause him pause. But, still, there it is, staring him in the mug, pause. Sure as hell it's there, and he doesn't know what to do with it. In the end, it's his gun which gives him confidence to go along with this rather unpopular plan, reasoning he can shoot his way out of anything if need be. He allows his thoroughly annoying smile to re-mount his face and makes light of his fears. "Christian, if you're fine I'm a Take-A-Bite-Out-of-Crime poster child. OK, let's get this show on the road," he adds to both of companions, "and remember, if you have to lie, lie big."

"How big?" Christian asks.

"Huge! Believe me, it works; I've kinda adopted it as the defining concept for my life."

"That doesn't surprise me," Christian replies.

"Always defer to the expert in his field," Tony says. He clasps them both on the back and walks them towards the counter.

There stands a massive example of a man, wearing a nametag brashly proclaiming, "My name is Gus." His stomach lives over his belt, and the heavy skin of his face hangs over his jowls and chin like a shroud. He fills the entire space allotted behind the counter; when he has to open the cash register he turns to one side. His voice rumbles like an echo when he chooses to use it. This is never for tourists, meaning anyone he doesn't know, and not all that often with the locals. Tony, of course, is a local; he smiles brightly and chirps, "Morning, Gus!"

"Mornin', Professor," he booms back. Gus starts to ring up their purchases, glancing from one to the other of them with equal interest. At Tony, because he's always so damn friendly as to make him untrustworthy. At Diane, because, well, she's Diane. She looks the other way, pretending not to notice his eyes on her (though she always does). And at the other two, strangers, standing close together and smilin' like sin. "You'll be lookin' for four bikes today, Professor?"

"No, just the two, Gus. The gentlemen here, their father was killed in a freak mountain biking accident in the Yukon. It kinda turned 'em off the sport."

Gus checks out the two of them again. "You two brothers?"

Joe brightens up another notch. "Hell yes! I love this man!"

"You don't look very much alike."

"Neither did our mothers," Christian says. This seems to settle Gus' mind for the time being, to Christian's great surprise. He is glad Joe's wisdom about lying is working to his benefit for a change.

Gus hands across two keys to unlock the mountain bikes out front; Tony grasps them gladly. He then takes his wallet from his pocket, but Joe stops him. "Please, allow me."

"Well, that's mighty generous of you."

With well rehearsed magnanimity, Joe replies, "Oh, no, it's the very least I can do."

Gus takes the card offered and maneuvers his way carefully to the far end of the counter, where the credit card machine lives. He mutters under his breath, cursing the strange people he has to deal with on a regular basis.

"So, when we get up there, Diane and I will ride up the path while you two take the chairlift. We'll meet up again at the Mount Baldy Lodge."

All nod their agreement. It's like the Brady Bunch on tour and it's making both Gus and I ill.

"It's about a mile or two from there to a spot with beautiful views, maybe we can have lunch up there. It's a step climb, so we should all be moving at about the same pace."

Gus returns, hands the credit card receipt to Joe. "If you'll just sign here, Mr.," he looks at the card again and attempts to pronounce, "van Rijn?"

"Please, call me Brant," Joe says, again with impressive amounts of magnanimity, in fact dipping into reserves of magnanimity he never knew he had. "All my friends do." And he signs with a flourish.

CHAPTER 45—PERSPECTIVE

You may have heard people say they have "Gained perspective" on a topic. This has always struck me as unusually, because to gain perspective you have to lose just as much,

Let's take our friends as an example. Christian and Joe, in traveling through the air in the syncopated cacophony of a cable car, are gaining and losing perspective by the minute. In the plus column must go seeing Tony and Diane about as large as lice, cycling laboriously up the dirt road which links reality and Mount Baldy Ski Lodge. The sight of these vibrant, eye-catching beings rendered insignificant by the über-smog, crystalline beauty along this tree-lined approach to the roof of the world gives the riders a snapshot of mankind's place on the planet. It requires the full workings of the imagination to see any bicycle-like gyrations of the riders; the unaided eye would sense only two points advancing slowly and smoothly against gravity.

At the ground level, however, the silky banalities of the big picture are shredded by sweat and dust. The deep treads of their tires greedily churn the earth, rearranging the *tabula rosa* into a rooster's tail. Muscles bulge and contract, arms levering against the handlebars until the front wheels get light, (wo)man and machine rearing up like temperamental quarter horses. Their thighs push forcibly dirt-ward, balling up their calves, lurching forward at first and then building to a tandem two step, their second favorite dance of power and pain.

Tony follows Diane up the hill. She's the stronger rider and more experienced at avoiding rocks, trees and other minor hazards. Then again, practical considerations are only part of the equation. Baser, animalistic echoes keep Tony drafting behind her. Hindbrain, he remembers, and smiles and she gets out of the saddle to clear a steeper slice of trail. His enjoyment of the moment is heightened when he lets out a low whistle; watching isn't a shared experience until you're caught. And it isn't erotic till she smiles, beauty alit in her sweet face, beauty inhabiting the churning, musky shell of feminine grace and guile.

So, paradoxically, the airborne observers see everything and nothing at the same time.

"This sucks," Joe volunteers.

"It looks like fun, don't you think?" Christian asks, referring to the ride on going below.

"Some people just don't understand the concept of modern technology."

"Yeah, but…"

"And what the hell are we doing out here, anyhow, Christian? Why's he got us out of the house, wandering around the damned wilderness? This whole set up makes me nervous." Obviously, Joe's good mood didn't last very long.

"I was already nervous."

"You both make me nervous," Joe informs him.

"And you make me laugh; Rembrandt van Rijn for an alias?"

"Well, I don't look like Picasso, do I?"

Christian smiles. This distraction is certainly proving effective for him; he hasn't thought about Marilyn in anything more than a passing way since they left the cabin. First he was afraid to be going back out into the world, back beyond where there be dragons, if you will. Then, there was the awkwardness of moving around handcuffed to Joe in that real world; now that keeps the brain buzzing. And now the triple thrill of being in the air, seeing a beautiful slice of Southern California (perhaps for the last time before going into exile), and trying to cheer up the suddenly manic-depressive Joe have completely occupied his mind. Even in the quietest moments, such as this one, he still retains a certain calm acceptance of the dangers of the day in the real world because of his heartfelt fear of the night meeting Marilyn.

"So what'd'ya think, Joe? He's called the cops and they're going to be waiting for us at the top of the ski lift? He's had plenty of better chances to nail our respective asses, if that's what he intends."

"I know." He sits silently for a moment, studying his shoes, lost in his fully enjoyable funk. "I don't know. I just have the proverbial bad feeling in my proverbial crotch about this."

That seems to sum everything up, from Joe's perspective. Christian shrugs it off and allows himself to get lost in the spectacle of nature unfolding around him. Tony and Diane continue their purposeful climb up the road, not keeping up with the insistent pace of the chairlift but making good time all the same. Not that he can tell it's them from this height, of course, but faith can go a long way in carrying you over your doubts and fears.

Diane keeps pedaling, enjoying the sensation of her heart thumping strongly against her rib cage. She needs the distraction of the journey as much as Christian does, being burdened with Tony's prophecy and all. The strenuous exercise hasn't calmed the racing of her mind in the least. Conflicting emotions and memories clamor about from one side of her brain to the other, fighting for attention like rabid dogs. Tony has treated her much better than any of her previous partners: caring, sweet, non-violent.

And, unfortunately, he is also alone in not causing a single spark of love within her.

She shakes a rivulet of sweat away from her eye, grinding her teeth together in anger and frustration, and acceptance. Whatever had created the association between being treated like shit and love, it had certainly done its job completely inside Diane's head. Love takes its own time, so time is what she needs (she tells herself) to accept Tony as a much better example of man than she has previously been attracted to. It hadn't happened yet, and she desperately needs it to happen. With each rotation of the pedals she further realizes she's been counting on this patient, loving man to be the example to carry her through this minor little psychological trap she's found herself in for years. And now he's telling her that he figures he'll be dead in a day or two.

Thank you very much.

She pedals harder, trying to clear her mind. The ride, think about the ride. She drops her bike into a higher gear and stands again, feeling the blood rushing to her legs. The anticipation of the scream her thighs will let out after a few minutes of this is a sweet syrup in her parched throat. Right on schedule, her thighs begin the full, long burn she craves, draining her energy and testing her will to continue. She pushes on, gulping up large slabs of the road with each stroke, gasping for air and pulling on the handlebars relentlessly. One more time around, she tells herself, and then when she's completed another revolution of the pedals, she says it again: one more time around.

The road levels out temporarily, and she sits back down, allowing herself the chance to catch her breath. The thighs will never be the same, though, not this biking day; it takes something out of them which is not immediately replaced. When she stands again for another hill, the pain will start sooner and the strength will be less. But that's OK, because the next time she rides she'll be stronger for longer. This, she realizes, may be an apt analogy for her farewell to Tony, if it occurs, which she's certain it won't. But if it does, it'll just be a temporary step back that will leave her stronger, healthier, and smarter the next time. Wanting Tony's presence she looks back, and Tony is nowhere to be seen, out of sight behind a corner, left quite literally in the dust.

Chapter 46—Mount Baldy Ski Lodge

At the lodge, Tony and Diane find the lazier pair waiting in the shade, sitting on a bench just off the back door. The view is not very spectacular; the hill top is pleasant enough, but certainly not a stirring vista, lush meadow or anything else predictably overwhelming for a mountain biking destination. Not that the view matters much, since they aren't looking anyhow. They both seem more interested in studying the design and construction of their shoes. Diane dismounts her bike and takes a long pull at the water bottle from the cradle on the frame of her bike. She passes it to Tony, who tilts it back for a long three count as well. He then smacks himself on the helmet. "Up and at 'em, guys. Let's get up the trail a bit and have a little lunch."

They stand grudgingly and follow along the path Diane is pioneering with Tony right behind. Joe is in the very depth of his latest mood swing, uncommunicative, seething, over what Christian hasn't been able to fathom. He stomps up the hill like a kid in mid tantrum, following orders but letting the world know he's not happy about it. In contrast, or perhaps in retaliation, Christian is feeling much better than he can remember feeling in ages, and it's not just because he's distracted. The fruitlessness of his occasional thoughts on what to say to Marilyn, when the time comes, has finally reached fatalism: he's accepted the fact he'll sound like an idiot when she arrives. And, perhaps, that won't be a problem; sometimes women really go for the hopeless, helpless effect. Maybe this will be one of those times, you never can tell. Besides, if fate is leading him to her, fate can damn well put some words in his mouth as well. The thrill of the great outdoors is also inflating his spirit, carrying him along in a state of good-natured acceptance of whatever the hell the day may hold. Tony, his best friend in the entire world, is there, with his beautiful mortician friend, working their way up a narrow path. He starts to daydream about the future, he and Marilyn, Tony and Diane, going out to dinner, sitting around playing cards, talking, relaxing, living life. Just finding out what life is seems like a worthwhile and perhaps even attainable goal to this iteration of Christian, at this particular time, in this clean and increasingly beautiful place.

This beauty gradient isn't just because of Christian's mood, either. The forest they have stepped into is lovely, pines and spruces making the whole place look like Christmas unplugged. The soft sweep of grass waving in the breeze to their left looks cool and inviting as they take step after step, or pedal turn after turn. "OK, hang in there," Tony calls over his shoulder, a few yards ahead. "This is a little steep, but it levels off soon enough."

"Excellent!" Christian shouts back buoyantly. Joe chooses not to respond.

They continue in silence, due to physical exertion and the disparity of their moods. Tony and Diane are in their lowest possible gears, struggling upward as if on stilts. On a steep grade like this the bicycle stops being a useful tool; racers of this breed of bike would be jumping off their machines and sprinting them to a more level playing field. Diane adopts this method as the angle increases again, stopping her bike and stepping over the bar. Over her shoulder a helicopter, painted traditional olive drab, flies deafeningly above the tree line, ruffling the waving conifers. They're all mesmerized by this machine long enough to realize it's en route to the clearing below, directly behind the lodge. Its influence on the air nearby turns Diane's hair into a waving mane and forces Tony to stop riding and rest one foot on the ground, the other still ready on the pedal.

"Fuck, I knew it!" Joe calls, pulling his pistol and shooting a single shot. The thunderclap of the gun echoes through the trees, momentarily drowning out the second helicopter flying overhead now. Christian, his hands convulsively covering his ears and shutting his eyes, doesn't immediately know who Joe is shooting at; he opens his lids in time to see Tony fall, tripping over his bike and pulling it down on top of him.

Their ears perceive an eerie pseudo-silence, the last chords of the recoil spreading out and fading slowly into the background. A full 30 seconds later no one has moved, and the sound of the slowly turning rotors of the earth-bound helicopter (the first 'copter landed in the clearing below) returns to their ears. Joe takes no further action, and wonders why exactly he'd pulled the trigger. Christian is telling himself not to believe what he's just experienced. Diane suddenly dives for the ground and crawls over to the fallen Tony, sees the blood soaking through his shirt and spreading out in a perfect circle.

The calm is broken by Diane's cry of anger and anguish. "God damn you!" Diane shouts in Tony's cooling face. "Don't die, you asshole!"

Joe crawls forward to where Tony has fallen, dragging the mostly inert Christian with him. "What are you saying?"

Diane turns her rage toward Joe, biting off her words with threatening contempt. "You get away from me, right now." When he doesn't move, she slaps his face with all her might, a round house slap which Joe sees coming and welcomes, suspecting he might deserve it.

The loud call of skin against skin snaps Christian back to real time. "What did you do, Joe?" he asks helplessly, his mind slowly wrapping itself around the events of the previous few seconds. "Joe?"

Then the shots start. The young men in green, black and brown pajamas begin firing from over a hundred yards out, marching rapidly up the hill after the bullets they've released. One wave of the men advances as another provides this withering covering fire; they switch roles and move on. Christian, Joe and Diane hit the deck, covering their heads with their arms, Christian and Joe being reminded yet again that they are attached at the wrist.

It was the last reminder for Joe. He can almost feel lead dancing on his receding hairline and doesn't want to wait for them to learn to shoot lower. He snaps the handcuffs off his wrist and launches forward to Diane's bike. He sprints up the steepest part of the hill, pushing the bike in front of him. Christian is again shocked into inaction; he forgets about the shots, about Tony, and stares dumbfoundedly at the handcuffs, now hanging impotently on his wrist. Only slowly, from a distance, but with great impact does he realize exactly where he now stands in these proceedings. A glance down the hill shows the soldiers spreading out and rushing upwards, seemingly on top of him. He turns and sees Tony, inert, making no response at all to Diane, crying uncontrollably as she covers her head with her arms.

Decisions like this shouldn't be rushed, but sometimes that's the only way it is. He leaps to his feet and grabs Tony's bike, having to untangle it from Tony's legs first. He then pushes up the hill, following Joe.

Chapter 47—On the Road Again

Joe gets to a lesser grade, hops on his bike and continues up the trail. Christian has made up a lot of ground; no more than 15 seconds later he mounts his bike at the same spot, calling "You son of a bitch!" at Joe's back with both feeling and emotion.

Joe, now free from Christian and high on adrenaline, is back to his patently obnoxious good mood. Whatever doubt he may have had about shooting is gone; Joe rarely spends much time doubting himself and quickly let the blame for the recent events fall back on Tony. For the first time today he is truly appreciating the great outdoors. He pedals wildly, getting further and further away from the enemy, and feels his mind switch back to its analytical mode.

"You son of a bitch!" Christian reminds him, from closer behind.

"Good legs, Chris! Which gym do you belong to?"

"Fuck you, fuck you!"

Joe takes a deep breath and keeps pedaling. "One day you'll thank me for this!" he informs Christian.

Christian's reply suggests he doesn't agree with the proposition. Tears stream down his face, blurring his view of Joe, who is looming always larger directly ahead of him. His overwhelming anger blurs out all other sensations: the wind rushing past his face and causing his tears to race off his cheeks in two small streams, the aching from his untoned legs, and the sudden freedom of movement after having become accustomed to being chained to someone he can't stand. Unaccustomed to riding, he doesn't immediately know what to do when he starts peddling so fast that his legs are spinning wildly without resistance. He reaches for the gearshifts and moves them in random directions until the resistance to his legs increases; then Joe really starts to get closer with each revolution of the pedals.

Thoughts are hitting Joe at an alarming rate, so fast he can't process them all. He starts to look for different places where they can get away from the blokes with guns, and finds precious little to work with. There is only one trail, and it seems to lead straight up the damn mountain. So they can run all the way to the top, but there won't be much to do once they get there. He remembers the scene from ***Butch Cassidy and the Sundance Kid*** where the lawmen are trailing them, and Butch and Sundance can't shake 'em and they keep saying, "Who are those guys?" They end up on the high ground and have to jump off a cliff into some rapids to get away. Though Joe doesn't know the area all that well, he doesn't think he can count on getting lucky enough to be in that suicidal position.

So he considers other options. His gun is still almost fully loaded and he could hide somewhere and make a stand. He feels a little low on firepower for that, though. He wonders if he can convince Christian to rush back down the hill and give him some room to maneuver. He looks over his shoulder and sees Christian gaining on him significantly, saliva spewing out of the corner of his mouth as he tries to scream at Joe and pedal like a Greek god at the same time.

Joe realizes that Christian may still be a tad upset.

Now, he can understand that. If the tables were turned and Christian hadn't told him the handcuffs were of the trick variety and can be opened at anytime without a key, Joe can imagine that he might feel a tad perturbed. But, after a few moments reflection, he's sure he'd understand this little omission in the truth couldn't be helped.

Christian can taste the dust from Joe's rear tires…

Chapter 48—Pastrami on Rye

The pastrami on rye looms large in front of the hungry eyes of Captain Smith. Both hands hold onto the bread, smashing it together to make it closer to the same size as his mouth. Pastrami and mustard spill out copiously, spreading over his fingers and dripping onto the sandwich's wrapping on his desk. The sandwich is from the same place I ate last night, so I'm convinced it's highly edible. His hands remain still and he leans forward, his jaws extended and his eyes wide.

The phone rings.

He freezes and allows his jaws to clamp shut again. The eagerness and hunger of his eyes disappears, and the standard police scowl returns. Disappointment mingles with annoyance in the pit of his empty stomach. He slowly sets down the sandwich, cleans his fingers precisely, and picks up the receiver.

"Yes?"

"Sir, that credit card tip was valid," says one of his eager subordinates on the far end of the line. He sounds like a puppy acts, standing on its hind legs, expecting to be rewarded after learning a new trick.

"Oh, good," Smith says without anything in the neighborhood of enthusiasm.

"The perps are headed up a dead end trail," the cop continues, dancing a little faster, arching his back, reaching out for acceptance a little further.

"Wonderful," he intones.

"We have troops coming at them from above and below. We should..."

"That's great, that's great," he interrupts, eyeing his sandwich carnivorously. "Could you possibly do me one favor?"

"Yes, sir!" he responds enthusiastically.

"Call me back when you nail the little shits, OK? OK. Bye."

"Oh, yes sir, we'll..."

Smith hangs up on him. He clears his throat, and takes a sip of his soda, in a paper cup, through a plastic straw. He extends his arms like the maestro calling for the orchestra's attention, and reaches out to his sandwich again.

I was in the room next to the good Captain when all this was happening. I'd eagerly verified the tip; the cops at least partially believed me when I said I couldn't tell exactly where they were, but that the words "Rembrandt van Rijn" was definitely in their consciousness at about the time the tip was phoned in from the credit card company. It was something; Smith was still being tolerant of me, and would still pay, but a little more information from me would be the icing on the cake to keep me out of trouble and employable.

So, here's my morale dilemma: Should I squeal on Joe for having shot Tony? I don't particularly want to be helpful; I know Smith is a borderline psychopath and a complete asshole, and you should see some of the things he fantasizes about while on duty! On the other hand, I've picked my favorite out there on the trail, too, and it's not Joe. I don't think squealing on him is going to keep me up at nights.

Now, of course, Smith won't use me at a trial, but you just know Diane will testify.

I walk next door to increase my credibility…

Chapter 49—Riding the Scree

Christian is close enough for Joe to feel him. They pedal up the trail without seeing any of their pursuers, unaware they are pedaling into danger as fast as they are pedaling away from it. In fact, thanx to the gravity assist the downhill blokes are enjoying, they're actually pedaling into danger faster, but that's not important right now. Christian continues to scream, to spit, and to curse Joe for all he's worth. Joe is becoming more cheerful by the minute, feeling that Christian's anger will help them both escape this little scrape and get them out of the country soon enough. He doesn't know where they're going, of course, or what they are going to do when they get there. He prefers to have a plan when he travels, but is willing to wing it when the situation dictates and feels this situation is dictating loud and goddamned clear.

They have reached the stretch of the trail that gives birth to the moniker The Devil's Backbone. The ridge is no more than a few feet wide with steep drops to both sides. The views down each valley are wonderful, giving a thrill which hikers usually never see: only rock climbers having this hanging in mid air sensation normally. There is an inherent feeling of risk, of danger in walking on a narrow footing with nothing but air and scenery as your handrails, even though a person of average coordination and sobriety can easily transverse the obstacle backwards. After this lovely stretch of open trail, it turns upwards again, leading to the naked peak of Mt. San Antonio, the complete lack of foliage leading to the better known name of Mt. Baldy.

Just as Joe reaches the spot, he hesitates for a second at going over this trail at full speed; he's not a cyclist, after all. Plus, he notices there are troops on the other side, obvious in their woodlands camouflage against the sparse terrain. They lower their rifles at him in what can only be regarded as a threatening manner. His instincts tell him to stop immediately, but he can't immediately find the brakes and his momentum carries him onto the ridge. Christian is only aware that his chase is over. He pedals directly up to Joe and wrenches the handlebars hard, slamming his front tire into Joe's back tire. This takes the saddle out from under Joe, leaving him hanging for a long moment in a balletic pose waiting for gravity to look their way again. Soon the poetry is over and reality reins them in, Joe and the bike go head over ass over elbows down the rocky slope away from greater Los Angeles. Christian, off balance from the collision, follows after pitching over the handlebars of his mount.

They tumble and fall, taking small trees and sharp scree along with them. Joe reaches out to try to stop himself several times without success; he also tries to free his legs from the increasingly battered bike with similarly useless results. He covers his head with his arms to avoid certain concussion and watches the world roll by, the scene switching from sky to dirt with troublesome irregularity. Pass large trees and boulders they manage to travel until their safe if somewhat painful landing in a small clearing surrounded by dense cover.

Joe lies on his back, thrown clear of the remnants of the bike at last. His chest heaves dramatically, gasping breath, his mind thinking over and over, "Just like Butch and Sundance." Christian tumbles to a stop face-first nearby. Joe looks over to him, still panting like a dog in the summer sun, smiling in an infuriatingly happy way. "Nice going, Chris. I think we lost 'em."

Christian comes to life and springs on Joe, going for the throat. He presses his thumbs into the soft recesses of Joe's neck, but even in his fevered angst doesn't dig in with any sort of seriousness. He doesn't have, and will never have, the instinct of a killer, the carnivorous desire to destroy life and taste blood; it's something that is not in his well-cultured, refined nature. That doesn't stop him from doing his best to inflict a little pain, though. "You son of a bitch!"

"Yeah," Joe agrees, letting the storm of violence run its course on top of him.

"You killed him!" Christian reminds him.

"He turned us in," Joe calmly replies, allowing a little of the being choked sound to enter his voice. He doesn't want his attacker to feel discouraged, especially not so discouraged he might want to try harder.

"You were using trick cuffs!" Christian spits out. His fury is starting to abate a bit; it sounds rather like he's just airing a laundry list of grievances now instead of making any point in particular.

"What sort of idiot do you think I am?" Joe wonders aloud.

"You son of a bitch!"

"You're fixating, Chris."

"Christian!" he yells, and starts to cry. "My name is Christian." Slowly he releases his grip on Joe's neck and rises, wiping the tears away with his dirt-caked hands. He returns to the crumpled heap of cro-maly and rubber that used to be Diane's rented bike and removes the small pouch from the front. "God damn you" he says to Joe, as a request.

Joe doesn't answer.

"You killed him." Joe nods his head, staring into Christian's eyes. "He was my friend!"

"He turned you in!" Joe responds with equally intense volume. He's had about enough of letting Christian's anger run its course and decides a little anger of his own is justified.

"Bullshit! We're two assholes in fur-lined handcuffs, anyone could have turned us in."

"He brought us outside."

"We followed," Christian points out.

"You followed!" Joe insists.

There is a time for talking and a time for not talking, as a sudden volley of shots from just beyond the trees reminds them. Christian looks in the direction of fire and asks, "Who are those guys?" Unfortunately, Joe is no longer in the clearing to ask; he's running like mad in the opposite direction. Christian takes off along the path Joe's selected. "What are you running from, asshole?"

"From the dudes with the guns, you shit!" Joe calls without turning around.

"Where are they, dickhead?" Christian asks.

"Behind us!"

Christian looks around as he's running, causing him to stumble over a fallen tree branch. "I don't see 'em," he tells Joe.

"Shut up!" Joe requests. "And keep away from me! Screw the damn Marines, I'm running from you!"

They run headlong through the forest, creating a new trail with their heavy footfalls and machete-like arm movements. A helicopter cruises by just above the tree line, the beating of the rotors shaking the trees and carbonating the debris below. "What was that?" Christian asks.

"Shut up!" Joe responds.

"You son of a bitch!" Christian retorts.

"Yeah, well you just keep you ass under cover of the shrubs or some gunner might rip you an extra orifice." Joe clamors over a downed tree and wonders where, exactly, they are going to come out by following the base of the hill like this. He hopes it will be near the lodge, because then they can get away from this forest and back to the more familiar smell and soot of the city. Then again, he hopes it's nowhere near the lodge, because that's the place the other group of guys with guns seemed to be setting up base camp. He takes this relatively quiet moment to wonder what the hell is going on with having all these very lethal, similarly dressed individuals after them; last he heard, the army, navy, air force and marines very rarely get involve in the nuts and bolts of law enforcement. He tries to figure out what it means briefly, for a mere moment, but it quickly shows itself to be wasted effort. Therefore, he immediately stops thinking about it, an ability that is truly a gift.

Christian does not possess this same ability. The words, "Son of a bitch!" keep coming back to his mind in relation to Joe. He hates him for all he's worth, and yet keeps following him deeper into the woods and further down this pseudo-path into who knows what. It occurs to him to wonder where exactly they're going, and what they're going to do when they get there to escape from the army following them, and why exactly is there an army following them, anyhow? "Hey dummy!" He calls out.

"Yeah?"

"What…" but the rest of the sentence is lost in the concussion of an explosion directly behind them. It flings them both to the ground like towels blown off a clothesline. They cover their heads convulsively, overwhelmed by the ringing in their ears. Bits of bark and branch rain around them, razor sharp and very painful in their backs and bottoms. Luckily the instinct to cover their ears also covers their faces, which saves their eyes for the time being. As soon as the air clears of these painfully imprecise missiles, Joe jumps up and runs, faster than before, driving forward with his arms. Christian follows him, pulling at the splinters in his ass and listing to one side due to inner ear strain. "What the hell, do they have a tank up there?"

"No," Joe answers in a relatively reassuring tone. Reassuring, anyhow, for someone running for his life. "Probably just hand grenades."

"Oh great, just hand grenades," Christian responds, ignoring the wooded shrapnel and running for all he's worth. "They're really trying to kill us!"

"What was your first fucking clue?"

"They're trying to kill us!" Christian repeats, still shocked at the idea. After all, he's just a bank robber. He imagines the relatively pleasant level of hell he figures he's bound for, the one with martinis and soda crackers, just no olives and the air conditioner is occasionally out of commission. Suddenly there is a well-trained, disciplined group of men lobbing death at him from over the last hill. He's having a little trouble understanding this concept.

"That's their job, man!" Joe explains. "Your job is to run like a mother!"

Christian catches up to Joe and they run along side by side. The forest clears out a little bit. This doesn't make their task much easier; it just means that instead of having to duck under trees and jump over things constantly, they only have to do so on a rather regular basis. They hear another grenade explosion, but it's significantly behind them and to the left, further out into the relatively flat terrain away from the mountain. Christian puts his hands on his head and continues to run like that for a pace. "What the hell are you doing?" Joe asks.

"I've got a stitch in my side," Christian informs him.

"So?"

"That's what happens when you forget to stretch out before strenuous exercise. This helps," he adds, indicating how he's holding his hands over his head. They suddenly come to the end of the trees and slam on their respective brakes; Christian hugs a tree to avoid rushing out in to the clearing. Joe immediately gets low to the ground, and Christian follows his lead. They look out on the clearing where the ski lodge sits, where the ski lift terminus is located: it's now also the home to a half dozen soldiers with M-16's, full clips, and unpleasant dispositions illustrated by their perpetual scowls. Their mirrored sunglasses glint in the noonday sun, creating a small constellation of binary, dazzling, lethal stars. The soldiers mill about, bored, aching for someone they can take a few shots at and carry off like a deer in hunting season.

"Oh shit, they're in front of us," Christian notes.

"Yeah."

"And behind us."

"Say something useful," Joe requests.

"We're shit," Christian offers.

"Thank you."

"You son of a bitch," Christian adds, returning to his previous but still overwhelming thoughts. Four of the soldiers go inside the lodge, leaving two of their number swiveling their heads constantly, looking for the suspects.

Joe smashes his head into the nearest tree, non-verbally releasing the scream building in his chest. Christian assumes it is a scream of frustration and despair, but Joe feels it's a war cry. "Look, Mister Destiny, I'm caught up in your fucking maelstrom here. I just wish you would've told me it's your god damned fate to die of spontaneous chest ventilation on top of a mountain!" Joe snorts for breath, and then wishes he hadn't been speaking so intently or loudly. There's nothing to be gained from releasing such anger right now. Anger and aggression are things to be saved up and channeled when appropriate. Save it for later, Joe says mentally, vent all you want later.

He has to ask Christian to repeat himself. "What?" he asks.

"I don't think so," Christian repeats.

"You don't thinks so? You don't think what?"

"I don't think we're going to die."

Joe is livid; Christian is not living up to his role in this partnership. He's supposed to be pessimistic and hopeless; what this shit? "What's this shit, Chris?"

Christian taps him on the shoulder and gestures towards the clearing. "Look," he says, pointing.

Chapter 50—In the Clearing

Diane. She walks out of the forest, Tony draped in her arms. Tony, dead but not yet buried, a sack of flower with eyes and limbs, carried from the spot of his murder to the ski lodge-cum-command post by his tall and limber lover. She grits her teeth together in concentration, the muscles of her face and arms strain with the dead weight they carry. The sweat on this hot day rolls off her brow like an artesian well in her skull, pure and sweet. She is dressed almost as before, having removed her T-shirt to soak up some of the blood Tony is still expelling. Every inch of her body screams her sexuality, the tightness of her biking gear enhancing the smooth striking lines of her lower half, the sweat soaked jogging bra clinging enticingly. Her gait is calm and unhurried, only slightly challenged under the burden she caries.

He ain't heavy, he's my lover?

Anyhow, Diane. Step after step she advances on the temporary fort in the woods. A few yards out she attracts the attention of the soldiers guarding the stronghold, men immediately torn between the instinctive desire to rush to her, added to by the chivalrous desire to help this woman in need, and the fear of approaching near her without an invitation. Even the strongest, best-armed man would think twice about approaching the intent scowl on her face. The ligaments in her neck are standing out and her biceps are quivering slightly in cadence with her stride. She stares at them mercilessly, challenging and warning with the same expression.

"Great, now we'll die quickly," Joe whines. "Small fucking consolation."

Christian makes a suggestion: "Shut up." He feels something much different in the air, something warm and fragrant. If Diane does indeed help them, he knows whom it's coming from (Tony) and he knows whom it's for (himself). The ultimate test of friendship is, in this case, posthumous.

A hundred yards from them Diane smiles, pleased with herself, catching small gasps of breath through her slightly pursed lips. She doesn't always need to be the center of attention and often dresses for anonymity, but there is a thrill to holding eyes when that's what you've set out to do. Her peripheral vision searches out the corners of the clearing as her head swings slightly as she walks, looking for other uniforms in her midst; she sees none. There are half dozen men visible at the ski lodge, though there are almost certainly others inside, the officers and comm people, coordinating the attack. It seems unlikely they'll need to step outside; of course, if they do then the two trying to escape will be screwed and it won't be her fault, she did all she could. That would be fine with her also; she'll gladly sing like a nightingale against them, singing out damnation for the two bastards as quickly and loudly as humanly possible.

Diane is fast realizing death wishes can be a real bitch, this one in particular causing her trepidation above and beyond the call of duty. On the one hand, she is willing to do what her lover has asked, because he deserves a last wish or two. We all do, after all. On the other hand she'd be willing to shoot both of the little shits with her own hand, if given the means and the opportunity. Well, maybe not both of them: just Joe. She walks a few more steps toward the lodge. Yes, Christian she'd be willing to just beat the hell out of, but Joe has got to go. So it's with a certain indecision that she advances, unsure what will happen when she must decisively act, one way or the other. Indecision plagues her, causing the greatest consternation; she simply can't consciously choose between the two options tugging at her soul, knowing she'll regret either action for the rest of her life, so instead decides to empower her subconscious to decide for her. She looks up and sees the soldiers are now a comfortable conversational distance away, decides to get the proceedings started and find out what she's going to do.

With the detachment of a disinterested bystander and a dramatic change of momentum, she stops dead in her tracks. The soldiers respond in kind. Her mouth opens and closes; not a sound breaches her dry, cracking lips. She knows if she can just keep the attention of the two dudes for 20, 30 seconds then the two bastards should be able to make their escape, if she decides to help them after all. She opens her mouth again, and suddenly words begin to pour out: "Friends!" tumbles out first, and loudly, resonating up and down the valley. "Now is the winter of our discontent. The best of times, and the worst of times." She feels utterly ridiculous, perhaps even terminally so. This stream of consciousness bit cannot possibly be working, can it? But the guys with guns are staring at her differently now, passing beyond the normal sort of attention men pay beautiful women carrying dead guys and venturing into the new, the unknown: they look like they expect her head to explode at any moment and large snakes to shoot out of her flaming ears and eyes. Faking insanity may not be the most elegant or dignified choice, but it certainly gets people's attention.

After all, no one ever said you could always provide a distraction with dignity, and at least she isn't having to strip to break the dudes' concentration.

Tony and Christian are close enough to hear her immortal words, and also wonder exactly what's going through her mind. They take a few hesitant movements to the edge of their cover and stare into each other's eyes. A brief, important message passes between them: if Diane is willing and able to assist, they'll take their chances with this opportunity.

"But enough of this simple-minded, half-hearted, indefensible balderdash!" then joins her other words, surprising Diane since she doubts she's used any of those words previously. Tony and Christian begin to low crawl into the open. "I've come here to bury Tony, not to praise him. I'm here to embalm and entomb and enshrine and…" and she figures that's about enough of that metaphor. "Though I've heard his spirit will always be with me, I can't help but feel a sense of loss at this exact moment. After all, doesn't everyone feel that way?" She stops and stares at the soldiers, figuring it might be a good time to make this an audience participation decoy. "Wouldn't you feel that way, at this time?" she asks, staring at the one on her right.

"Listen, Miss, why don't you just calm down, and…" he starts, taking a small step forward; Diane convulses backward, protective of the body she carries, and freezes the solider again. He then decides to play along with her, try to gain her trust a little more. "Yes, I suppose I would."

"Of course you would! Anyone would feel that way, and since everybody thinks that way, I'd be a damn fool to think anyway else, right!" The soldier's nod; Christian and Tony are a little over halfway to safety, but are entering the most dangerous zone: directly behind Diane, where the soldiers are most likely to catch a glimpse of them by accident. Diane isn't too worried about that, and not just because she can't see exactly where they are in relation to her; she's got problems of her own, in that she'd run out of material. She continues on with her most recent reference. "That's the catch, you see; Catch-22."

And that's it. Diane finds herself running out of anything even vaguely literary or coherent to say. Oh well, she tried, she can tell herself that for the rest of her life: she tried. She did her best and it won't be her fault when the sons of bitches are caught. All she has to do is stand there for a few more seconds and wait for the soldiers to spot the two vermin slithering across the meadow on their bellies.

Suddenly, a helicopter of the LAPD, which had been up at the top of the mountain monitoring things up there, rushes over Diane's head, heading for the lodge. Both soldiers look up and following it across the sky, turning around to do so. They've been tasked to keep the press well out of the area, so they have to follow the craft long enough to see the LAPD markings clearly. As soon as they turn, Christian and Joe jump up and run wildly for the cover of the far side, diving head first into the dense branches and out of sight.

The soldiers turn back. Diane is pissed off, and tired, and wants to just get the hell away from people for a little while. She lowers Tony gently to the ground. The soldiers approach and bring her slowly to the lodge (promising to return for the body momentarily). It occurs to her suddenly that lowering the body was probably all she had to do to provide the necessary distraction; the beautiful solutions are never the first to mind, somehow. As they walk, she surreptitiously gives a one-finger salute to the two rushing off into the thickening forest, her middle finger running down the seam of her pants.

Chapter 51—Sex

The rush down the hill is nothing too dramatic. A scramble here, a slide there, and a completely welcome lack of gunfire everywhere and they begin to return to civilization. They avoid the main road in deference to the helicopters and so tear randomly through the underbrush and tree limbs, continuing downward whenever possible. Each little scratch, each poke striking frighteningly close to an eye, causes Joe to smile in martyred joy and Christian to growl in righteous anger.

Christian unfairly figures it's completely Joe's fault that they are on the run again, forgetting the guys with guns showed up and fleeing was inevitable no matter what happened to Tony along the way. But he is miserable, and a distinctly un-magnanimous part of his brain insists on blaming someone. Each step he takes on the uncertain terrain bothers his ankles, each change of direction wrenches one or both knees, and each breath causes his lungs to scream with a slightly sharper version of agony.

But more than the physical discomfort of this afternoon, there's the shooting of Tony. That's not an easy thing to forgive, no matter what distractions life has recently presented him. Christian muses that even if Joe had felt justified in executing Tony at the time, the part Diane played in their escape must surely change his mind about whether or not Tony was to blame for their loss of anonymity. Tony thought of them to the last, or thought of Christian to the last at least. It's inconceivable to Christian that anyone would think of saving Joe. No, Tony had saved Christian, not turned him in; there's no room in his mind for any other explanation.

In reality, Tony really did ask Diane to save both of them, but there's no means for Christian to actually know that like there is for me.

All in all, "Bastard" summed up all Christian's thoughts of his partner. "Bastard," is the word running through his head over and over again, with occasionally monotony-defying emphasis: "Bastard. Bastard. Bastard!"

Joe is feeling pretty good, actually.

The trees eventually thin out a bit. Christian and Joe rush towards a line where they disappear entirely and stop suddenly upon reaching this invisible barrier, the beginning of a steep drop into a parking lot cut out of the hillside off the main road. Joe remembers driving past it this morning; good, they've come a long way, baby. After scanning for signs of life he hops over the edge, sliding a few feet to the right then zigging back left for a few feet more. Christian follows his example, albeit slower and less enthusiastically. Their final few steps of their wholly uncertain descent leaves them teetering precariously, looking for support from any solid object; they both find themselves leaning on the low slung hood of a Porsche 911.

"Your destiny is getting classier," Joe tells him.

"Shut up," Christian suggests.

Joe makes a move to the driver's side; Christian grabs his arm without a hint of playfulness. "I'm driving. You just start the bastard."

There's that word again.

"You sure you want to…"

"I'm driving," Christian repeats, and Joe doesn't want to take any more time to discuss it. Joe rushes to the driver's door and tries to decide how exactly he's going to gain access to this machine. Grand Theft—Auto isn't exactly his line of work, after all. He doesn't have any lock-picking tools, and wouldn't know how to use them if he did. The glass is probably breakable, but it looks rather thick to take a swing at with his elbow. He decides to hope for the best and just try the door, which opens immediately. Not bad, not bad. Now he now wonders how exactly it is people hot-wire these things. He then notices the keys are in the ignition.

"Hey, Chris, will you look at…" he begins, but is rudely interrupted by Christian pushing him out of the way and climbing into the seat. Joe reminds himself to be offended later when they have time and Christian has cooled off a bit, and rushes around to the passenger door as Christian brings the car to life.

The passenger door is locked.

Joe realizes this may not go well. Christian puts the car in gear as Joe knocks in what he hopes is a confident, manly and effective manner. Christian reflexively reaches over and unlocks the door and then tries to lock it again, realizing what an opportunity this is to have a little solitude. His instincts kick in too slow, though, and Joe has already yanked the door open and climbed into the passenger seat.

Christian spins the rear tires dramatically on the gravel of the lot. Before the brakes can complete their task, he's forced the car into first and is starting the wheels spinning in the opposite direction. This sort of behavior is bad for the tires, but excellent for a bad case of badly repressed anger. The owner of the Porsche scampers out of the woods and up the embankment, his pants grasped around his waist hastily, trailed by a partially undressed friend. His friend is calling him bad names.

"I locked my side," his friend informs him as she puts her breasts away. This does little to pacify his mood. At this point you have to conclude (or at least I had to) that sex seems to be doing everything it, as a force of nature, can to save Christian and Joe.

CHAPTER 52—PORSCHE VS. BMW

Christian had never driven a Porsche before; he'd always told himself he's much more a BMW man, someone who wants power but in a comfortable and somewhat unreliable sedan for well over $40,000. But this little test drive might just prove to be enough to change his mind. With each hairpin corner down from the rarefied air of Mt. Baldy he throws the car into it a little bit more, until he has to get the front wheels turned completely akimbo to counteract the skid he's creating and he's carrying 40 miles per hour through each. The thrill of it actually causes him to completely forget the reason he's driving the car in the first place.

Until Joe speaks, of course.

"Uh, Chris?"

He brings the car out of a corner and accelerates down the hill. He expectorates his words through the corner of his mouth, staring straight at the road ahead. "I don't want to hear another word out of you. Not one, got it?"

They make it through the next corner, though the car's tires are just never going to be the same.

"Christian?" Joe tries again.

"That's one," Christian replies, though he's surprised this is the one that Joe has chosen. Using his proper name is a surprise, no doubt about it. Christian's anger at his partner doesn't decrease, but for one moment in time it doesn't increase, either.

"Might I suggest one little thing?" No reply, so Joe continues. "You might want to slow down to the limit to avoid the cops that are almost certainly coming up to help look for us. The cool part of the road's over, anyhow."

Both of these statements are true, Christian realizes. They've survived the sports car enhanced section of the road and are now steaming through boring corners a few miles above the suburbs of L. A. Coming out of the next corner (which Christian notes he took twice as fast as the highway sign advised) he brakes, downshifts to second and lets the car putter along at something resembling the speed limit.

"Thank you," Joe says softly, in a voice resembling a whisper.

"Sure, you son of a bitch," Christian responds. He starts to drum his fingers on the steering wheel out of boredom, and tries to consider how to get away from Joe, the man ruining his life. After all, he has a lot of living to do.

This last thought takes Christian by surprise. He's never been one for death wishes, but had never thought of his time on the planet as precious until a few days ago. Christian wants to live his life now; it's a strange but entirely pleasant sensation. But there are some conditions on his happiness, he sees, and that means the whole darned thing will require a little planning, a little strategy. First of all, think of a way to get rid of Joe; nothing immediately occurs to him, so he decides to accept there will be some way to do this, and he'll do it once he figures out what it is. Second, stay out of jail; again, no immediate, foolproof plans leap to mind. Third, find Marilyn again; at least he knows where she works, so that's something to tally in the plus column. Fourth, convince her he had nothing to do with killing her brother and live happily ever after.

Well, nothing directly to do with killing him, anyhow.

So, it'll be an uphill battle. He stares at the road and lets his mind muse over these thoughts for a while.

"I have another suggestion," Joe informs him.

"Eat it."

"I know the ultimate hiding place."

This line hangs in the air between them for many minutes. "A hiding place," Christian thinks, "that's a good idea." He doesn't want to answer, in case he finds he has no ideas of his own to turn to instead. Joe takes his silence for a softening of feeling and places his hand conspiratorially on Christian's shoulder. "You'll be glad you let me in the car, I promise."

Christian, of course, doubts this. He doubts this enough to roughly shrug Joe's hand off his body. "Shut up. Take your suggestion, eat it, digest it, and shit it. I don't want it."

They drive on in silence past homes which, in this market, just aren't worth what they used to be.

Chapter 53—Test Your Psychic Powers

The phone takes to ringing again. As I believe I mentioned previously, Captain Smith actually has quite strong if underdeveloped psyche powers, but he doesn't utilize them due to a lack of faith. However, he's just psychic enough to avoid answering this particular call on its first, second, third rings, rather convinced it is bad news. He doesn't admit he won't pick up the phone because he's psychic, of course. He doesn't believe ***he's*** a freak, and that's fine with me, because that way he still needs me around from time to time.

I'm not thrilled with that word, by the way.

Ring.

Ring.

Captain Smith, instead of answering the telephone, is doing something he finds much more pleasant and less likely to disappoint: he's eating an ice cream cone. Vanilla. His tongue reaches out to the cone slowly, each time a short turn around the scoop so that he eats it evenly, pleasantly, thoroughly, with a minimum of mess, muss and fuss. The white globs of vanilla are thereby shoveled efficiently into his mouth, and he savors each quickly and completely, ready for the next addition to the summation of sensation.

If only he had slightly better concentration, or more confidence in the powers he denies and therefore underutilizes, he probably wouldn't bother to answer the phone at all. But, alas, the ringing annoys him each and every time, and he's not ***sure*** it's bad news, so he stares intently and precursorally at the telephone with its light blinking for his line.

Ring.

His right hand holds the cone off at a safe distance, and his left brings the receiver swiftly to his head. "If you're calling to tell me that you lost the assholes and have no clue where they are, just hang up right now."

The phone goes dead in his ear.

He nods his head slowly in the general direction of the telephone, whose receiver is still held helplessly in his left hand.

Wait just a second, though, before I tell you what happens. I bet there are several of you reading this who have psychic powers you are currently unaware of or have noticed but don't trust enough to rely on. Can you tell what's going to happen? Guess for yourself, and see if you're right.

Go on, give it a try. You've nothing to lose but your dependence on only five boring sense. And, as I'm sure you can imagine, sex is much better when you have extra senses…

Have you guessed yet? OK, here we go.

Captain Smith chucks his ice cream cone off into the back corner of his office with a flick of his wrist. His left hand brings the receiver down disastrously but dramatically against his desk repeatedly, causing the earpiece to hang limply by a few threads to the rest of the device. He then starts licking the earpiece, rotating it slightly after each lick, nearly convinced he's eating his ice cream cone still, efficiently and effectively.

Chapter 54—Foster's (a.k.a. Donutman) in Glendora

At the bottom of Mills Avenue, Christian is suddenly presented with the Claremont Colleges, which normally wouldn't have had too much effect on him except for the fact they are built solidly across the path Mills once took. Presented with the choices of left and right, he chooses the more expedient one, to the right. The Porsche now tools slowly along Foothill Boulevard, content to wallow in the slow flow of Sunday afternoon traffic.

"Can we stop at Foster's Donuts?" Joe asks. He refers, of course, to the shop now know as Donutman, in Glendora. It used to be known as Fosters, though.

"No." Christian doesn't look in either direction. He's not particularly looking at the cars in front of him, either, and only brakes when the car in front of him gets significantly bigger and speeds up when it's become very small. This technique meets the basic intent of traveling from Point A to B, but add this unconventional technique to his unfamiliarity with the clutch and you're left with a rather rough driving motion. The car enthusiasts who see this display curse whatever god lets assholes afford cars like that and leaves them driving Toyotas or Fords or whatever.

"They're great donuts, Chris. The best..." Joe speaks in a voice meant to create such a curiosity in Christian that he'll leave the car pointed donut-wards.

Christian slams on the brakes to avoid the stopped car in front of him. "Is this donut shop your ultimate hideout?"

"What? Hell no. There are cops around there all the time, driving in from as far as Santa Monica. But who gives a shit about a hideout when we're talking an apple fritter as big as a football." Christian looks at him skeptically. "I swear!" Joe's hands sit approximately football distance apart for dramatic effect.

"No donuts. Which way to this hiding place?"

Joe smiles wide and wicked. "Couldn't think of anywhere to go yourself, eh?"

Christian doesn't bother to nod. "I hate you."

"I know. Turn left."

Christian begins to look around to make a panicked lane change, since they are on their way into the intersection, or nearly so.

"Not necessarily here, Chris. Anywhere." Joe smiles.

Christian turns through the intersection from the right lane, leading to more single-digit finger pointing and horn honking. No actual accident, though. And Joe does stop smiling for just a brief, pleasant few minutes...

Chapter 55—Emphasis

There is, or so it's been noted in the past, something magical about Disneyland. What exactly that something is has never been adequately defined or displayed, but people persist on saying it anyhow. "There's something magical about Disneyland," they say as their kids are heaving their guts out into garbage cans after too much sugar followed by Mr. Toad's Wild Ride. But, what the hell, if they want to say it, I say good on 'em.

So, let's accept it as popular opinion (or perhaps even an unverifiable fact) and move on: There's *something* magical about Disneyland. There are also a whole heap of cops about Disneyland; not cop cops, of course, but the Disney Police. To serve and protect and blend in is their motto, apparently, since they wear the same uniforms and friendly badges as all the other employees. They smile and smile, offer directions to lost guests, and even pick up the odd piece of litter. But let someone try to moon a friend while halfway down the Matterhorn and see how friendly they are; they'll throw you out of the park much much quicker than Goofy can complete a sentence.

Not that anything like that has ever happened to me.

Anyhow, the Disney Police are also the blokes responsible for going through the park every evening, as each area shuts down its little corner of exquisitely forced happiness for the day and everyone's funneled either to the exits or Main Street for the Electrical Parade. Take Treasure Island, for instance, sitting peacefully in the middle of the Sea of Tranquility or some such nonsense. You can't be out there any later than 7 o'clock in the summertime; they will find you and escort you off the island. And don't even think about trying to hide out behind some bushes to be able to kiss some young thing out there when you're both struggling through puberty and her tightly bound breasts are as inviting as the Welcome Wagon. You won't be in their Small World for very long, let me tell ya that.

OK, I'll admit I've got a few issues with Disneyland.

Every evening two Disney Policemen have to take the "canoe" out to the island and make sure everyone has left, and then go back and continue their rounds (scare up guests in the Haunted House? Shiver some Timbers in Pirates of the Caribbean? Use your own twisted imagination). On the particular evening we've been talking about for such a great number of pages now, the gentlemen are named Alberto and Skip. It says so on their nametags. Skip is driving the boat, and Alberto is riding shotgun. Al hops out on the island, walks once around (checking all the secluded spots, of course), and hops back in the boat. "The island's clear, let's head," he says to Skip, who paddles them back to shore.

Not literally, of course. Paddling would be work, and Disneyland is about animation and happiness, not work. Hidden motors are left to do the "work." Skip hits a button and they glide back towards the mainland, an innocuous hum and a small wake left in their, well, wake.

As the sound fades into the warm night, Christian and Joe dig themselves out of the damp sand under which they had hidden themselves moments before. Looking like Creatures from the Sand Lagoon, they shake like damp dogs and breathe in the wonderful night air in hurried gulps. You don't have to be particularly claustrophobic to dislike being buried in the sand and breathing through a straw, and Christian disliked it quite a lot. He continues to shake himself to try to eradicate the last vestiges of sand from his body in general and his face in particular;

he figures he may never want to go to a beach again. Joe didn't enjoy the experience all that much either, but recovers more quickly, pleased that his plan for a good hiding spot is working out so astoundingly well. He takes a quick look around in the gathering darkness of mid-spring and likes what he sees: nothing of any note.

"Aren't there surveillance cameras all over this place?" Christian asks in a sotto voce.

"Yeah," Joe says normally, yelling by comparison, "but the one on the island is notorious for breaking down. The fact that I stepped on it shouldn't draw any attention until maintenance shows up in the morning."

"How the hell do you know this stuff?"

"I was Minnie Mouse here for awhile, during a different phase of my life."

They sit. Christian plops his bottom down first, and Joe takes a spot relatively near him, almost as close as they were forced to sit when shackled together. The remnants of that phase of their lives still hangs on Christian's wrist. Joe considers offering to remove the memento, but decides it's probably best not to bring up that particular topic again. Joe looks startlingly like a puppy dog seeking approval from his master after making a mess on the living room carpet.

(Joe is forgetting that most dogs end up having their noses stuck in it before forgiveness can be sought, but a boy can't think of everything, all the time.)

Christian notices the intrusion into his personal space, but doesn't say a thing about it. What is there to say, anyhow? Get your sleazy ass away from me, something like that? No, not worth it, there are more important things to do right now. He opens up the small pack he took off of Diane's bike, which had become Joe's bike in the course of things before they were forced to abandon it, twisted and broken, at the bottom of the very steep hill. At the time, he was trying to be considerate: he should return this back to Diane at least, since he had pretty much insured she wasn't going to get the deposit back on that bike. Now he realizes there are other things which are a bit more important. In the pouch he finds her wallet, which causes a moment's hesitation. He shouldn't be looking through her things at all, but definitely not her wallet. That's almost on par with reading her diary or grabbing her bottom, an invasion of privacy somewhere along those lines. But, desperate times can call for desperate measures...

Diane has $37 in her wallet, a number Christian commits to memory in a small measure of security against Joe's thieving ways. Despite both being bank robbers, Christian feels he maintains some semblance of moral superiority over Joe: he won't steal from friends, just from clients. About Joe he's not so sure, and besides Joe doesn't have any actual friends as far as Christian knows.

Joe feels left out of the conversation going on in Christian's head. He tries to get a little attention with, "Well, we're tired and hungry, but safe."

"Sure we are," Christian sarcastically replies.

"Sure!" Joe chimes back, smiling at his cleverness before even delivering the line. "Nobody fucks with Disneyland!"

Christian bypasses her credit cards but stops to glance at the pictures. Family shots, a dog with a young girl who certainly could have been Diane, a prom picture from the cocktail dress era... and a picture of Tony, sitting on his couch. There is sereneness to his eyes, in reality and in photography, which is disconcerting and reassuring in the same moment. Collective guilt waves over him, realizing he's in many ways responsible for the end of this man's life, even though he didn't actually pull the trigger. He quickly flips the picture over and out of sight. "I've had enough," he tells Joe.

"So have I, believe me."

"I've had damn well fucking enough," Christian adds, for emphasis. He looks in a deeper pocket of the wallet. "I have a deal for ya."

Joe eyes him warily. "Now, Chris, I'm not much of one for making deals."

"You keep the money."

Joe thinks about this for a moment. "OK…"

"You keep every damn dime, every fucking fiver…" Christian continues, again, for emphasis. He leaves something unspoken hanging in the air.

"And…"

Christian finds what he's looking for, and shows it to Joe: a business card for Diane Ramsden containing a large, gaudy logo for Forest Lawn Cemeteries. "And you drop me off at Forest Lawn tomorrow morning."

Joe understands what Christian is saying to him. "You really fell for that guy, didn't you?"

"I will never fucking forgive you," Christian says, his anger showing more than he would like, though he still enjoys adding the emphasis. "Never. He was a great man."

"I agree."

"He didn't turn us in."

Joe frowns. "Now, I just happen to disagree, given the evidence available, but…"

"Fuck you," Christian concludes (with emphasis).

Neither says anything for a few minutes. Christian's mind is racing, one thought pilling up on the next, each clambering for his full attention and unwilling to leave him alone for a millisecond. Like someone attacked by a swarm of mosquitoes or dive-bombers his rationality is under attack. Who will be at Forest Lawn? What will he say to Diane? Marilyn? The police? How will he get away from Joe? What will he do once he has? Will Joe turn him in, or will he turn in Joe? How the hell did he end up like this?

That's really the question to consider, of course, since it seems to have so much to do with all the others. How the hell did he end up like this? He was a successfully unhappy lawyer, like all his friends and even his family before him, and he threw it all away. He was a psychotic asking an inane question of complete strangers, and then he finally meets a completely wonderful complete stranger who he's been seeking for years and years without having any clue why. His life is somehow associated with hers, and yet he can't figure out how or why or… maybe he should have just been happy with his miserable life. It doesn't occur to him there were many choices beside a life of crime or a life of lawyer, many other paths he could have chosen. He hasn't quite seen the big picture and couldn't care less, because he's happy with the conclusion that he's being screwed. He wails and laments about the rotten hand he's been dealt in life without the slightest capacity to bluff, when really he's just made some very stupid choices of late.

"Fuck me," he adds, in summation.

"You really should do something about your language, Chris, especially around here." Joe is occupying himself by throwing small rocks into the water and watching the rings spread out slowly into the darkening sea.

Christian turns to him. "You get me to Forest Lawn tomorrow and I swear upon your worthless soul I won't turn you in."

"All I have to do is get you to the mortuary on time?"

This clears up Christian's mind in a hurry. All he can think of now is how much he hates Joe, hates him now and forever more. "Good night, you son of a bitch" and he lies down in the still warm sand.

"Aw get on!" Joe exclaims, leaning over the prostate form of Christian. "You're tired, you're hungry, you're suit is more trashed than any of Kathleen Turner's dresses ever were and you're a little pissed at me. Fine! But…"

"Don't say it," Christian tells him, though he has no idea what Joe's going to say. He's merely predicting that whatever it is, he probably doesn't want to hear it.

"But tomorrow's another day!"

"Good night," Christian repeats (without any particular emphasis). "If you swim for it, I hope you drown." He lies down again, sulking in silence.

Chapter 56—Me

I'd been listening to the thoughts of Christian and Joe from when they'd gotten up that morning till Christian attempted to retire for the night. Exhaustion wasn't living all the far away from me at this point, but I was still listening.

The four walls around me are starting to feel a bit confining. I stand up to stretch my legs, maybe even make the sojourn to the urinal and then coffee pot for about the twentieth time since arriving, when it happens. Remember what I said at the very, very beginning, about lives turning on particular moments? Well, that moment, that exact specification in time, my life turned. It knocked me on my ass, to be honest; I was sitting again, after, and didn't even remember looking for the chair my bum is placed upon. If I had walked a few more feet first, I'd have been sitting on the ground instead.

I'll tell ya all about it later.

I got up, walked out of the station and haven't been back since.

Chapter 57—Plausible Deniability

Joe takes a couple of rather pointless laps around the island. His mind is not exactly focused; there are many things to decide. Yeah, he could probably swim off the island by himself, but getting the money across with him would be a bit of a trick. No, it's better to wait till morning and drift out with the gathering crowds. Then they could just leave the park and go wherever the hell they wanted to, after stealing another car.

He. He means he could leave.

There is still the small difficulty of getting out of the country, but a drive to Phoenix should be far enough away to safely board an airplane under his assumed papers. Yeah, the deal Christian is offering him just might work; he'll ditch their car after dropping him off and leave town in an unknown vehicle hell bent for leather, whatever that means. They could be lying on a beach by mid-week.

He. He could be lying on the beach.

Why does he keep thinking of the two of them as a couple? For some strange reason, he doesn't want to be rid of Chris. Christian. Whatever. Despite his best efforts to the contrary and for absolutely no logical reason, the annoying, mostly useless son of a bitch has grown on him, like a fungus. A broad smile at his metaphorical cleverness keeps him warm for his next lap. Joe starts to feel very guilty about what he's done to Chris' life, what with the severe depression about Tony and losing the woman he thinks he's been looking for, and he wants to make it up to him. Maybe he can talk him into coming with him, without doing something as crazy and out of control as telling the truth.

He interrupts his circular pacing and sits down next to Chris again. Christian. Whatever his name, he's pretending to be asleep.

"Chris-tian," he begins, not well, "why do you want to go to the funeral? Is it to say good bye to a friend or are you still continuing that stupid mission of yours?" No answer, but he can see the muscles of Chris' jaw tightening, so he's pretty sure his listener is keeping up with him. "You're going to try to get with Tony's sister at the funeral, ain't ya?"

Christian clenches his eyes shut, angry, but feeling he has to answer. "Don't even think of trying to make something disgusting out of this. I'm being drawn towards her by events I never could have imagined and never should have survived."

"Big deal!" Joe almost screams, although he sees Christian's point. He tries a different tact at this point. "So..."

"Shut up," Christian says, and not for the first time. "I need to know whatever she knows. And, I'm willing to give you three quarters of a million for that chance. So what the hell do you have to complain about?"

That, too, is a good point, Joe realizes. He is beginning to run out of options. Wait, that's not true; he's completely run out of options. He may as well tell him, then. Either the truth will set him free or it won't, and Joe is ready to find out which it's going to be. He's pretty resigned to his fate, whatever it may be. "Chris, I really didn't want to tell you this..."

"Then don't. Good night, you..."

"It was me, Chris." The words wait between them for a long, long time before crashing down on Christian's tired mind. He rejects them with a shake of his head. "Yes, Chris, it was me, that voice you heard, years ago, when we were kids, that voice that told you to ask that stupid question, that was me with a megaphone."

"Bullshit," he responds, but doesn't sound convincing. Christian rolls over on his side again. "You have no right..."

"It was."

"Bullshit. It didn't even sound like you."

Joe takes a deep breath and then grabs his throat with one hand and shakes his larynx back and forth. A thin, warbling voice seems to escape from the vicinity of his nose: "It didn't even sound like me."

Christian's eyes signal that he's heard the voice before. Unable to cling to any plausible deniability, he is faced with a couple of unsavory choices: try to gather even more anger for Joe, or just shrug it off, one more log on the fire. He tries to shrug it off, though he can't stop a quick, "God damn you" in Joe's general direction.

"It was a joke, man! I thought you'd ask a couple of people, someone would answer and you'd wet your pants, the end! Big deal! I'd completely forgotten all about it until you told Tony the question yesterday! I never dreamed…"

Mentioning Tony doesn't bring Christian and Joe closer together. "Shut up," is all he can say to Joe.

"I never dreamed it'd ruin your whole fucking life!" Joe shakes his head in wonder at how things work out sometimes. "Even I'm not that much of a dick, Chris. I swear." Joe stares at Christian's back, pointed distinctly and resolutely at him, his shoulders chillier than the Anaheim night. "Aw come on, Chris. We'll go to Rio, party every night, look back on all this shit and laugh, OK? Deal?"

Indistinctly and under his breath, Christian mutters, "Yeah."

An honest and jubilant smile crawls across Joe's face. "Hot damn! We'll get off here in the morning and…"

Christian rolls over to face him. "I mean, my deal stands. You take me to Forest Lawn, you keep the money, I keep quiet."

One of the most amusing of all human traits is this: people can be completely convinced of diametrically opposed things. Isn't that a hoot? Take this situation. Joe has just told Christian that God had nothing whatsoever to do with initiating the mission he's spent so long trying to complete. Nothing. Nada. Zilch. And yet, Christian refuses to stop, now that's he's met someone who can answer The Question. You might imagine that Christian doubts Joe's involvement; he does not. He accepts it, and feels a right idiot for not having thought of it himself, years ago. He's just being obstinate, stubborn, unswerving: in short, human.

Joe, faced with this situation, wants to continue a logical argument to convince his opponent of the validity of his point. But, in the face of this sort of resistance, logic is useless. It can't even get in the game. "Chris! I told you, it was me! Me, damn it, not God!"

"I know; thanx for telling me." Christian is being overwhelmingly, infuriatingly polite. To add to the effect, he throws in, "Good night" with a smile might be considered sweet in other circumstances. He then rolls away from Joe again.

Joe correctly interprets this as a knife between the shoulder blades. "This mission of yours is bullshit! It's garbage, it's…" The anger, the acrimony: yes, folks, Christian and Joe's points of view and their strategies for expressing them are working together marvelously. "It was me, god damn it!"

"It's still fate," Christian informs him over a shoulder.

"It's not fate! It's me! No divinity, a poorly planned, executed and then forgotten joke!" He wants to hit him desperately; that's the next step, after this sort of talking. The bastard deserves it for not agreeing to Joe's way of thinking. But he doesn't hit Christian. Doesn't quite have the anger for it, anymore, he's tired and if the idiot won't listen, well fine. He turns to fatalistic sarcasm for a big finish. "Fate… you are so fucked up."

"Thank you," Christian replies with equal sarcasm.

"You wouldn't recognize reality if it walked up and fucked you," Joe tells him.

Christian does not reply. Joe opens his mouth a few more times, but can't come up with anything better to say to Christian's back.

CHAPTER 58—WHEN IT'S DARKEST

It's been remarked that's it's always darkest before the dawn. *Always*, mind you, not just something which occurs with a high probability. Always means always. Joe, being the experimental sort, decides to test this theory. Well, OK, it's not really why he's sitting up, awake, on a very small island with his boyhood pseudo-friend sleeping soundly next to him. But, as long as he's up anyhow, he may as well kill a couple of birds with one really big rock.

A few minutes before midnight, it's really dark. Damn dark, a bank of clouds becoming entrenched over the small sliver of a moon. Joe can't see his hand three feet in front of him, or at least wouldn't be able to even if he tried. A few hours later on it gets a little darker because one of the lights on shore burns out (something else for maintenance to deal with in the morning). Then it's ***dark***; Joe stares into it, his face a mask of concentration and determination. Even without much of an imagination it's easy to see the world as a very empty, meaningless place, on a night like this.

At this time, surprisingly, Christian is dreaming about salmon. This is a little unusual in that he'd never even thought about salmon before (except in seafood restaurants) let alone dreamt about them.

About salmon: Salmon begin life with a long roller coaster ride down a river, their aquatic birth canal. They swim around the open ocean eating and playing and enjoy the good life for years until one day an overpowering urge to reproduce starts to control their lives. Filled with this mission they didn't ask for and don't understand, they struggle back up the very same river where they were born for the moment of blissful spawning which their hormones tell them is the end all, be all, life-fulfilling moment of salmon-dom.

Then they die.

In his sleep, Christian smiles. Why, you may ask? Christian smiles, and feels he knows what the salmon know. His mind is filled with salmon dying somewhat miserable deaths in shallow Alaskan creek bottoms and he doesn't feel pity, just empathy. Maybe spawning isn't about hormones; maybe their epic salmonillic struggle is not about sex and procreation at all. If they're anything like Christian, maybe the salmon just get so damned bored in their oceanic lives they are willing to try anything to shake them up. For a long weekend now, Christian has been swimming up a river where perhaps great experiences and death await him because that's what it takes to feel free and in control again.

Then Christian starts dreaming about Marilyn. Understandably, this has the effect of knocking salmon way the heck out of his mind.

Anyhow, about 4:30 or so the clouds clear, and the young moon dutifully reflects a few photons at the sleeping planet. The features of the park around them are dimly visible again. Any observer could make out Cinderella's Castle and the Matterhorn and they stay similarly observable for the rest of the night, up to and including just before the dawn. But Joe, unfortunately, has finally succumbed to exhaustion. His thoughts didn't let him sleep, but they couldn't keep him awake, either. Therefore, the witness sleeps and another untrue saying is allowed to live on for another millennium or so.

Day Four: Monday

Chapter 59—Santa Monica

It's still dark, about four a.m. on Monday morning. Since last I talked to you I've been driving around downtown Santa Monica and trying to decide what sort of person I am. Am I a selfish, uncaring, Machiavellian sort, or a compassionate and righteous dude?

Don't answer too fast, I beg of you.

I drive past the First Federal in Santa Monica for at least the thirtieth time tonight, and turn down the street next to it. There it sits, the beautiful BMW which has been abandoned a few blocks from the bank since the preceding Friday. If the police were of any use at all they would have picked up this car days ago and searched it in an effort to track down Mr. Whitney; they have not done so, obviously. I hadn't thought to go looking for it until Christian thought about his car while sitting on the wet sand of Treasure Island. I drive on about three blocks and find a good alley to leave my car in for a few hours; I don't want to leave any clues in case the police become more vigilant in the future.

I turn off the ignition and sit in the darkness. The question basically comes down to, am I the sort to go and steal Christian's car? I know where it is. I know where the spare key is hidden, underneath the right rear wheel well in a little magnetic box. I know what's in the trunk. I know I can get away with it. All I don't know is, can I live with myself after taking it?

Minutes tick by. Joe is asleep by now, as Christian has been for hours. I get out of my car and walk back towards the BMW, unsure if I'll get in, and unsure what I'll do once I take it home. I mean, if I take it home.

Chapter 60—So Far, So Good

And now, a reading from the book of Meat Loaf, Chapter Six, Verse Three:

So now, I'm praying for the end of time
To hurry up and arrive
'cause if I gotta spend another minute with you
I don't think that I can really survive.
I'll never break my promise or forget my vow
But God only knows what I could do right now
I'm praying for the end of time
It's all that I can do do do!
Praying for the end of time
So I can end my time with you....

It's funny, the things which float through people's minds when they are nervous. That clip of a Meat Loaf song came to Christian the second he saw the tombstones and brilliantly green grass and the gaudy fake Colonial facade of the main building at Forest Lawn. It sits comfortably off the 10 Freeway on top of a hill, so it wouldn't be the choice of folks whose eternal rest might be disturbed by a little traffic noise. Joe had dropped him off at the bottom of the long drive, fearful there may be the law enforcement element lurching about somewhere. Christian therefore has a sweaty, heart-pounding, musically accompanied climb to the Big House.

No cops anywhere to be seen. So far, so good.

(I'm now tuned into all this from home, eating Lucky Charms in my underwear; or is that a little more information than you really required?)

Christian had convinced Joe to stop at a florist on the way over. He had picked up six long stemmed red roses (a dozen is rather blasé and looked like an awful lot to carry). He didn't know exactly who they were for, but he felt more prepared, somehow, by having them as a shield. The florist had carefully wrapped them in thick paper for him, keeping him safe from the thorns contained within.

Again, so far, so good.

There were several things to consider, of course. What if the funeral isn't today, if Tony's off-handed comment about a speedy funeral was merely the retelling of a favorite joke between him and Diane? Or maybe Diane had meant it literally, but some force beyond her control (scheduling at the chapel, lack of grave sites, police interference) had kept the funeral from occurring expediently? What if Marilyn couldn't make it? What if…

The list, of course, goes on and on.

As he gets closer to the chapel he sees there are indeed a large number of people in both somber and formal attire parking their cars and entering the building, so at least there's a ceremony for *someone* today. Mourners pretty much all look alike, though, so it's impossible to say who might be responsible for bringing out this sort of crowd on a Monday morning. But, at least things are looking promising.

So far.

More meters nearer and the outline of a tall woman can be seen meeting the bereaved as they arrive. She helps the older ladies and gentlemen up the steps and shakes hands with one and all. She wears a tasteful but perhaps somewhat overly attractive black pinstripe suit with a skirt that cuts off at the calf. Her general build, height, and form suggests Diane to Christian immediately.

So good.

He walks around the circular drive, honing in on the front door and his future. It is Diane; their eyes lock as he starts to climb the grand (yet, God help me, hopelessly tacky) stairway. She gives him a blessedly tender look, which reminds Christian of all he's been through in the last couple of days. And reminds him of how he must look, and smell, at this point in his adventure. But, destiny waits for no man or his hygiene, so he continues on.

Besides, Diane has plenty of reason to be angry with him, so any tender look, for any reason, will certainly do.

At the top of the stairs he cuts one rose from the herd and hands it to Diane. She wraps her arms around him for a brief moment, and then releases him. "Good guess on the time," she says, smiling.

He shrugs. "It's fate. It is just fate."

"I asked the police to stay away. Told them guns are against Tony's religion."

"Thank you," he replies, though it feels inadequate. "I can't thank you enough."

"Thank you." She looks over the rose and stares into his eyes. "Your friend is an asshole."

Christian nods his head. "He's not my friend."

They both are satisfied with this, like spies passing the correct code word before getting down to business. He offers Diane his arm and she accepts; they walk past the columns and into the church.

Tony is in an open casket near the altar, lying very still. All corpses look serene and peaceful, but you can sense a special sense of affection that Diane used in preparing him for his last big day. There are a few dozen people in the pews, some in tears, some with solemn, expressionless faces. Christian scans them all in search of The One, and finally sees her in a back corner. Marilyn is a vision in black silk, her high-necked dress a perfect demonstration that you can be grief stricken, fashionable and tasteful all at the same time.

A man in a dark suit walks up to the front of the room, near Tony. "Hello to you all. This ceremony will be simple and honest, a valid tribute to the man lying before us today in the place of honor. Anyone who wishes to share his or her feelings with your fellow mourners, please rise and do so. Those who wish to share their stories of Tony, please do. Those who wish to share their money, I'm afraid you're at the wrong church." There is a polite laugh for this line, several knowing nods. "I miss him. I'm sure I'm not alone." He then walks solemnly back to his seat.

Christian stares at Marilyn but doesn't move. Diane looks at him expectantly. "Well?"

Christian stammers a few syllables, but can't find the words to express the fear, anticipation and need he feels at that moment.

"She'll never need anyone more than she does right now."

That makes sense, Christian admits. He takes the one, most perfect rose from his bunch and hands the other rejects to Diane. Diane sits on a nearby pew alone as Christian walks to Marilyn warily. He's vaguely aware of a male voice in the background offering his tribute to Tony, saying, "Tony was a beautiful man. He expressed his tenderness for life and each of us with a strength unrivaled by any."

Christian sits down on Marilyn's pew, a few feet away. In her grief she doesn't notice him. He slides the last exquisite inches across the smooth pew until he's sitting comfortably next to her. He's not comfortable doing it, mind you, his heart's pounding like mad and his brain is searching desperately for anything vaguely appropriate, memorable or erotic to say, but he's sitting a comfortable distance away. His mouth opens and a faint sigh-like tone says, "Marilyn?"

She glances his way. There isn't any big reaction, nor is there any anger or resistance. The change in her expression hints at the smallest glimmer of recognition as Christian being one of the guys from the other day. "Oh, hi."

"May I?" he asks, though he's already seated. She nods politely. He hands her the lone rose, eliciting a smile from her that he is afraid will make him swoon. It lights up the room and causes the birds to sing, and several other wonderful things smiles are capable of. What it mostly does, though, is make Marilyn look completely, unequivocally, and sensuously beautiful in that instant in time, an image which is frozen in Christian's memory forever.

Somewhere, in the distance, Christian hears a different voice. "I'm sorry this kind, gentle man had to die. But, if he did, the fact that it was so dramatic was quite fitting for him. He deserved no worse, he could hope for no better."

Marilyn looks away from the flower to Christian's unsteady eyes. "I heard you were coming. Nice handcuffs."

His heart leaps a bit, skips a beat, whatever inaccurate platitude you prefer. "Thanx; really?" he asks, convinced that perhaps she is impressed with his fashion statement.

Another voice: "Tony and I went fishing once, up on Bitter Creek. He never uttered a word he didn't mean."

Marilyn is acting just a shade impatient. "Diane didn't tell me why, she just said you were coming."

Christian wants to rush headlong into an explanation of what's happened and why he's here, but can't find the proper transition. Instead, he makes a sound resembling, "Oh."

"And it's always nice to see *the* Christian Whitney."

He turns away, shy and unable to speak. He's grateful when another voice covers his embarrassment: "Professor Tony taught me more about life than any college student deserves to know. He even gave me an extension on one of my papers. The man is a saint. I mean, was a saint."

Subtlety not working for her, Marilyn chooses direct. "So why are you here, Christian?"

Again, he has no words to work with. He says, "Well," and then, "I don't…" but they are not exactly apropos. He even threw in an "uh…" or two.

Marilyn pats his hand gently, almost matronly; Christian's flushed reaction is not the kind matrons usually engender, however. "That's OK, I'll give you a moment to think." She stands up and speaks loudly enough to be heard throughout the large room. "I'm sure that Tony, upon seeing you all, is smiling right now, wherever his soul may be. Even if we hadn't been born in the same family, I still would have loved him like a brother."

She sits down next to Christian again. He manages to say, "I'm so sorry about Tony."

Marilyn shrugs. "He lived as he wanted to, and he did what he had to do; who could possible do better?" Christian nods, but her bravery starts to dissolve and tears start forming at the corners of her eyes. Christian feels himself starting to tear up. She leans to him and he gladly accepts her in his arms, holding her lightly, supporting her shoulders with the width of his chest.

Not exactly the seduction of the century, but it's a start, you know?

Now or never, Christian my man, now or never, he tells himself. And he believes it. "Marilyn, can I tell you something?"

"Please," she says, with a slight catch in her voice from the crying.

"I… I…" I sound like an idiot, he thinks. "This sounds silly."

"So what?"

Deep breath and off he goes. "It's just that I've always had the feeling I'm looking for someone, and…"

She leans back and he releases her from his grasp. Her eyes, still producing the odd tear, have lit up like the Las Vegas strip. "Oh my God… really?"

"Yes." Christian stares into her beautiful eyes, trying to figure out what they're saying.

Then she says some words he didn't expect. "I though I was the only one."

"What?"

She takes the tissue she's been holding and gently wipes her eyes and nose. "I've been prompting people forever, waiting to hear the right response from anyone."

Christian now lights up. "Me too! Me too!"

"Sometimes, I feel like I should just give up," Marilyn laments.

"Oh, don't do that! I didn't, and I found you!"

The excitement that had been in her eyes starts to fade away, but Christian is too wrapped up to notice. "Well, that's sweet of you…"

"You!" he says, too loudly for the circumstances, but Christian doesn't realize he's being inappropriate. Several of the closer mourners turn to see who's shouting, but Christian doesn't notice that, either. "You are the one I've been searching for. You answered my question in the bank on Friday, and…"

"I did?' Marilyn asks, surprised.

"Yes, you did!" Christian repeats, enthusiastic for both of them.

"Oh, Christian, I'm so sorry…" she says, taking his hands in hers.

The brakes have suddenly been applied to Christian's mood. "You're sorry?"

"You see, I prompted you also, and…" She shakes her head slowly, slowly no.

This is not at all what he had expected. His disbelief keeps him from noticing that a rather large number of policemen, lead by Captain Smith himself, have entered, walked over to him, and placed a hand on his shoulder. "There you go, you shit! I've got ya! I took that anonymous phone crap, I ran with it, I got ya! Book 'em, Danno!"

"But, but wait!" The cops handcuff him behind his back, his fur-lined cuff still dangling from his sleeve. "Marilyn! I love you! Wait!"

Captain Smith is cackling with excessive glee. The service is completely brought to a halt, all eyes focused on the ruckus at the back. "I knew it! I nailed him! I knew we shoulda been here!"

The cops are dragging Christian up the aisle now, Marilyn following at a safe distance, waving good-bye. Christian continues to shout her name, but it's not improving his standing in these proceedings in the least. Captain Smith follows them all out towards the real world, pausing just long enough next to Diane to shout, "Ha!" in self serving triumph, the lone syllable echoing off the far walls over and over again.

Epilogue

The Aftermath

Oxymorons, like it or not, are a constant in this life. Christian, after several months in jail spent in constant resistance to this idea and others, has picked today to accept it. When the cell doors slam shut with a sound of utter finality for the umpteenth time since his freedom had been handed to the State his soul gives way and he believes: there are oxymorons in life.

After all, it's difficult to be a man of principle under these conditions.

The sun is going down in the west, over an ocean Christian can no longer see, but he accepts its reality all the same. His mind can still vividly remember the sun boiling away the aqua blue of the Pacific until its heat is dissipated and the cold ember of a star disappears forever. A new fire is lit hours later, appearing over San Bernardino, but it's nowhere near the spectacle and doesn't receive as much press.

He looks old. He isn't, of course, but the straggly beard and the gaunt cheeks have transformed him into an elderly gent before his time. His prisoner's denim hangs on him like a gunnysack. At least weekly he reminds himself he should become one of those prisoners who works out in the yard constantly, creating a body that'll be the envy of his peers, until he remembers he's in a minimum-security facility with a golf course but no weight room. Oh well. Still, it's valid as a concept, maybe he can just do push-ups and sit-ups in his cell, that sort of thing, except the floor looks rather hard and the carpet is a bit bare in spots already. All in all, seems like too much effort to Christian's bedraggled mind.

He's fairly content to waste away, anyhow.

OK, so this evening he's accepted oxymorons into his universe, such as "military intelligence," "bad sex" or, the one Christian is particularly thinking of, "white collar crime." All this thought on oxymorons is just stalling anyway, a distraction from the fact that he's damn near done with the only project that has thus far occupied his mind and he's got three years till his first parole hearing. Finding another activity to change his minutes into hours then days will not be easy; his only idea so far is memorizing "The Rhyme of the Ancient Mariner", and his guards fear it may be deemed cruel and unusual punishment even if undertaken voluntarily.

So there are oxymorons, Ancient Mariners, and nearly complete projects, but Christian's problems run deeper than that. There's one more fact about life, or at least life as he knows it, to accept and he doesn't want to do it.

Well, he thinks he has to accept it, anyhow. Who, after all, could live through his recent life and not accept that fate is carrying us along? And, who could walk those miles in his loafers and not conclude that some higher power out there is a real asshole? It'd take a stronger man than I, Christian admits. A much stronger, more stubborn, stupider man. Christian looks around his cell, admiring with pride the two banners he's scrawled in red crayon on reams of fax paper he smuggled out of the prison library: "I hope the asshole missed Rio and hit North Dakota" and, more succinctly, "Fuck Fate." This overwhelming, practically debilitating anger with Joe is understandable, but he must let it go if he is to move on with his life and reenter society.

Or at least that's what the prison shrink said. He also said something like, "Just because he called the police on you doesn't mean you have to obsess about him for the rest of your life."

Christian doesn't buy it. "Fuck that," was his exact response, and his first step to ending his analysis. His righteous anger (another bloody oxymoron) is the lone possession he intends to honor and cherish for the rest of his days, wherever they may be spent.

He resigns himself to the fact that tonight is the night he finishes his project. He takes up a yellow legal pad and his Monte Blanc and flips to the back. There's one blank page left, after the corporate raider next door borrowed a sheet to calculate his dividend income for tax purposes. That's OK, though. One page will be enough; it's just the epilogue, anyway.

At the top of the page he writes: "Scene 75, Interior of a prison cell—Day." A brief moment is spent in silent contemplation, and then he begins with a brief description of the scene:

> Fade into the sound of a cell door being slammed. The camera zooms in over CHRISTIAN'S shoulder. We see the following words, hand scrawled on a sheet of yellow legal paper:
>
> "I'M SITTING IN A CELL, WRITING ON A YELLOW LEGAL PAD. ON THE WALLS ARE THE WORDS, 'I HOPE THE ASSHOLE MISSED RIO AND HIT NORTH DAKOTA,' AND 'FUCK FATE.'"

Satisfied he has sufficiently captured the moment, he moves on to a bit more directing on paper. Curtis, the agent who's doing two to five for fraud and handling all the screenplays by inmates, has warned him about doing that, that it annoys directors and producers and other real players. But, damn it, it's Christian's story, he's the bastard that knows best how it should be captured on film for future generations to see, learn from, avoid. So, on his screenplay-within-a-screenplay he damn well includes more of what should be seen on film:

> "CUT TO my face, tired, angry, a bit pitiable. Fade to Black.
>
> The End"

And then, for the kicker. The bit that'll really grab people's hearts and won't let 'em leave the theatre until they've read every last credit, and when they finally do find their legs and walk away, that'll make them question their assumptions. Was it fiction? Was it fate? Would a just God allow what has transpired to occur? Yup, this is what you get the big bucks for, mate, the big finish:

> Rotate camera until it faces towards CHRISTIAN's face. It is tired, angry, a bit pitiable. The camera slowly moves in and slowly fades to black.

Can you say Oscar, baby? Filming himself finishing his screenplay—outrageous! Christian wonders if they'll let him go to the ceremony. Oh, he almost forgot:

> Cue "Free Will" by Rush.
>
> The End

Music is very important to a film, you know. Very key, Curtis had agreed when Christian pitched the story to him. And then it hits him: he has finished it. His face is tired, angry, a bit pitiable, and he likes it that way. He puts aside the legal pad; Jerry (Curtis' assistant, serving eighteen months for aiding and abetting) will type it in the proper format tomorrow. You've got to love the typing class. Well, love may be a little strong but at least you have to appreciate them.

He goes to the door of his cell and tries it. It's locked again, as usual, but you can't blame a guy for trying. "Hey guard!" He calls down the darkening cellblock. Fred, (two kids, a mortgage and a 401k plan, getting lessons on his short game from some of the 'mates) pokes his head out the office door, three doors down. "Hey ya, Fred. I need some more paper, OK?"

"Yeah, in a minute."

Sitting on his bed, Christian watches the last rays of the dying sun leave the patio below. He remembers something Tony had said to him, the night before that sweet soul was whisked away from this reality forever: whatever you decide, you'll be happy. And, even though he's loath to admit it, he's enjoying feeling sorry for himself, he's reveling in hating Joe for the remainder of his existence, and the angel hair pasta here on Thursdays is to die for. He is happy, damn it.

Happy or not, he decides next time it will be free will. Though, of course, this time it was free will, too.

Footsteps slowly approach his cell door. Fred, the middle class man guarding the formerly rich and powerful, walks ups and chucks in a roll of Charmin toilet tissue. "Here ya go."

"Thanks," Christian nods. "It's just what I needed."

OK, he's had his say, now I get mine.

I've been tapping into Christian for the last few months, of course. I knew he was writing his story; it's what gave me the idea to write it down also. I have several advantages over him, after all: I can get into the heads of all the protagonists, antagonists and apathetic-agonists; I have a much more poetic writing style; and, best of all, I know the ending.

I know who read Christian's mind when he was thinking of one more way to get rid of Joe: offer him more money.

That was Christian's secret all along, and it answers the question, "How could Christian plan to live the rest of his life on $780,540:" he didn't. The bank robbery was for show and statement, to demonstrate his resolve to change his life and keep him from changing his mind. The cash he really needed was already in his possession from the sale of his house, and stocks and bonds, and a pleasant inheritance.

I know I eventually convinced myself to start up Christian's car. He was absolutely correct, it's a joy to drive.

I know, therefore, who got the 1.7 million dollars in perfectly clean cash hidden in the trunk. Some people just haven't heard about traveler's checks, I guess. Or Swiss bank accounts, for that matter.

I know who then called Captain Smith and told him Christian was on his way to Forest Lawn. Once I talked myself into taking the car, it was easy to keep taking things from him, especially when I figured he'd blame Joe for it when Captain Smith claimed it was an "anonymous tip."

*For the grand finale, for the true icing on this wonderful cake, I know who went into the First Federal in Santa Monica on Tuesday, who waited for the lovely strawberry blond teller to be free, who walked right up to her and when she said she's pleased to meet, "*The* Mr. Wonderful" (not my real name) I know who responded correctly. The correct answer was something else she had thought when I was listening to her mind while she watched M*A*S*H re-runs.*

I therefore also know what a look of utter and complete ecstasy looks like.

I also know who's going to turn off his computer, go to bed, and find the enchanting and perfect Marilyn Green waiting for him there, ready to wear that ecstatic look again and again. I have become, for most practical purposes, Christian Whitney. I have his money; I have his car; I took his freedom; I'm taking his life story: and I have taken the woman he loves and always will.

I should probably feel bad about at least two of those things, and I may, someday, if I ever get tired of being so darned happy all the time. But, in many ways, it was just fate, right? What's the use feeling guilty over what I was able to make meant to be?

Read that sentence again, it makes sense, I assure you.

Good night. I hope all of you sleep as well as I do.

About the Author

Mary Jane is a graduate of Harvey Mudd College in Claremont, California. Her fans can reach her at mary_jane@alumni.hmc.edu and read her short fiction on www.aidtopia.com (the ideal spot on the web). She is currently living abroad.

9 780595 189854